# *Stalking*

# *Nightfall*

Mike,

Thanks for making the art of writing so interesting to me when I was only thirteen years old and thought that

**Jesse Carter White**    it was 'easy'!

Thank you for all of your support!

Jesse Carter White

*Stalking Nightfall* was self-published using Amazon-owned CreateSpace™ and was submitted for publishing on May 24th, 2013.

ISBN-10: 0985506504
ISBN-13: 978-0-9855065-0-6

Library of Congress Control Number:   2013909697

White, Jesse. *Stalking Nightfall*. Massillon, OH: 2013.

www.fabricatedautumn.com is owned and operated by Jesse Carter White and is hosted by ipage™

*For my mother, Cheryl, for her persistent encouragement and openheartedness.*

*For my father, Brian, for his unmatched dedication and ceaseless hard work.*

*For my brother, Zachary, for his brotherly support and artistic investment.*

*For my wife, Samantha, for her loving companionship and understanding.*

# Contents

# STALKING NIGHTFALL

JESSE WHITE

*Prologue*
*Unknown Author*
*Unknown Date*

How easily the years drift away from us. I watched decades fall from the clouds and drip down the clogged gutters of neighboring homes. Time slipped through the teeth of manholes, bathed the rats and fled with the sewers. Filth sits upon filth; grime intoxicates any loose, willing decency. The world I loved, the one I once knew, has been gone for years.

The pillowing fog from the chimney tops has turned the sky rotten. If heaven is alive, it is missing several teeth. Humans strive to destroy their own kind. Any hope that I once had for the future of mankind no longer waits like a starving owl does for its cleansed rodent. I wait, and wait, and wait . . . but what are we all really waiting for? How do you define the idea of the word *tomorrow?*

We all sit and wait for something better to come along; and it never does. So in the realist's eyes, aren't we all simply waiting for death? Can we help but count the seconds until a new minute begins; the minutes to the hours; the hours to the days, weeks, months, years?

Must every thought have a purpose? Must every second fill up an hourglass? Who knows what's stirring in this used up body of mine. My name is of no importance; it never has been and it never will be. A name is just a label; a cue for us to turn our heads when a master calls. A name is a way to identify yourself and a way to generalize yourself. Your parents gave you a name so you'd listen. People never stop and think that perhaps it's their own inner self that needs the attention.

Crazy, psychotic, idiotic, egotistical, vapid, crude; I've been called many names before. But what do they really mean? Do you ever wonder how many petals are on a purple lotus flower? Did you ever take the time to count? Hmm . . . you probably never will.

Man has bickered with time since his own origin. So many botched, limbless attempts to better mankind's future; I admit that I was no different. When the world cried, I held a bucket for its tears. Alas, I am a different person now. I have tasted revenge; both dealt it and received it. It should not shock you to learn that I have no family. I am a crippled, aching, whining old man. I could say that I've seen better days, but does every new day not make us long for the past? When tomorrow is finally today, are we not stuck dreaming of yesterday?

Our limitless personalities tear us apart, and when they collide, it is either ugly or beautiful; we never know until it is behind us. Regardless of the outcome, we are always the wiser. Do I consider myself a wise man? Well, we are all wise in our own ways, aren't we?

The following is a collection of journal entries, or literary recordings if you will, that I happen to have in my possession. The stories of many are now wrapped together under one neat, little bow. Now, they are my gift to you. One can learn quite a bit through the mistakes of others. Sometimes the obvious is not what its name implies. Sometimes one's assumptions are proven wrong with a tweaking of the brain.

Mankind ruins itself; our origins left up to our own personal beliefs. We claim to see signs from God and ghosts, believe in miracles and karma that have control over our actions; but is this all a form of reality? Or is it merely a mirage; an oasis in our minds that is full of tainted water and reflections of another world? Who in this world, or in another, holds the strings above our heads? As my body grows weaker, I realize that I have yet to find an answer.

My innards have begun to deteriorate, and any day now the dirt will swallow me whole. Take these entries as you will, but always look backwards while stepping in the right direction. The mistakes of others are valuable lessons. As another day dies, I

can still hear the years drooling over the rooftops.
My galoshes fill to their brim, and memories pour
out into my living quarters. My brain grows tired
and my eyes yawn. If I am to find sleep, I wish the
same upon you. Sleep well.

Signed,

With a Smile

*Chapter One - The First Recording*
*From the Journal of: Harold Elway*
*December 12th, 1905*

My name is Harold Elway. I live at 418 Pryer Drive; the stone-grey house that cowers between two imperfect lamp posts. One bulb flickers on and off half the nights; the other hasn't worked in over a year. I am left sitting in the darkness again with the feeling that a knapsack full of spiders has come unraveled behind my neck. Tonight marks my sixth month of nearly sleepless nights. Sometimes the smile of dawn is enough to knock me into slumber. At other times, a straight shot of whiskey and the light of a lantern can blur my vision. Some nights, I don't sleep at all. I am caught in the storm of another walking nightmare. My trusty pocket-watch, though long-rusted now, reads a quarter 'till two. The room screams silence, but I feel *its* presence amongst my own. I have run out of kerosene oil this night, but I've noted to pick more up at The Wax Parlor before the new day's end. Even my trusty pillar candles have all burned flat. These useless puddles of wax won't stay lit for more than a moment. A lone tea-light flickers on the end-table near the kitchen. My name is Harold Elway, and I am a poor, poor bastard.

The piffling flame of the tea-light disorients me, sometimes creating illusions in the space between myself and the fire. Web-like splotches weave across my eyesight, and speckled dancing figures appear at the far end of the room. When I reach out to them, I grab only darkness. I return to my seat, forgetting instantly about the figures I swore were real moments before. Short minutes pass before the candlelight plays with the shadows once more. I pause, spotting another figure embalmed in cyan-blue particles hovering down the stairwell. The wind whistles, and it is gone. I am not quite sure what to believe in any more. Trust is both an enemy and a friend. I sleep through the fogged mornings and the stretching afternoons, often waking to the town's clock tower crying at noon.

The pen trembles in my fingers, rattling against sweaty skin and tired bone. To this day, it frazzles me that everyone I know grips their pen with three fingers. I use only my thumb and index finger to scribble onto the paper. Alas, I already begin to digress in a cowardice attempt at dodging the true subject of this literary recording. I am not afraid to admit to this empty notebook that I have presuming fears of someone finding this entry and thinking I am a mad man. The simple truth is - I've been seeing and hearing things after darkness falls. I've told no one.

The research documents I've checked out of the nearby library tell me it is merely my brain playing tricks on me. The articles tell me that my mind is deprived of sleep, running in an awkward state that is trapped between the living world and the dream world. Notorious doctors write that my waking mind fills in lapses of consciousness with the physical images of randomized figures from my subconscious. They *all* say that my sight is radically impaired, as if I have a disability. I say they're wrong. I say they're all wrong. God, London is quiet tonight.

What I have heard in these walls cannot possibly be fiction. When I am calm enough to sleep, I dream untamable, unimaginable nightmares. Some visions are potent enough to wake me, while others send me deeper into the torment. Believe me, I'm not crazy. I'm not bloody crazy.

It might seem like I'm being a bit particular with my words, and for a damn good reason. I swear there is a curse placed upon me. The very religious might even call it a test written by The Heavenly Father or a trap laid by the hungry Devil. How am I ever to know if the spirit never answers my calls? Nothing feels real anymore. The days are manageable at best. Daylight muffles the horrendous sounds that I hear in my living quarters; which is where I sit now. I sit at the same crooked, termite-ridden coffee table I've been at every night for the past many months. Never did the phantoms haunt me like this before. The nights were never this unbearable.

As the calendar runs onwards, it becomes increasingly difficult to elude the demons. I am rightfully afraid to tell anyone of the apparitions I see. They'll yank me from this condemned house and throw me into the loony-bin, they will! Thus, I shuffle around my purpose for beginning this journal yet again. Whether they find me dead by morning, or they toss me against padded walls to live amongst the manic bastards, *someone* will find this entry and know the truth. Last night's haunting is fresh in my mind, and I suppose there is no better place to begin.

I flipped up that aged pocket watch I've had for years now - I couldn't tell you where I got the damn thing. How sad that my ticking companion corrodes a little more each with each passing day. Last night began with nothing out of the ordinary, but quickly transpired into something lavishly fresh and fiendish. It began around 1:30 in the morning. The house donned its black cloak as usual, struggling to keep the frost from crawling up its skirt. I sat up in the same wooden chair that I do now, it's brittleness as unwelcoming as ever, reading more of the previously mentioned documents I'd recovered from the library. The parchments fluttered under dimming lantern light, the last of the kerosene burning off into the overweight air. The ink of the documents appeared dry, if not lightly tortured. The pages crackled at the sound of my incoming guest.

The voice of croaking footsteps cluttered the stairwell. Mind you, I have always lived alone in my house. Never married, I am a twenty-eight year old bachelor who embraces his privacy with welcoming arms. My home is a rather modest structure. I have but a small living quarters, narrow hallway of a kitchen, and alcove of a bathroom on the ground floor. The upstairs holds only my bedroom and an attic space that's essentially a pint-sized closet. It certainly is no lush mansion. The footsteps spoke from the crest of the staircase.

The parchment fell from my hands, narrowly missing the fire's spittle and landing in a pile on the tabletop. My patient chest anticipated the next footstep, but was left weirdly disappointed. I rose, lifting the chair behind me as to not pinch out a sound. As I crept towards the front door, a crescent of moonlight cracked through the window pane at the peak of the stair set. The natural light revealed a pitiful fog tumbling down the steps. A regular illness brewed in my gut as it became clear that my night was young. Retrieving the lantern from the coffee table, I walked from the living quarters into the kitchen. I peered into the shadows in search of a mug, my eyes catching the dishware that hadn't been fully scrubbed in weeks. This is truly a sad way to manner myself considering I am part of the sixty percent of folks who has running water in their homes. I have the luxury of being able to wash the dishes at my convenience, yet I can never seem to ration out the time. Pitiful, if you ask me.

Yet again, I find myself beside my point. Good Lord. I must convince myself that no one will find this journal until this is all over. As I said, I stood in the derelict wasteland I call a kitchen. I spotted a mug in the far left alcove of the countertop. Grabbing the cup by its fat lip, the grime of whatever had been inside of it days beforehand brushed against my finger. The volcano of dishes in the sink was parted a bit to the side; just enough to slip my mug underneath and give it a half-hearted wash. Rotten egg, or some other indistinguishable and slimy relative of its kind, clung to one side of the outer-lip. The liquid doesn't touch that part of the mug, so I found no harm in leaving it as it was. I pounded the mug's insides with a dishcloth and dried it on my nightwear.

I set the gas burner of the stove to its highest setting and filled my mug with lukewarm water from the sink. The water fell into the same teapot I've been using for weeks now; its new permanent home the wires of the burner. That old bit of pestering moonshine came through the curtains of the kitchen window just above the sink. The light appeared skewed as it filtered through one end of the glass and met a tower of dishware at the other. I turned for the pantry and heard it again.

Two footsteps this time; they were nearly above me. I ripped open the door of the pantry and reached for the bottom shelf, retrieving a tiny silver packet. These glistening pouches are my prized possessions; a gift from a trusted friend. Possession of these packets is not illegal in any form, but they are indeed quite hard to come by outside of Japan. I held in my hands the simplest, most efficient way to brew coffee; an absolutely divine water-soluble solution that produces java in an instant. This powder has barely been patented for a year now, but my old friend Johnny has a way of getting things for me. Reading back my own written words in my head, it sounds as if I am writing about an illegal narcotic of sorts. Friends, it is merely caffeine and warm water to you; but it is sanity to me.

I shuffled to the stove, catching a light breath of steam leaving the teapot's spout. The water was warm, but not quite ripe. I tore off the head of the coffee pouch and dumped it into the beckoning mug. The powder never smelled all that great; much like a fertile dirt patch in fact. The drug kept me awake, though, and for that I was thankful. From the moonshine came the arcane spirit. *BANG, BANG, BANG:* an impatient rattle upon the kitchen window.

The thunderous fists resonated through the window's glass, wobbling into the still barren kitchen. My toes nearly tore the roof from my slippers as my legs fumbled backwards. In instinct, one hand grabbed for my heart while the other searched for stability. Mid-inhale, the oxygen was sucked from my tender chest. I coughed, wiping

dried crud from the corners of my mouth. Tiny
pigments of dead skin united with rotten remnants
of my nightly cigar. I was crouched now, hidden
behind the unstable comfort of the dish volcano. A
slight gap existed between the lip of a bowl and the
plane of a full-sized plate. Putting the grime of
uncooked chicken into my peripheral vision, I peered
through the narrow window of dishware to the
actual glass window that lay behind it. Particles of
dust filtered through the thinness of the curtain; a
slim finger of an oak branch jabbing for my attention
to the left.

Silent echoes of the knocking ricocheted in my
head, pinging from ear to ear. As the noise slowed to
a quiet, I heard only the flat, bubbling chords of
gurgling water in the teapot. Self-interrogation began
once more. This was my third haunting of the week,
and my sanity grew tired of fabricating excuses for
its own many faults. I stood now, adjusting the collar
of my unwashed nightwear. Reaching for the curtain,
I assured myself there would be only London fog
behind it. And there was. The yard lay empty aside
from familiar desolation.

My back lawn is truly nothing spectacular; only
a small, fenced area with a round-wired table and
two adorning chairs in the eastern corner. The
remainder of the yard is covered by copper-yellow
grass; none of those shimmering emerald blades that
Johnny grows in his yard. Even for December, the
grass screams for an artist to bathe it in forest-green

paint. The oak branch that had stretched for my awareness revealed its decrepit body, appearing as if it was on a sickening deprivation diet. The tree is a horrid sight; disgustingly slim with the limbs of a leper. December had never looked so bleak. Snow has yet to fall in the city this year. The light drizzle of rain from earlier in the day had left the lawn a grimy marsh. Taking a final glimpse around the yard, only the chipping paint of the charcoal-grey fence caught my eye. Relief slid itself back into my throat as my hand released the curtain and met my side. Before I could swallow the much needed dose of solace, *BANG, BANG, BANG*; I spat it back up.

My slippers shuffled with the hair of the crumpled rug beneath me. I tumbled backwards, my shoulder blades slamming against the ridges of the kitchen table. Knees hitting the stone floor, my hands scraped to comfort my back. The footsteps interrupted again; half-way down the stairwell now. Further *croaks* and *bangs* rang from unclear corners of my home, filling it with the sounds of a filthy brothel. Pain shot through my legs, trickling from my kneecaps to my toes as I forced myself to stand again. A consecrated carving knife glistened on the kitchen table, its handle warm as my palm wrapped around it. The footsteps grew louder as they neared the base of the steps. I pressed my back against the doorway to my living quarters, the tomato-stained blade clenched in my hands. The footsteps grew heavier, the creaking wood beneath them putting splinters in my fear. An ultimate *thud* rang out before the silence. The phantom had reached the ground floor of the living quarters. Rationality raced circles in my mind, attempting to convince my feet to turn the corner. The knife suffocated in the sweat of my palm. My breathing was shunted by pathetic wheezing and helpless anxiety. I shouted aloud; an unintelligible wail as I spun around the doorframe to face my demon at the stairwell.

There stood only moonlight; just how it had been in the rear of my yard. Once again, questions of torture had gone unanswered. My shoulders ached with the ripeness of pain. The house was quiet once more, even through frightened, rattled ear drums. A familiar dancing figure appeared by the front door in all of its blue, shimmering glory. I scoffed at the illusion. The webs of blotchy light were attempting to trick my mind once more. A drawn sigh escaped me, until I was sharply stricken with the remembrance that I'd left the lantern in the kitchen.

"Who's there?" I called out to the shadows. There was no reply; it never replies. "Who's there?" I called again. The spirit, demon; whatever it may be, remained silent. "I grow tired quickly tonight," I warned. My feet moved closer to the stairwell, my eyes watching the sky-blue specks of dust twirling at the bottom step. This was no lunar trick. "I know you can hear me, spirit. What is it that you want?" I stammered. "Jesus, what do you want from me?! I can't stand it any longer!" Sweat again bathed my forehead, and the sadly familiar parade of spiders crawled from underneath the front door. "Leave me be! I have not done anything to deserve this!" My arms swatted drowsily into the darkness, helpless as the bloodthirsty arachnids took over my skin. With dripping, gnashing teeth, the spiders commanded their armies down my spine. Marching and droning, a thousand piercing legs tickled my stomach like a feather made from thorns.

Desperate to shake my body of the spiders, I ran to the stairs and collapsed to my back. Like an old washboard, the ridges of the steps ripped away the eight-legged monsters as I grinded up and down the staircase. If only I could have seen myself; a desperate dog with an itch he can't reach, and no one else willing to scratch it for him. As I stood, I knew I'd find only the weak light from the window around me. There was no aftermath save my own steep breathing; no pool of crushed arachnids or blotches on my skin. I felt the spiders settle themselves between the ridges of my vertebrae, where they would nest for the remainder of the night. The faint ticking of my pocket watch was all that remained. *Tick, tick, tick.* The sound of rotating hands beat into my skull like a stubborn nail does to a coffin. *Tick, tick, tick.* Darkness and light were still. *Tick, tick, tick.* The taste of the night was flavorless in my mouth.

*BANG, BANG, BANG.*

The specter rattled at the ribcage of my front door. Time was an annoyance; too confusing to understand in my state of mind. Out of options; out of patience, I ran to the door. The top latch was cold to my hand as it came unbolted, the chain falling into the wall behind it. The second latch jammed midway; nothing a nonsensical punch and a bit more force couldn't fix. With the twist of my thumb, the final lock gave in and the door swung open. "Goddammit, what do you want?!" I bellowed out into the tumbling nightfall. There was no poltergeist anxious or capable of replying. There was only London; the gag of factory pollution and an awkward minty aroma in the air.

The black houses across the cobblestone street had all been sleeping until the noise opened their eyelids; no doubt my outburst had lit them up. In fear of being reprimanded by strangers I'd never met, I moved quickly to shut away the night. The moans of the door hinges were shortened by a sharp *slam* and re-bolting of the chain lock. I felt like the city fool; a headless chicken loose in a luxurious five-star restaurant. This hadn't been my first outburst. In fact, I've woken the neighbors a handful of times now. I'm not even sure if they can hear the shouts coming from behind my closed doors. I try not to vocalize my distraught if I can help it, as my brain typically relies on impending daylight to save itself from such embarrassment. Alas, I fear the shadows grow more impatient with each passing night. The knocking and footsteps squeal louder with every haunting. When this all began six months ago, the ghosts were nearly as proper as I. They would perhaps give my shoulder a gentle tap, or breathe a bit of ice down my neck. No longer are they as polite. Now, they strive to devour me.

My hand remained on the top chain for a moment, the metal now warm. Embarrassing moments like these force me back into reality. Each cranking brain cell reminded me of the atrocity that I'd become. Sweat pooled over my skin, clumping select hairs on my forearms. Still, there was malice in the air. There was something behind me. Its peppermint breath chilled the nape of my neck. The trembling skeleton of the man I was turned to face the demon I had feared all these months.

Now-familiar blue fog churned before me. Illuminated particles struggled to form the shape of a human. A short figure began to emerge, long-flowing hair masking its face. My lips parted to speak, but the phantom interrupted with a lowly growl. It was a slow groan that shook the ringing from my ears. The silhouette lost structure quickly, twisting within the fog to escape solid form. Lord knows I saw the phantom; it had never revealed itself to me before now. The quiet snarl blew into a screeching whistle. The spirit lurched for me in a jumble of aquamarine dust. The knife in my hands still willing, I stabbed blindly at the specter. The blade cut mere pockets in the cursed mist. Whatever this atomized spirit was; I was helpless in harming it.

The particles fluttered around my head, much like a colony of bothered gnats. My hands fought to swat them away, but a misplaced galosh caused me to once again stumble to the frigid, unforgiving floor. In a novice action stunt, I rolled around to my side and hurled the kitchen knife into the fog I had escaped from. The ghastly swarm had left me, my hand already embarrassed as it heard the metal blade *clink* against the stone wall behind the stairwell. The blade hit the floor, wobbling a moment before settling. The piping whistle of the 'spirit' remained. The water in my teapot had finished boiling.

I wobbled to the kitchen, slamming into the writing table and knocking a few medical documents to the floor along the way. The teapot quieted as it left the coal-like wires of the stovetop. Steam erupted from the crusty mug as boiled water filled its hole. The aroma of bold, virgin coffee filled the air. Resting the pot on the grey neighboring burner, I twisted the stove's knob to its *off* position. With the lantern in one hand and coffee in the other, I drug myself back into the living quarters. Setting both comforts on the table, I bent over and shuffled through the spilled documents. There were snippets from magazines, excerpts from books, and recent notes from local doctors; something that Johnny had so graciously provided for me.

I may have stretched the truth a tad when I wrote that absolutely no one knows about these inexplicable haunts. I trust Johnny. I've known him since the week I moved to London more than eight years ago. In all truth, I am a natural-born American. I spent the first two-thirds of my life in the glorious land of the free. I woke up one day, and that freedom had suddenly grown stale for me. The air soured my lungs with every breath, and there appeared to be nothing left for me there; so I packed up my wits and moved here to London. Ever since then, I've been living at 418 Pryer Drive; the stone-grey house in-between two twinkling lamp posts. I've made a few friends during my time spent in London, but I pride myself in privacy. When I say *a few* friends, I of course mean Johnny and Johnny alone.

I've brought up my 'condition' to Johnny on a handful of occasions. He chuckles at me at times, saying that I am merely sleep-deprived; pretty much the medical textbook answer I'd expect from most. He consistently gives me the old 'filling in missing gaps of memory' and 'scrambled brainwaves' speeches every time I bring up the matter. My response is always that he is mistaken; that there has to be more to it all. So to prove me wrong, what does he go and do? He goes to damn near *every* doctor in the surrounding ten miles, collecting random diagnoses and notes from each one of them. I've picked through about half of them so far, and they're all a bunch of hogwash. Upon returning to the table last night, I couldn't help but stare emptily at the bottomless pit of medical reports. My eyes travelled the words, but my ego wouldn't read them. My pocket watch clicked open, ticking nearly five in the morning as my body finally went limp in the chair. I woke this afternoon to the routine chiming of the clock tower that I wrote of earlier. A stiff neck accompanied crusted eyes.

As for tonight, all has been quiet save for a few sightings of the blue dust. I am beginning to think that the phantom will grant me an evening free from extraordinary anguish. I'm not sure what time it is now, and I honestly don't care to check. Perhaps I've miraculously written myself through the night. Recording my encounters has made my condition appear a bit worse than I previously thought, but I realize how important it is that I keep writing. One day the doctors will come to drag me away, and I will present these logs; recite everything to them in immaculate prose. They'll have no choice but to let me go. But before that happens; before I *let* that happen, I vow to discover what this spirit requires from me. My greatest fear is that I cannot do this alone; and that is why Johnny has promised to help me uncover the truth. He judges me; of course I know this. But I know that he will not speak ill of me to the neighborhood. Though he tells me that I suffer

from a combination of insomnia and bad luck, I am
confident that I can convince him otherwise.

As I close my first entry, I cannot help but think
of Johnny's words and question what in life is left up
to chance. Some people carry a rabbit's foot for good
luck. They swear it does wonders for them; brings
them fortune and riches, meaningful love and
bulging inspiration. Excuse my language, but I call
steaming horseshit on this logic. I've never crossed
one too many black cats or stepped under another
man's ladder. I've not once cracked a mirror or
opened my umbrella in my living quarters. Luck is a
fable, illuminated by mere coincidences that appear
in rapid succession. Such an idiotic person will ask,
"Why has my luck been so terrific lately?" and they'll
ponder for days and days until they gasp, "Ah yes! It
is because I ate potatoes with a spoon instead of with
a fork last Tuesday!" They'll conjure up absolutely
any ridiculous thing they did differently in the last
month or so to *invent* a reason for their luck.

And so now, every Tuesday, this fool of a man
eats potatoes with a spoon. Any time he has bad
fortune after making a ritual of this behavior, he'll
blame it on the way in which he conducted the ritual;
thus leading to the development of yet another rule
for reliable good luck. *Now* every Tuesday, the man
eats potatoes with a spoon *and* he always remembers
to scrape his utensil against his bottom set of teeth.
Now, do you understand where my frustration
comes from? Ridiculous rituals, really! Yet, I see

these folks who carry a rabbit's foot in their pocket or around their neck as if it is a trophy. Can you imagine how ridiculous it would be if the roles were reversed; if rabbit's wore a human foot around *their* necks? Implausible. Well friends, I put no faith in the severed limbs of once sprite, helpless critters. I wear formal black pants and a well-pressed white button-up shirt. I throw on my black suit coat and button it up to the top. Then, I grab my short-stacked, dressy top hat and I'm out the door. I never leave the house without my faithful pocket watch in my suit coat pocket and my wallet in the rear-right slit of my pants. I sometimes carry a pocket knife and a book of matches, but I've never had need of them. My trusty umbrella is always prepared for the rainfall in either hand. I carry no rabbit's foot. *I* am the footless rabbit.

With no clue as to the time, I can be certain that I've rambled myself throughout the entirety of the night. The sun's fingertips begin to pull at the blanket landscape. Last night's visit from the spirit is not easily forgettable, but a few puffs of my nightly cigar remain to comfort me. I may in fact catch a few winks of sleep when the stick has burnt out.

There was a scraping sound out back a few moments ago, but when I went to look, I saw it was nothing more than a grey squirrel dancing up the old oak tree. The sunlight quarrels with the darkness, creating blotches in my weary eyes. Sadly, my cigar has lost its taste for the night. An hour or two of sleep should be easy to find now; no doubt my body needs it before tomorrow. Wait, is it not tomorrow already? Do you see now why I bicker with time? The whole concept is an enigma; a puzzle that I can never quite seem to finish. Everyone else's tomorrow is still my today. This pocket watch is different though - It and I seem to have a sort of understanding that I cannot quite explain.

My thoughts are a stewed mess. My hands shake without a comfort to hold onto. The stone floor I've fallen to so many times is the only place comfortable enough to sleep. Being upstairs after dark is anxiety-ridden; another unexplainable fear that I've developed in the past few weeks. It feels like an entirely different form of darkness up there; something I don't want to tangle with. This can't go on. This isn't living. I must talk to Johnny. I must tell him everything. My name is Harold Elway, and I am in dire need of help.

*Chapter Two – Fruitless Endeavors*
*From the Journal of: Johnny Tappling*
*December 13th, 1905*

Johnny Tappling here, checking in for the first time. Today, my good friend Harold Elway informed me that he has begun keeping a journal on the highly questionable interactions he has been having with the spirit world. The idea of a logbook sounded foolish and primitive to me at first, but the concept seems to have grown on me as the day carried onwards. My meeting with Harold today has inspired me to keep my own records of how these illusions haunt the lonely man I've accepted into my life. Woefully, this journal is a recording of what I see as Harold's inevitable demise. I want to help the poor bastard; I really do, but he tends to worsen near every day. I fear that I am out of answers for Harold at this point. It seems odd writing in this notebook with no clear recipient to my words. To better explain, allow me to advert my thoughts back to the beginning of the day.

I awoke at six and promptly began my morning rituals. A brief shower turned warm only after I had finished with it. A freshly washed towel rubbed frigid droplets away from my body as I decided on a pair of tan slacks for the day. Married with a tan overcoat, a burgundy sweater completed the outfit. A hearty breakfast awaited me downstairs; one that my wife, Annie, faithfully prepared for me. Every morning, she hands me a piping plate of Canadian bacon, eggs over-medium, and a slice of freshly toasted bread. After devouring the familiar meal, my lips tasted the perfume on Annie's neck just before carrying it to her lips. My son, Thomas, finished his breakfast as I gave him a light pat on the shoulder. He would be off to school shortly after I left the house. Thomas is a bright lad. Nine years old now, he brings home shockingly high marks on his report sheets. To be quite honest, I couldn't tell you where the boy gets his uncanny intelligence from. Though bright, Thomas still has quite a bit of growing up to do. His tenth birthday shortly after the New Year should add a bit more discipline to his shoulders.

I smiled as my wife and son sipped white juniper tea with their meals. With a nod goodbye, I buttoned up my overcoat and began the brief walk to work. No one in my family drinks coffee; and for good reason too. I am the owner of Tappling Teas, a homey little herbal shop that sits just a few blocks from my home. I open for business at 7:30am every weekday and Saturday, excluding holidays of course. Since early November, it has been difficult to spend adequate time with Annie and Thomas. I've been finding it necessary to keep the shop open late the past few months in order to prepare for Christmas. Thomas handed us quite the extensive list of new toys and gimmicks he wants to have this holiday season. He won't receive everything on his list, of course, but Annie and I decided we needed to make it up to him for last year's inadequate amount of gifts. My mother was sick during last year's holidays and it took near all of our saved funds to pay her medical bills. By the Lord's will and my own coin, she has recovered and is still with us today.

Annie and I have found it challenging to recoup financially. Spring and summer were manageable with the additional income from selling a few extra homegrown herbs, but these winter months are proving much harsher on my wallet. There is also the fact that I have spent a good deal of money in attempt to prove Harold's sleep deprivation to him.

Mere days ago, I tried speaking to the fool about filling a prescription for sleep-aid medication. He didn't fancy the idea in the slightest, saying that medication would only serve as a temporary and unreliable fix to his much more cryptic problems. He babbled on, as he usually does, intensely growing more defensive. "Why choke on manmade pills?" He bickered. "So the unknown can murder me in my sleep?" Paranoia is always the period at the end of Harold's sentences.

I am both curious and fearful for Harold. He continues to deny reason and modern medicine. I may just have to get the sleep medicine myself and invite the chump over for dinner. When he's off in the washroom, I'll break up the pill and slip it into his meal; much like a master does to a disobedient mutt. But of course, therein lies another problem. No doctors will write a prescription for Harold without actually *examining* the man for themselves. Not to mention the fact that deception between friends does not typically strengthen the bond of the friendship. My struggles with convincing Harold to see a doctor have been worse than pulling a rotten cavity with a pair of rusty needle-nose pliers. Faith tells me that he will come to his senses, but doubt weighs heavier than hope these days.

I order the bulk of my tea leaves through a local distributor on a weekly basis. As I wrote a moment ago, I even grow a few of the herbs and leaves myself in the warmer months. As for my rarest and best-selling blends, I order them from a middle-man who's got connections with a few gents in Japan. How do you think Harold came about those instant coffee packets? I of course recommended caffeinated teabags to him in the beginning, but he scoffed at my suggestion. "Not strong enough," he said, waving his hand impatiently at my finest homegrown green blend. "Not bold enough, Johnny!" I swear, the only thing that bloke does is complain.

I take no pride in supplying Harold with the exact opposite drug that he actually needs. He sees caffeine through different eyes; calls it a 'natural aid' to his problems. Poor guy practically *begs* me to keep instant coffee on my order form. Hmm . . . yet another quality that equates Harold to a dog. I sense an ill-conceived pattern here. In any case, I can often slip a few extra items into my shipping order as long as I've got the coin. I plan on speaking with Anthony, my international connection, about acquiring some sleep-aid pills to send over in the next shipment.

Finances, relationships, business; they all swarmed for my attention as I arrived at my shop sharply at 7:15. Fishing for the store key in my overcoat pocket, I realized I had trumped the sun by more than a half-hour. December days bring lagging sunlight and early darkness. The lock snapped in the cold and I gave the door a hard push. I stepped into the shop and reconnected the bolt with the woodwork behind me. You really can't be too careful these days; even one's own neighbor will betray you if given the chance. I retrieved the cash till from the safe in the back room. As I secured the drawer in the front register, I noticed how badly the storefront needed tidying. The cobwebs of shivering spiders demand I clean each night before closing, but one tends to slack when he works twelve hour days with no other staff by his side. Admittedly, the place still looks quite beautiful aside from the dust gathering on the lighting fixtures. The layout of the shop itself has not changed since my father opened it for business decades ago. Domestic teas are displayed on shelves against the left wall and atop the front counter, whilst foreign blends are organized alphabetically to the right of the doorway. The center table contains a few combination gift baskets I invented myself, as well as a dwindling supply of leaves I grew by hand earlier in the year. The rare teas are kept in the back room for my 'special' and 'interested' customers. The best of these foreign treasures are too ingenious to write off without a proper description.

The peculiar blends sometimes come pre-packaged, but the best of them are handmade by yours truly. I take the time to meticulously break down each ingredient with a mortar and pestle. My favorite of the homemade blends is titled *Hazed Forest*. Each carefully prepared, potent tea bag contains a mixture of green and black teas direct from Japan. A bit of nutmeg and a pinch of yerba mate leaf are mixed into each pocket-bag as well. The most delectable of the ingredients is salvia divinorum. This precious psychoactive plant is near impossible to come by in London, especially during the frigidness of bastardized winter. Once ingested, the plant wastes no time seeping into the bloodstream. The all-natural chemicals shoot through the body, providing an innocent yet glorious, euphoric sensation. This item is a best seller of mine, as the effects of salvia divinorum are short-lived and scientifically proven to have no addictive properties. When taken in properly portioned liquid form, the drug has a much milder effect that is rarely accompanied by severe hallucinations. I do not advise my buyers to steep more than one bag at a time; nor do I advocate that they remove the contents of the bag and smoke them through a pipe. Whatever happens after my product leaves the store is entirely out of my hands. Through my eyes, I am simply selling my buyers a dream-inducing tea of hypnotic proportions. The idea of offering this blend to Harold has crossed my mind, but I'm not sure if the effects would help or harm his already potent hallucinations.

Another of my best-selling teas is titled *Mauby Marmalade*. White tea leaves are dipped in Mauby syrup, which is made by boiling buckthorn bark and adding cane sugar amongst various other unrefined spices. The tea itself is quite bitter, and is best softened with the squeeze of a lemon wedge. The tea bags contain a mixture of clove and cinnamon, with a light dab of vanilla extract for taste. The formula results in an acquired taste that provides unique sensations of calmness and warmth. Customers often comment that they are spellbound by visions from their past.

I do not consider the distribution of these blends a means of putting a smudge over my own name. I am by no means an experimental drug distributor. Rather, I am a simple tea merchant looking to reach all potential customers. I've already noted my poor financial situation, and any honest business man in this day and age can understand my notions. Alas, these writings are not intended to dabble in my own troubles; they are meant to tell of Harold's.

I stood in the back of the tea shop combining a new batch of *Hazed Forest* this morning when I heard a knock at the front door. Gazing at my wristwatch, I saw that it read only 7:25. Opening my doors a few minutes early certainly couldn't hurt my credibility any. After drying my hands, I stepped out from the back to find Harold standing outside the shop's window. His hands pressed against the glass, he was hardly recognizable through the frost of piping breath. Harold's usual attire gave him away; a well-pressed black suit and subtle top hat behind the clouded glass. I approached the front door, immediately noticing the trouble plastered on Harold's face. He looked terrible; like he hadn't slept a wink since I saw him days ago. I flipped the store sign to read 'open' and undid the impatient lock. Harold squeezed his way through the still-opening door, brushing past me before resting his umbrella upon the center display table.

"Johnny, I need to talk to you" he said as the door clicked behind us. "Harold, we've just been through this," I reminded him. "It's different this time," he said, removing his top hat and resting it upon the handle of his umbrella. His rapidly thinning hair sat as a flat, drenched mop-top from all the sweat and anxiety that his hat had been holding in. "I saw it the other night, Johnny. It revealed itself to me; reached out to grab me." "Wait, wait, wait," My hand shot out to interrupt him. "You saw *it*? What exactly did you see?" Harold scratched at his chest as if he were picking my comment from it like a bothersome thorn. "The ghost," he replied shrewdly. "Or maybe it isn't a ghost. It's . . . it's . . . *something*." His eyes darted from side to side, searching for a better explanation. "The spirit that has been haunting me; I saw its silhouette for the first time. Part of it swarmed around my head, as if trying to enter me. There was hellfire on its breath; vengeance in its cries. I tried to escape it, but tripped on a boot I'd foolishly left in the walkway. My carelessness nearly cost me my life. I need to take better precautions in the future." Harold was exasperated, nearly wheezing as he stared emptily at the handle of his umbrella.

I rested my hand on the door frame, rubbing over a hole that a nail had once called home. "Harold," I began. "I honestly think that it's time you see a doctor for yourself. If you won't do that, at least listen to the medical advice that I've gathered for you. Did you read the notes?" "Yes, I read the bloody notes!" Harold snapped, banging his fist against the tabletop and sending a few of my homegrown white blends drifting to the floor. "And they're all the same shit, Johnny! The same jargon in every one of those damn notes! How am I supposed to find sleep when *it* visits me nearly every night?! "Harold!" I shot in. "Calm yourself, please! No one is coming for you here, alright? It's morning now; you're safe in my shop." He stared with white eyes for a moment before shaking his head in his hands. There was a bitter silence as he bent down to pick up the tea that he had spilt. "Sorry Johnny," he grumbled beneath cigar stained breath.

I walked over to Harold, bending down to help pick up the tea bags. "There is no cause for your outlandish behavior, "I said. "You and I have been good acquaintances since the week you moved into the city. You can trust me, Harold. I simply feel that you need to look into every possible explanation for these sounds and images that you are experiencing." We stood up straight, Harold with a knot in his neck. If there is one thing I've learned about Harold when he is in this panicked state, it is to never accuse the haunts of being imaginary. He'll act is if there is cement in his ears if you do. What I *have* been trying to do lately is act as if these haunts are in fact real. My reassurance tends to calm him down enough so that he can rationalize his own thoughts. I never speak in a manner that puts doubt into his sanity. If I keep moving forward from here on out with this mentality, there is hope that we will one day see progress in his behavior. "So you saw the figure, then?"I asked. Harold nodded.

Harold told me the tale of what he'd witnessed: the banging upon the window pane, the supposed footsteps coming increasingly closer, and the lightly colored dust particles he called a ghost. If you ask me, the crazy bastard got spooked by his own shadow in the moonlight. I've heard of talking to one's own shadow before, but of attempting to fight it? No, no . . . I can't say I've heard much mention of that before. Of course, I couldn't tell Harold that. *'Reality'* I kept thinking to myself. *Encourage Harold that the ghost is a reality. With reassurance, maybe he can move past this.*

"Why didn't you come to me yesterday?" I asked Harold. We sat behind the counter now. "Yesterday was Sunday," he replied. "You weren't open for business." I threw my hands up, letting my pants catch them as they fell. "Jesus, Harold. Are we all business talk these days? What's going on in that cluttered head of yours? You should have come to me yesterday; you no doubt know where I live." Harold paused a moment, clearing his throat before replying, "I didn't want to bother you at home with such private matters. Sunday is your only day away from the tea shop, and I didn't want to ruin it with my burdens. Annie and Thomas don't need to be bothered with my problems either." He paused for a moment longer, rubbing at the corners of his lips. It was a habit he'd formed whenever he felt anxious. The light perfume of tobacco was vaguely present. "But I suppose I could have asked you to lunch or something of that nature . . . and we could have talked then," he finished, flicking dark bundles of dead skin across the room. The front door opened as I gave him a playful smack on the shoulder. "You should have; and you will from here on out."

It was nearing eight o' clock now, which is usually the busiest hour of the day. The first customer bought a few pre-packaged tea bags, which is admittedly odd for a morning purchase. The next few clients came in a stampede. I'd been so busy talking to Harold that I'd forgotten to fetch the vacuum flasks from the back room. These wonderful inventions, created over in Germany, were made available for public purchase nearly a year ago. Since then, they've allowed me to keep my tea bubbling hot for elongated periods of time, thus bringing in more business and saving everyone from having to drink lukewarm tea. I asked Harold to fetch the three brews I had been steeping in the back. He did so, and I guess I got so caught up in the morning rush that followed that I forgot Harold still required my attention.

My establishment is one of the most conveniently located tea shops in all of London. Neatly packed in the western corner of Central Square, it is I and three other shop owners that box-in the town's clock tower. Nearly everyone in the area passes through Central Square on their way to work at dawn, making us prime locations for business. Honestly, what is better than a fresh, piping cup of tea to warm your walk to the factories on a frigid December morning?

There were a few moments of downtime here and there. Harold assisted me by handing over cups when customers wouldn't bring their own. I figure he must've gotten bored after a while, as he picked up his top hat and umbrella before disappearing into the back room. When the morning rush finally slowed, I called out for him. "Harold!" I shouted once more, but he neglected to return the call. I peered out the front door, grazing for any inbound customers. It appeared clear for the time-being. I grabbed the handle of a near-empty vacuum flask and stepped into the back.

There, I found Harold gazing into a shipping crate in the far left corner of the room. "Harold," I said again. "Find something you like back there?" Harold reached into the container, wrestling with the straw before bringing out a fistful of instant coffee packets. "No, no," I said, setting the flask down on the blend preparation table. "You have enough of that stuff. I just sold you an entire box two weeks ago. You can't possibly be out." Harold stared at me with a mischievous glare, still clenching the packets tightly in his fist. "Jesus, Harold!" I called. "You drank them all already?" I turned and dumped the garbage-like filth from the flask into the trashcan. The smell of minty garbage overwhelmed my nostrils. "That stuff isn't very easy to come by, you know. When that crates gone, I'm not sure when I'll be able to get another in. Regardless, you know that sleep deprivation is a huge concern for your condition."

I gave the flask a quick but thorough rinse and took the nearby teapot off the boiler that Harold had thankfully put on for me. "You know I believe your stories, Harold. I don't think you're insane or anything of the sort. All I'm saying is that you could benefit from getting more sleep. You can't rely on caffeine for the rest of your days, you know?" Pouring the water in the flask, I threw a handful of brotherly teabags inside and twisted the lid back on. I gave it a good swirl before setting it back on the preparation table. I turned to find Harold standing there in the same statuesque pose, giving the same hopeful grin. "How much?" he asked.

Harold dropped the packets back into the crate and reached further down into the straw. With a shuffle of the hands, he brought out one of few prepackaged wooden-boxes of instant coffee. Each box held forty packets. "I'm not out of them quite yet," he said. "I've got about four left in the pantry, but I don't want to run out like I did with candles and kerosene last night. I was unprepared." I stood with my hands at my hips. "You were unprepared?" I asked. Harold nodded and walked closer with the box. "And what happened?"

Harold stopped, looking into the eyes of the doorway. "Nothing," he said solemnly. "Nothing horrid happened last night. But tonight . . . tonight is still to be decided by what some call fortune. If you want my advice Johnny, toss that disgusting peppermint tea into the garbage pail and brew something with real flavor. The smell alone is enough to make me choke. Now I think you have some impatient customers waiting out there." He brushed against me, slipping a few bills and coins into my shirt pocket. I'm not sure how much it was; I threw it into the register without ever counting it. Despite Harold's wishes, I returned to the front of the store with the freshly brewed flask of peppermint tea. Three customers stood at the counter, none of whom looked very happy. Harold was gone. I set the flask back on the counter and returned to my post. "Sorry to keep you waiting," I said. Thus the monotonous chores of everyday life continued.

The remainder of the work day dragged on in an all-too familiar blur. I enjoy creating new teas and providing them to my customers, but honestly, the slower part of the days really get me down. I did quite a bit of thinking about Harold during these slower times. There must be some other way that I could help him. I'd tried reasoning with him, I'd tried making paid doctor's appointments for him; I'd even gotten him dozens of diagnoses and written notes from local doctors. But then I had a wonderful idea; one a bit out of the ordinary. I closed the shop up at 7:30, leaving the flasks to sit stale overnight. I figured I'd come in a few minutes early in the morning to clean them.

As I wrote earlier, my home is only a few blocks from my tea shop. Doing a bit of a jog up the steps to my front door, I greeted Annie with an eager smile and a kiss on the cheek. "Honey," I said to her. She looked up at me with those auburn eyes, setting a hotplate of scalloped potatoes on the dining table. "I'm going to need that to go tonight." Annie looked up at me, a bit of a puzzled expression at first. She caught on quickly though, giving me a lip-covered sigh. "Harold?" she asked me, though she already knew the answer. "Harold," I said.

It isn't betrayal if a man tells his own wife a secret, is it? I mean, she *is* my wife. We are supposed to share everything together, so why not this? I just didn't want Thomas to catch wind of it and grow concerned; after all, he'd grown quite attached to young Harold. The fact that Harold was so great with children always seemed quite odd to me, especially considering he was now twenty-eight years old and didn't have any of his own. Actually, Harold had never even spoken of any sort of love interest to me. I'd tried to set him up with a regular customer of mine before, Margie, but he didn't seem to be interested in the slightest. Anyways, I have confidence that Annie would never blab Harold's secret to anyone.

Annie wrapped my meal in a blanket of tin foil and kissed me goodnight. I stepped into the living area and briefly asked about Thomas's day at school. He's a bright boy; never failing to impress me with his grades. "Where are you going?" he asked, noticing my still-fastened boots. I paused in the doorway, my back against the doorframe "I have to work overnight tonight, son. I'm running out of homebrewed teas and I need to make more before the morning rush." I moved for the front door, but was interrupted by Thomas's shrill, childish voice. "How come you didn't do that today? Like when you didn't have any customers?" I was at a loss for an answer.

"Your father had customers all day. It was a busy day for tea-drinkers, I guess!" I said with cheer. I knew how corny and weak of a lie it was, even before it left my mouth. "But I heard you say something to Mom about Harold?" he asked as I opened the front door. "Um," I hesitated, looking to the floorboards for an answer. "Yes," I said, finding one. "Harold's a bit sick, Thomas. I have a new batch of tea that came in today. If I get it mixed up tonight and bring it to him, he can hopefully get a good night's sleep and feel better by morning." Thomas looked at me with fooled eyes. "Oh," he said softly. "Can I come with you to see Harold? I want to wish him a speedy recovery; I've been learning . . ." "Thomas!" I interrupted with accidental sharpness. "You know your bed time is in less than an hour. I will tell Harold that you wish he felt better. After school tomorrow, come down to the tea shop and we can talk about whatever you wish to then: school, Harold, tea, anything."

I hated to disappoint my own son, but I certainly couldn't tell him the honest truth; it would break his heart. And so I left. It was nearly 8:00pm then, and Harold would be leaving work in a few short minutes. He worked seven hour shifts at the printing press, stamping newspapers from 1:00pm through 8:00pm. It didn't pay much, but it was enough for a single man to get by comfortably. My timing was perfect, as both Harold and I had about a fifteen minute walk to his house. I remember he'd said that he had run out of candles, so I swung into The Wax Parlor on my way over. The over-perfumed atmosphere gave me a nauseating high. I picked up a few unscented long-stick candles and hurriedly made my way out of that clustered gas chamber. My feet carried me a bit faster in order to make up for lost time.

When I arrived, Harold's house still appeared dark inside. I leaned against the flickering lamppost just off to the left, resting the Wax Parlor bag beside me. The place looked horrible, like he hadn't done a bit of work on it in months. Then again, my judgment could have been swayed by the hideous, swampy winter that surrounded me. Thus far, we've seen no trace of snowfall this year. As I pondered the unusual weather pattern, I realized just how cold the night had gotten. The thermometer couldn't have read more than negative six degrees Celsius by now. Just as my body began rattling against my coat, I spotted Harold walking towards me from down the street. I picked up the bag of candles as he stopped in the sidewalk before his house. A bit of frost escaped my lips as I waved to him. Harold fumbled in his pockets for a moment before retrieving his house key. Key in hand, he turned and walked towards his front door, leaving me standing alone by the lamp post. He hadn't even seen me.

I jogged up behind him just as the key was meeting the lock. "Harold!" I called out with another raised hand. He jumped, dropping his house key to the stone pathway below our feet. He spun around with the face of a frightened rabbit. "Jesus Christ, Johnny!" he screamed. "What are you trying to do to me?" he chuckled, shaking my hand. He bent over, hurriedly swiping the key from the freezing stone. "What are you doing here?" he asked. Harold faced me now, his eyes squinting heavily under his top hat. "I'm here to stay the night with you." I replied.

Harold looked at me for a moment, unmoving. "You're here to . . . what?" He chuckled again. "I'm here to stay the night with you." I reassured him. "You told me how unbearable the haunts are, so I want to see them for myself. You won't take advice from me, or from any actual doctor in town for that matter. I want to help you pull out the roots of these haunts. I'm only here to watch tonight; to make sure you stay safe. I'll stay up all night, giving you the freedom to finally get a good night's rest. Nothing can harm you as long as I'm looking out for you, and . . . and . . . shit it's cold out here, Harold. How about inviting me inside?" He stared blankly for a moment longer, a bit of a smirk on his face. "Of course, of course," he said. "Where are my manners at?"

Upon stepping inside the home, I could immediately smell the pile of rotting dishes that Harold had been talking about earlier in the day. It reeked of spoiled chicken marinating in stale lime juice. Walking over to the small writing table, I set my bag down on the chair and lit a small tea light that rest on the tabletop. The table's surface was covered in articles and notes; many of which I'd provided him with. "Well at least you've been reading these," I called out to him as he hung our coats by the doorway. "I've been *reading* them," he said. "I just don't believe them quite yet." "Aha!" I snapped with my tongue and fingers, "You said 'quite yet!' That's progress, Harold! You didn't say you'd *never* believe them; you just said you didn't believe them *yet!*" He shot me a smile, kicking off his boots without untying them. "You don't have to do this, you know," he said, walking over to me. "I know that, Harold," I said. "I want to help you." I turned and reached into the bag I'd brought with me, pulling out the two still-wrapped candles. "You said you were out of candles," I said, motioning for him to hold out his hands. He shrugged as I tossed both wax lights across the room. Harold embarrassingly failed to catch either one of them. "Oh," he said in a drone. "Right, I sort of . . ."

"You sort of *what*?" I asked, leaning further back into the tart, dank odor of the atmosphere. He walked over to a small end-table by the kitchen and pulled the drawer open. As I brought myself out of the comfortable position I'd found, I saw that the drawer was filled to the brim with at least twenty-five identical unscented candles. "I stopped as soon as I left your shop this morning," he said. "I wasn't expecting you to come by so I stocked up. I didn't want a repeat of last night; having to rely on nothing but a single dwindling tea-light." He shut the drawer, recovering and hastily unwrapping the two candles I'd just purchased for him. "But that's alright," he said. "We'll use these two tonight and it won't cut into my supply. Thanks, Johnny." There was a certain frigidness in the room I'd never quite felt before. "Sure," I said, blowing out the tea light I'd just lit. "Sure." I suddenly found myself wishing I'd bought scented candles instead; maybe a calming ocean breeze, or perhaps a soothing lavender bouquet.

"Well let's light these so we can actually see what's going on in here, shall we?" Harold said. He struck a match, setting both candles ablaze on the first attempt. I watched as he picked up the articles from the tabletop and moved them to the end table near the kitchen. I retrieved my dinner wrapped in tinfoil from the bag and laid it out before me. "Have you eaten?" I asked as Harold rested the burning candles around the food. "Yes," he said, taking a seat across from me. "I picked up a cut of prepared fish during my lunch hour today. I ate the rest on my walk home." "Are you sure?" I asked, motioning to the greasy potatoes that had been bathing in a pool of butter.  "Annie made these." He declined again. "How is Annie?" He asked. As I ate, we took quite a bit of time to catch up with each other. I told him about Annie's newfound interest for fine cuisine, and then moved on to talk about how wonderfully Thomas had excelled in school. He filled me in on life at the printing press, dodging around specific details. "Still no romantic interest?" I asked him, wiping my lip with a partially used napkin. Harold exhaled, sending the stale aroma of his earlier fish dinner out into the thickness of the air. "No," he said solemnly. "I simply have no interest right now."

I guess I understood where he was coming from. After all, it would be rather embarrassing to invite a woman over for dinner, only to reveal to her that you thought spirits were haunting your home. There would also have to be mention of who would step up for night-watch duty. I really shouldn't make light of Harold's problems; it's just unbelievably easy at times. "I see," I said, crumpling up the tinfoil and hurling it across the room. It made a light patter as it sunk into an empty waste bin. "So, now what?" I asked. We stayed up another three hours, chatting and laughing together. We hadn't done anything of the sort in months. We even took a break to clear a chunk of those dirty dishes Harold had sitting in his sink. He refused my help at first, but I jokingly made him smell the mug he'd been drinking out of the last few nights. That seemed to convince him. It neared midnight before either of us had realized the hour, and I was already tiring. I get up at six in the morning, so naturally I am typically asleep shortly after ten in the evening. Once our conversations had spoiled, we were both left sitting at the table once more.

"When do the footsteps usually start?" I asked, finally coming to the topic of the haunts themselves. Harold shrugged, taking a swig of water from a freshly washed glass. "I never know," he said. "Sometimes they've already been going on for hours now; sometimes it isn't until four in the morning." "I see," I said, pausing to look at the veins running atop my hands. "And what if nothing happens?" I asked him after a moment. Harold shrugged again. "If nothing happens, then nothing happens. The only reason I'm not scared out of my mind right now is because I have company, Johnny. I hate to tell you this, but this nice gesture of yours probably isn't going to work. I'm not sure why I wasn't visited last night, but I'm positive that whatever this spirit is can sense your presence. It longs to have me all to itself. It wants to get me alone; devour me from the inside out." I twisted at the nail of my thumb. "I see," I said again. "So if you don't think anything will happen tonight, how about trying to get some sleep?" I asked. *Snap*, the hangnail tore loose. A shallow river of blood followed.

Harold stared emptily into his glass for a moment. "Come on, Harold," I pleaded lightly, smothering my thumb. "Wouldn't it be nice to rise before noon for once? If you try and sleep now, you could get a full seven hours rest and still be up before the sun. It couldn't hurt to sleep until eight or nine even." He looked at me cautiously. Now it was he who was playing with his hands. "I suppose you're right," he said at last. "I am quite tired. I haven't had any caffeine since the coffee I drank last night. You know that this means you'll need to stay up all night, don't you?" I nodded at him. "Yes, I know." I replied. "It's alright. I want you to get some rest tonight." Harold rose and retrieved a blanket from underneath the end table. "Just don't fall asleep on me," he said with a light chuckle. He moved to the stone of the floor, laying the blanket down first and then putting himself down on it as the fabric wrapped around his body. "Aren't you going to sleep in your bedroom?" I asked him. "That's where it walks from," Harold said, turning away from me and facing the wall.

He didn't waste any time finding sleep. I asked him roughly five minutes later if he was positive he didn't want to sleep upstairs, but he didn't respond. I'm glad I could help Harold catch some rest tonight. I hate to see a good friend of mine suffer from such paranoia and insomnia. Harold may be a bit crazy at times, but that certainly doesn't make him a terrible or helpless individual. It's just after three in the morning now, and he hasn't stirred from his sleep once. As for myself, I'm finding it a bit difficult to stay awake. The writing has kept me busy for quite a few hours, but I fear I am out of events to record for now. I haven't noticed any supernatural activity whatsoever, which just confirms my suspicions that Harold is merely seeing creations of his subconscious. His brain is so devoid of sleep that it does not know what to do with itself whenever it helplessly drifts off for a mere second or two. His brain scrambles to compensate for these short dozing gaps by creating the very sounds and images that he's been describing to me.

I was going to earnestly try and stay awake the entire night for Harold, but it doesn't look like he is going to be waking up any time soon. He hasn't flinched since he found sleep more than three hours ago. I could convince myself to drift off for an hour or two before I am required to rise for another day of work at Tappling Teas. I don't plan on waking him when I leave in the morning. Harold will be just fine between my departure at six am and the sunrise just before eight. In fact, he doesn't have a choice really. I must open the shop on time, especially if I am to clean the vacuum flasks before the morning rush.

I can only hope that my findings, or lack thereof, will help Harold find some peace with this demon of his. I have faith that I can change him in the next coming weeks. Faith has carried me far these past couple of years, and I hope that I can gift that comfort to Harold for the holidays. I'm not quite sure how to appropriately end one of these journal entries. I suppose there really is no proper way in doing so. Signing off for now, this is Johnny Tappling.

*Chapter Three – Repaying the Favor*
*From the Journal of: Harold Elway*
*December 14th, 1905*

*8:45am*

That son of a bitch; that *Goddamn* son of a
*bitch* Johnny! I should have known better than to
trust that impoverished tea merchant with my own
life. He vowed to watch my house for activity last
night, and let me tell you; he far from delivered on
that promise. Just when I began to think that our
trust was measurable, he leaves me as an offering to
the damned phantom itself.

Last night, Johnny had assured me that he
wouldn't take his eyes off of me while I slept. I
wasted no time in accepting his offer, as I haven't
had a decent night's sleep in months. I've never had
someone make such a ridiculous proposal to me
before; I'm such a fool to think that he could follow
through with it. With my back turned away from
*dear* Johnny, I was shaken from my slumber by a
sharp itch between my legs. Clouds of apple-scented
dish soap tickled my nose as I moved to escape the

blanket. The cloth only wrapped tighter around my body, constricting me and forcing my back against the floor. With a sudden white flash, my vision left me. No longer was I seeing through my own eyes, but through those of a spectator hovering above my own body. An article from the library had described this as an out of body experience. My torso flailed in the cocoon I'd created for myself, only serving to tighten the armless jacket. The familiar black spiders came from all directions; I was helpless to escape them. In mere seconds, they had smothered my squirming body with their army. A powerless spectator with a foggy brain, I could not save myself.

Swarms of the bastards crawled over my neck and entered the blanket. Still, I watched my physical body kick and swing. My mouth opened to scream, but was quickly filled with arachnids and the taste of peppermint. Without warning, I lost my spectator's view and my vision was sucked back into my own body: Only I could not see the outside world.

The following is unlike anything I have ever experienced before, and is far beyond anything I ever believed to be fathomable. I could in fact see *inside* my own head, as if my eyeballs had spun around to be a spectator to my own brain. The inside of my skull looked as if a depression-era artist were painting it as I dreamt. The entire right side of my brain appeared to have been painted a sparkling cyan blue; the same color as the spirit I'd seen nights before. Spiders clung to the bone and tissue around my head, spitting webs to weave bridges to the right half of my brain. The left half was grey, appearing lifeless. As the spiders worked, snow-like particles drifted down from the ceiling. The flakes that touched the right side of my brain immediately engulfed in flames. As for the left half, the snow melted as soon it made contact. I could do nothing but stare in tranquility, as if my brain understood and accepted what was happening. This phantom snow appeared to have no purpose other than to comfort me. Without warning, the familiar ghost emerged from a ridge in the lifeless half of my brain.

The spirit twisted in its cyan smog, somersaulting into itself and appearing to vomit its own body back up. The figure was again faceless; having no physical form apart from the atomized fog. *Tick, tick, tick.* The sound of my pocket watch reminded me that I was not fully dreaming. One eyeball spun around, kicking my eyelid open to watch the darkness in my living quarters. The sound had not been enough to fully wake me. I was still partly dreaming; seeing reality through one eye and the dream through the other. The spirit twisted itself into the shape of a lanky hand; a form I had seen before. With a nauseating tickle, it stretched its fingers across the entirety of my brain. A quick, filthy massage turned violent as the spirit's fingers clenched together. I tried to scream, but felt only hot air reach the brink of my throat and reverse back into me. The taste of peppermint was now stale; the smell of dish soap non-existent. My mind begged for me to shout, "Johnny, Johnny, wake me up!" But my open eye could see only the dark ceiling of the real world. I then feel my stomach tighten; my spine crack into a thousand pieces. The spirit releases its hold on my mind, acknowledging the spiders' presence. It grabs at the strings of silk and rips them from my brain, and I fully wake; screaming.

I let out an exasperated, horrific shout as my sight returns completely to the living quarters. Sleep paralysis releases its hold on me, and I scramble to my still-numb feet. I notice Johnny asleep in the dining chair, his head resting on his shoulders and his mouth wide open. I take an angry step towards him, but my feet are not ready to walk. I crash hard to the floor with a *BANG, BANG, BANG*, at the front door. "Johnny!" I yell, but he does not move. The clatter comes again without patience. "Johnny!" I scream once more.  Johnny snorts a wad of thickened snot into his nose, but he does not wake. *BANG, BANG, BANG*. I crawl to wake him, but something pulls at my ankles. I kick the numbness and the perhaps imagined hands away. I fear for death, adrenaline pushing myself to my feet and into a full sprint for the front door. My hand grasps the handle; the spirit rattles. *BANG, BANG . . .* I thrust the door open before it can finish. A cold breeze coats the sweat over my arms. The figure stands before me in full human form, its face hidden behind sheets of long-flowing hair.

The figure releases a long moan of pain, barely forming a word at its end. *"Harold."* A woman's voice calls my name, her breath more frigid than the winter air. In a trance, I reach out to part the demon's hair. "I . . . I . . ." There were no words to be found within me. She brushes my hand away, whispering something inaudible beneath her breath. The spirit drifts backwards. With a wave of her fingers, she beckons me to follow. As I step forward, she lashes her hand out and grabs hold of the door handle. In convulsion, she pulls the barrier shut. The door slams in my pasty face, the chain-lock banging against the wooden door frame with a heavy *clack*. Johnny wakes at the table with abrupt snorts and yelps.

Johnny's arm had slipped throughout the night and knocked a candle on its side, creating an eerie puddle of wax that had dripped down to the floor. "Johnny!" I shouted, latching the door and bolting to the other end of the room. "What in God's name happened?!" Johnny asked with a yawn, rubbing the bags of his eyes. He noticed the spilt candle but did not move to put it upright. "Harold, Harold, I . . ." he began. "You fell asleep!" I screeched, reaching for his shirt collar. Before I could grab him, he knocked my hands away and shot to his feet. "Harold, I'm sorry," he apologized with a note of shrillness. "What do you expect? I haven't slept in over a day. I work twelve hour shifts. Besides, it seemed like you had dozed off pretty deep. I was up until three in the morning, or somewhere around that hour." Johnny continued pitching excuses to me, but they were all nonsense. I trusted him with my life last night, and that mistake nearly got me killed. I showed him the way out of my house shortly after five this morning, luckily before my anger got the best of me. I'm not sure if he went home for a quick hour of sleep before work or not. He was already wearing his best outfit from the day before, so I imagine he just walked to Tappling Teas and did a bit of tidying up. He complains enough about never having the time to clean.

Alas, that was all hours ago. It is nine o'clock in the morning now. Since the early hours, I've been feeling a bit of guilt for what I did to Johnny. It's not like it's his job to protect me. But he offered, didn't he? And when someone extends an offer and you accept it, they should follow it through to the end. I suppose I do give him credit for staying up until three, despite the fact that I've been exceeding that hour for the past few months now. Still, I feel as if I should apologize to him; perhaps at the end of the day. For now, I am going to make a mug of instant coffee and think things over a bit. I've already had a cigar burning for the last half-hour now.  I may leave a few minutes early for the printing press and stop for a revitalizing cup of black tea. Oddly, part of me wishes to see snow today.

*9:00 pm*

Old Johnny seems to have his head stuck up his own rear about last night. I strolled into his shop just after noon, an earnest smile pasted onto my face. Now, I've been given the cold shoulder before; but that uppish bastard wouldn't even recognize the fact that I'd walked into his shop as a client. I stood in line like every other customer, and when it came my time to place an order, I asked for a cup of his finest black blend. He poured the brew for me, and then proceeded to hold out his hand without ever saying a word. Johnny never makes me pay for tea, but I could understand his bitterness. I reached in my pockets and hunted for a single coin, but that apparently wasn't good enough. He motioned inwards with his fingers and waited until I'd placed another coin into his greedy palm. I paid nearly twice as much for my tea as anyone else. As he slid the mug to the edge of the countertop, I asked, "Johnny, why don't we talk a bit later in the day?" You know what he said to me? "Next customer."

I stood off to the side for a moment, patiently tapping the floor with my umbrella until the store had emptied. "Listen, I'm sorry I lost my temper this morning," I said to a still oblivious Johnny. "You can't possibly understand what it meant to me that you offered to stay awake, but you put my safety at risk." It was still as if I didn't exist. "I was visited again last night. The haunting began in my sleep and carried itself into the real world. I saw the phantom again . . . it revealed itself to be a woman." The door opened, and Johnny immediately greeted the customer with cheer. The door opened again, and then once more. Before I could continue, Johnny had yet another long line of thirsty customers; many of whom flocked to the homemade blends at the center table. I bit back a grin the best I could.

The lunch rush put me short for time; I needed to get to the printing press before long. Johnny's behavior had once again angered me. "You act as if you are a child," I said, my patience gone with a swing of my suit coat. "Thomas is much more an adult than you." The remark was intently snobbish. I cannot deny that in that moment, I was trying near my hardest to fill Johnny with anger. My ironically childish insult seemed to do the trick. Johnny dropped his coin-begging hand, letting it slam against the already splintered wood of the countertop. "I am a child, Harold?" he stammered, the smell of creamy body odor hitting me hard. "I'm a child because I offered to help a good friend? To push my personal health to the backburner and completely disregard the wishes of the family that I hardly ever see? I sacrifice a well-deserved sleep to put *you* to bed; would you rather I had read you a fairytale too? You'll have to excuse me, Harold, if I am a tad bitter for being tossed out of your home before dawn on the coldest day of the year thus far. I was at the shop more than an hour early this

morning, not to mention the seven hours that still lie
ahead of me before the day is over. I twist my own
arm to help a desperate, supposed friend; and I am
the child?"

I admit; Johnny's fiddling lecture caught me
off-guard. Stale whiskey stained my lips, buying me
a moment of time to conjure up a rebuttal. "Is a man
not supposed to keep to his word? You made a
promise to me, and you couldn't even follow
through with the simple task of staying awake. You
failed me, Johnny." He interrupted me then, "And is
man not supposed to be able to sleep in his own bed
without fearing imaginary monsters? What do you
know about fulfilling promises? Have I not done
enough for you, Harold? I bit my tongue ordering
that crate of coffee for you, yet I let you practically
steal it from me for next to nothing every single
week. You want the rest of it, Harold? Go ahead and
take it; go ahead and rob me blind!"

Johnny's insult had sent an echo rattling
through the room. Where there was once malt, I now
tasted blood on my upper lip. The customer at
Johnny's counter, an older gentleman, had been
caught in an awkward position between the two of
us. "There's no charge. I'm sorry," Johnny said,
handing the tea to the gentleman. "Can I help you?"
he asked the middle-aged woman standing next in
line.

"You think we're bloody finished?" I
snapped. "I do," he returned sharply, twisting his

torso to face me. "You're costing me business. I've done nothing but try and help you, Harold. And now I don't know if there's any one out there that can do that. Maybe you can't be helped. Maybe there's a reason you're seeing this horrific spirit. Maybe your hat sits too tightly around your enormous head; or perhaps your umbrella's shoved a bit too far up your own back end. Or maybe; maybe you're just bloody crazy."

They say that everyone has a boiling point. *They* surely aren't mistaken, because Johnny had reached mine. Lucky for him, the tea in my hands had been boiled much earlier in the morning; because I dumped the entire lukewarm cup over his fat, balding skull. As busy as Johnny was, you'd think he'd like to keep his products warm for his customers. Isn't that the point of using vacuum flasks? The only reason he even *had* hot water the other day was because *I* put it on for him. I expected Johnny to throw himself into a toddler's tantrum, but instead, he actually mannered himself quite well. Honestly, I didn't give him much time to react. I left the spillage for him to clean up on his own time. With a mocking tip of my hat, my hand met the glass of the door and I was on my way to the press. As I left, I could hear the woman at the counter yelling something awful. I truly hope she was beyond pissed at him.

The walk to the press was the most beautiful I'd ever had. Everything felt so real, as if the blank white sky revolved around me. I embraced the arctic air, letting it fill me; cleanse me. For the first time in a long while, I felt hopeful. Sadly, the misguided adrenaline left me as soon as the printing press came into view. Work was only part of my reality. This spirit, this woman; *she . . . she* was my reality.

I get along with the guys at the press, but I suppose I don't know any of them well enough to invite them out for a drink. The gents asked me to meet them at the pubs once, but I'm really not much of a beer-drinker myself. I prefer my whiskey straight and my gin and tonics with a generous amount of gin. I wouldn't quite fit in with a crowd of factory workers. Imagine them carrying on in their grimy slacks, me sitting in the middle with my best suit and a diluted spirit in my hand. Any choice beverage of mine costs nearly double what they'd all be drinking. Besides, liquor always offers me a different state of drunkenness than beer. Beer leaves you feeling light and carefree; specifically stupid if you ask me. Liquor, on the other hand, tears open your mind. It allows you think about the world and its origins; the leaves in every tree and how they came to be. Simply put, liquor tends to brighten my vitality. Beer usually leaves me through the very same hole I shoved it down.

There is one gentleman I work with, Abel Anderson, who has the qualities to be a fairly bright and potential friend. He is a few years younger than I; a lonely bachelor as well. He only began working for the press about eight months ago, but I've shared more intelligent conversations with him than anyone else in that ever-rusting hole.

Industrialization is now on the rise, and I'll admit it's leaving tensions high at the factory. I fear not only for my own job, but that Abel will be left without a job to support himself as well. Word around the factory is that soon, the presses will not even need the touch of a human hand to operate. Of course, they will still need to be monitored and maintained, but that leaves a large portion of my coworkers out of a job. I suppose I am not terribly worried about myself. If I were to be let go tomorrow, then I would just find another job; or perhaps take up agriculture.

Oh, who am I kidding? I couldn't grow anything in this forsaken lot of a back yard. That grass has been sick ever since I can remember; at least it and I have something in common. I think I may ask Abel to go out for a drink with me one night soon. If I learn that he is someone I can trust, I will let him in on the secret of my haunts. Still, I have bickering hopes that all of this turmoil between Johnny and I will blow over. I bet that by tomorrow we've put this all in the back of our minds.

I am going forward from this point in time with a bit of a different attitude towards the spirit. This morning, I nearly opened the 'practically stolen' box of instant coffee I got from Johnny to restock my pantry, but then I had quite a different idea. The beginning stages of rest last night were luxuriously pleasant, until the sleep paralysis and visions kicked in of course. I think I will take my chances this night with the phantom; but I'm not going to do it alone. I sort of *borrowed* something from Johnny while I was at his shop yesterday. He'd gotten so busy with customers that I became bored and found my way into the back room. There, I saw he had just finished mixing up a blend of tea that smelled inescapably inviting. A handful of tins sat next to the pestle; some of which had already been filled with bags. The blend is a little something Johnny titled *Hazed Forest*. I am examining a filled, borrowed tin now as I write this description: "An enthralling concoction of green and black herbal teas combined with nutmeg and yerba mate. The shining light in this tea is the inclusion of the plant Salvia divinorum. This psychoactive plant increases alertness to the outside world just before easing the user into an effortless night's sleep."

After last night's activity, I am certainly more frightened of the spirit than I have ever been before. I have hopes that the out of body experience was nothing more than an ill-placed coincidence. I can be positive now that there is only one demon. Whoever this poltergeist is, she has much more to tell me, and I believe that she will not attempt to harm me until she has gotten her message across. I am headed downstairs now to boil a pot of water and steep two of these teabags for five minutes. Hopefully matters can be sorted out with Johnny, but I fear he may have noticed by now that I've borrowed a tin of his rare herbal blend. I'll pay him back later. I always do.

*11:15 pm*

The night creeps onwards. An hour ago, I drank a double dose of *Hazed Forest* tea. The effects have been dissatisfactory to say the very least. Squinting eyelids made me believe that I was growing drowsy for a moment, but it turned out to be nothing more than an incoming sneeze. I wonder what all is in this tea exactly? Is Johnny required to list each and every ingredient? I ran some tap water down in the kitchen sink earlier and the liquid appeared to have mercury-like qualities. It looked remarkably thick; a bubbly paint texture with a shimmering silver hue. Upon letting the water run across my hand, it felt the same as any regular old water. All I know is that I am left severely disappointed with this 'enthralling concoction'. How does Johnny get away with marketing this trash as sleep-inducing euphoria?

Boredom and senseless pacing lead to the sorting of the medical documents I'd taken from the library. Amongst the books was a guide to medical botany; the medicinal uses of natural plants and herbs. I looked up salvia divinorum in the index and found its dedicated page. This medical encyclopedia advocated the psychoactive effects of the plant much more than it mentioned its restful qualities. But I suppose at this point, I am desperate for any sort of help. The book said that if I were to smoke the plant rather than drink it, the effects would hit me at a much faster, much more aggressive rate. I have an old corncob pipe in the nightstand beside my bed. I admit that I am bit leery of going up to my bedroom at this hour, but I will carry a candle in each hand. I've never been much of a pipe-tobacco user, but I have used the pipe from time to time in past days. I know that satisfaction all boils down to personal taste, but the robustness; the masculinity that accompanies a cigar can simply not be rivaled by a petty hollow vegetable. The hours are dripping by again. As long as I am able to find more peaceful sleep than I did the previous night, I will consider this experiment a success. I hope to write in the morning about a peaceful night's rest.

*12:05am*

The words in the page . . . are dancing for me! How wonderful! It looks like that big 'H' is waving at me! Hello H! Hello! H. H. H. H. Haha! Look at all the friends I've got waving to me now! I thought I saw a bloke skipping his way down my street just a few moments ago. The streets, of course, are made of stone; cobble stone. Corn on the cobblestone; how dirty would that be? What if all the roads were made of corn kernels? Surely they could survive in winter, but summer? Oh no; never summer. There would pieces of roadway popping up everywhere! Since I mentioned air, mine is beginning to get a bit thick. Oh; oh my. It feels like I've got kernels stuck between by gums. I'm trying to dig them out with my big nail. You know; the big finger. The uhhhh . . . thumb that is attach . . . Now I am bleeding - All over the table; all over the pajamas. The same pajamas I've worn every night for the last . . . how did I come to the subject of corn kernels? Damned corncob pipe. I need to clean this bloody mess up. But how great is this?! No fear of that washed out phantom! No cowering in the rat holes for me tonight! This tea is best drunk through a pipe in the form of smoke! This is the best idea I have ever had! No, really; I need to clean this up. There really is blood flooding my mouth and it's just awful. I'll be back! I will return! Do not go anywhere! Of course you can't go anywhere; you're a book.

*1:30am*

This has been one of the worst ideas I've ever had in my entire life. One moment I was dancing around the living quarters; the next, I found myself sprawled out all over the filthy kitchen floor. The sweet lady moon beyond the window tried her best to comfort me. Spinning like a hypnotist's coddling watch, that great big orb stretched her arms out to embrace me. My own arms left the cold, worn floor to greet her. As we almost touched, the limbs of that

anorexic oak swatted my lunar love away. Her
curdled milk eyes spurt a tear as I waved goodbye.
My sleep paralysis from the other night was like
child's play compared to the effects of this blasted
salvia. Jesus, I have never been so paranoid; so
insecure, so . . . disconnected from what is real.

      The moon left my sight as I stumbled through
the doorframe and into my living quarters. The
staircase was embalmed in a canary-yellow jelly
mold. I was weightless; free to bounce down them
and nearly touch the ceiling. All else around me
appeared as if it were made of paper mache. The
possibilities of what could exist outside my front
door were far too tempting.  Unfortunately, it was
this very temptation that sparked the quick
downward spiral into sickness. I do not know if it
was the sudden rush of frigid air, or if it was due to
the head-wrenching appearance of that damned,
flickering lamp post; but I fell drastically ill once
more. Tar had been tossed across the entrancing
world that had been crafted for me. All that was
beautiful to these glazed-over eyes had been taken
away.

      I spent the next five minutes lying on the
stone by the open front door. The ceiling spun
around my eyes, much like a cyclone of twilight stars
that I knew could not exist. There were blotches of
whiteness, and then suddenly; a sea of tenant black
spiders flooding the stairwell. I could smell the
sizzling poison of their venom; taste the hair of their

legs as they grazed my tongue. With numb feet, I sat up to reach the banister; but the drugs would not let me. My back hit the floor again, hard. I was a shell-less turtle rocking back and forth, fully exposed to let the swarm crawl up my pajama bottoms. Stability argued with the floor, but I didn't have time to wait for the first punch to be thrown. Rattled hands grabbed at my waistline, thrusting my pajama bottoms down to my feet. The hair on my privates and legs were indistinguishable from the clusters of arachnids. My nails broke skin, drawing blood from the abused scars on my thighs. My left foot beat itself senseless into the banister until it was numb with redness and bustling with sores.

As the forgiving paralysis quickly swept itself from my body, the taste of my own regurgitated air welcomed a slew of coughs and gags. Feet still willing, I stood. My pajama top had been torn open, leaving my drooping bare chest exposed to old man winter's breath. I cut the coldness from the room just before searching the stairwell for the march of spiders. They were nowhere to be seen. The room spun around me, as if I had mounted the blades of an over-clocked windmill. Using the banister railing to keep myself upright, it was a slow, miserable drift back into normalcy. God, I must have looked so foolish; standing stark naked with war gashes all across my legs and feet. Johnny really ought to put a warning on that salvia stuff that discourages buyers from removing the tea from the bag. Perhaps I should have read closer into the book on medical botany and waited more patiently for the *easing* effect it described via liquid ingestion.

Alas, the worst is over for now. As I slump into my writing chair, my brain cringes with delirium. Sometimes I feel as if my mind whispers to me; tells me that it fears paranoia but has nowhere else to sink into. I am afraid of sleep, but I know that I cannot prevent it in the coming minutes. I have already dropped my pen twice now since I began this update. Though paranoia bickers with better judgment, I am going to rest in my bed tonight. I could not tell you when the tightly tucked sheets were made last, I only understand their seductive calling. A candle will burn brightly on my nightstand and fill the entire room with safety. It has been only moments since the intensified visions left me, but I still feel the smoke spinning around inside of my lungs. I have the stark feeling that my night is far from over, and that those precious satin sheets are nothing more than a deathtrap.

*Chapter Four – A Hypnotic Warning
From the Visions of: Harold Elway's
Subconscious
The Early Morning of December 15th, 1905*

*Harold.*

Hehch hesch . . .

*Haaaarold . . .*

Eeeeeeeeeeeaaasy. You don't want to;

*HAROLD!*

*That seemed to wake you, didn't it?*

I told you not to wake him like that.

*How else am I supposed to do it; a gentle kiss on the cheek?*

Well maybe that wouldn't be such a bad idea.

*Jesus, no wonder you make him so soft.*

*Well, I . . .*

*Enough; please. I'll have to disappear if you won't hush up.*

Alright, Alright.

*You agreed to let me talk to him; he has to know.*

Well I just can't believe the damn fool hasn't figured it out yet.

*That's what I'm here for you bloody idiot.*

But really, how does he not know? Ha; heh . . .

*You can't answer that for yourself? Of course you can't; not in that state anyways.*

What do you mean "Not in that state?"

*Look at yourself; you're blazed out of your damn mind. Well you really don't have a mind. You sort of . . . are his mind; his conscious one anyways. You know what I mean. Why am I wasting my time talking to you anyways? I don't know how long I'll have with him.*

Oh was it the tea then? The stuff he tore outta that porous bag and jammed into that veggie pipe?

. . .
*I told him not to do that. I really did.*

*Well he did it alright; and that's why you're a rambling mess right now. Why don't you give it a rest while I try and speak to him?*

*Harold! Can you still hear me? Hell, I don't know if he can or not. It's so light up here where you live. I don't know how you stand it.*

What do you mean? I thought it was quite nice. I . . . I need to sleep for a bit.

*Yes, do us both a favor.*

Listen to me, Harold. I am everything that is bad within you; everything that is stinking, rotten, and sinful. I am the feelings you long to forget and the hearts you've forgotten about breaking. Every bad decision you've ever made has stemmed from my hands. Every ounce of guilt that has seeped through your pores or tickled from the corners of your eyes; I put there. You may call me a bit of an irrational genius.

I am in every ounce of liquor you've ever downed. I enter your lungs through every obese nightly cigar. Your body can't cleanse me or filter me out. Why, Harold? Why can't you simply forget that I exist? Because you've been letting me out quite a bit lately. You seem to enjoy playing with the hands of darkness. And I know that you have every reason to hate me; to despise me even! But we seem to find ourselves lost in the thickened fog of a decision. You're standing on the railroad tracks just waiting for the five o'clock train, Harold. Yes, I am the one that put you *there; but now I need you off of them. Harold, you have to listen to me! There's nothing I enjoy more than watching you make poor decision after poor decision. But I need you. You're my . . . host. You're like that old haunted home that I can't seem to move out of; that old, useless dog that I just can't seem to shoot. If you die; I die. We all die: You, me; even the old religious conscious that's sleeping over there in the corner.*

*Sometimes I can't even control myself. There are times that I have no authority over the thoughts I send through you. But you, Harold; deep down inside of us; you know what you need to do. You know the reason why you're being haunted. You have forgotten that I hold every single one of your repressed memories. All of your darkest secrets swarm within my body. But if you cannot accept that these images are real only to you and no one else, then you will never live to see thirty. It will continue to haunt you until the day you die; and even then the groundskeeper will swear he feels a cold breeze every time he passes your grave. You must find it, Harold. Deep within yourself; you must find it. Apologize to it. Be sweet to it; kindly offer it your hand. Impress it, caress it; move closer to embrace it. Then slit its throat and watch your freedom gush from its windpipe. Through remembrance you can kill it. Through repression and forgetfulness; it kills you first.*

Hech Hech . . .

*Goddammit. I thought I had longer until he regained his senses. Tell Johnny, Harold. Tell Johnny! But before you*

*can tell him, you must remember it for yourself!*
*Remember the bliss -in an envelope beneath the fourth*
*stair from the floor. You haven't forgotten; I know you*
*haven't. It awaits your apology, Harold. Even if that isn't*
*good enough for it, it's worth apologizing to. Both of our*
*lives depend on it. You wouldn't have tucked that envelope*
*away all those years ago if you had intended for us to*
*forget everything that brought us here.*

*It's a bit funny, really. As I sit up here in the*
*conscious light, watching your eyes dart back and forth*
*through the frantic workings of sleep, I can't imagine it*
*any other way. I don't mean to be an ol' pansy, Harold,*
*but sometimes you need to love your imperfections in*
*order to survive. No matter how much it pains you, the*
*consequences will only get worse from here on out. The*
*haunts will get worse; the voices will get louder. The*
*banging at your window panes and the crest of your door*
*will grow stronger each night. What you saw at the door*
*the other night was a gift from yours truly, friend. You*
*must stare your mistakes in the eyes before they let*
*themselves back into your reality. Just because you packed*
*up what little belongings you had and fled from*
*responsibility does not mean that you have evaded guilt.*
*Guilt is a powerful, relentless bastard; and it does not play*
*fairly. Guilt has driven many men insane. Guilt becomes*
*your God. You can't let that happen, Harold. If it does, I*
*will be powerless to help you. I would no longer be able to*
*control myself, nor any part of you or what visions you*
*see. You must emerge from the fog. Acceptance . . .*

*Hech Hesch hech . . .*

    *I can feel my voice becoming increasingly distant from you. Your eyes are slowing down a bit. It is almost morning. I doubt you will weaken your conscious mind with drugs enough again so that I may speak to you further. Remember, Harold; fourth step from the floor. You know where it is. The thousand nails you've hammered there can't keep you from it now.*

    Harold? Harold. Jesus Christ, Harold! Wake up! How could you fall asleep in your bed? The sunlight is coming through the kitchen window now. The phantom could have killed you last night. What were you thinking?! You know it always comes from the stairwell.  You know better; you should have known better. Tell Johnny you slept up here. It might comfort him. It might give you something to start the conversation with. God, you should probably apologize to him. Are you still sleeping?
    What if Johnny never speaks to you again? What if he's so pissed at you that he won't care to listen? Who will you talk to then? Do you have enough candles in the downstairs table drawer? Oh shit, Harold! Shit, shit, shit! The candle's burnt out over night! You are beyond lucky that it didn't come for you last night, you know that? And you still haven't gotten any kerosene, have you?! You'll have time before work today; don't worry about a thing. I'll take care of you as I always do. Maybe you should invest in a phonograph? Hearing some big band music

might keep you awake through the night, you know? Those machines aren't too hard to come by now. Still asleep - how incautiously rude of you. Wake up Harold! WAKE. UP!

## Chapter Five – An Unmannered Gentleman
### From the Journal of: Johnny Tappling
### December 18th, 1905

It has been more than four days since I last spoke to Harold. From what I hear, I'm not the only one whose been missing him. Harold must have mentioned me to his mates at the printing press, as one of his coworkers came into the shop asking if I'd seen him this morning. Abel Anderson, I believe his name was. Nice enough fellow with only himself to watch out for; reminded me much of Harold actually. Abel told me that Harold has not shown up for work at the printing press since Monday. His coworkers are growing concerned, and frankly quite annoyed with Harold's disappearance.

I must admit that this news causes me to feel a bit uneasy as well. After all, I think I am the only real friend that Harold has. He confided in me with his embarrassing yet deepest secret, so our friendship must amount to *something*, right? I can't even fool myself; I miss the poor bastard, even if he *is* slightly insane. I closed the tea shop for lunch today and headed over to Harold's house to see if I could speak with him. I know it wasn't the wisest decision in these poor financial times, but sometimes personal matters are more important than pants weighed heavily down with coin.

I picked up a small container of kerosene on the way over to Harold's. Though I was sure he had gotten the oil for himself by now, I saw it as a bit of an apologetic gesture. The walk to his house was purposefully slow, my nerves scrambling to form an immaculate apology. You see, I'm not very good with sappy, dreary rhymes or speeches. By the time I got to his house, I had come up with nothing more complex than handing him the kerosene and giving his hand a firm shake. The apology would be mutually understood, I thought. The town's clock tower struck two in the afternoon as I approached the front door.

Within a few short steps, a clamber of jazz music pummeled my eardrums. I hadn't noticed a phonograph when I was over at Harold's earlier in the week, but perhaps something had convinced him to purchase one since then. *Whatever* he had playing sounded God-awful to my poor ears; so much so that I thought they might begin leaking blood at any moment. Still, I approached the door and set the kerosene to the side of the doorstep. A whiff of stale shoe polish blew up from under the cap. I cleared my empty throat; you know, one of those fake, placebo gargles of air that calms the nerves. It would have been easiest to simply leave the kerosene at the door for him to find later. I mean, he *is* the one who dumped a cup of lukewarm seaweed tea over my head for no good reason. My conscious reminded me that he could desperately need my help, though. After all, I am his only real friend. Before my angels and demons could bicker any further, I took a final whiff of the kerosene air and beat my fist against the door.

There was no answer. Once more I struck the wood, and then again. Three times total my fist beat upon his door. "Harold!" I attempted to break the vocal barrier between us. "It's Johnny! I must speak with you." My voice felt muffled; lost in the ricocheting waves of the phonograph. So again I banged upon his door; *BANG, BANG, BANG*. The force sent a quickened numbness through my wrist. And then Harold screamed.

"I've said my apologies!" He hollered. "I told you long ago to leave me be! I remember Goddammit; I remember! What more do you ask of me?" Thick, buzzing trumpets added rampage to what could be heard of his suffocated voice. What a crude way to manner himself. Here I am at his doorstep with a mouthful of apologies and he doesn't even have the decency to crack his door. I was angry now; beyond pissed. I gave the door a final, judicial *smack* before walking away in a mist of my own violent steam. Harold began yelling again, but I couldn't make out what he was saying. I didn't care to. I left the kerosene at his door, which I'm sure he's found by now. Now that I think about, I should have kicked the tin over and soaked his patio in lamp oil. If he has any sense at all, he's on his way over here to apologize to me at this very moment.

It is quite discouraging to realize that today has been less than eventful; a complete failure, in fact. Most other fathers spent this beautiful Saturday at home with their faithful wives and tireless children. But as for myself? I was glued to the store all afternoon, selling room-temperature tea to other lonely folks who poked their heads in my door just to see a forced smile. I didn't profit more than a pen's width of bills today, but it is still *some* compensation I suppose. Abel was at least kind enough to buy a fresh cup from me. He stayed and chatted awhile, mainly about Harold. Abel is a tall man, maybe a few inches taller than I. He wore a red and black checkered flannel shirt that was torn down the right side a bit. An impressive beard embossed the better-half of his face. He kept a few single bills in his shirt pocket, and I did not see any bulge in his back pocket from a throbbing wallet.

Though Abel questioned Harold's whereabouts, I didn't give into his inquiries about his mental condition. Abel mentioned that Harold had been acting a bit strange around the factory lately; being even quieter than he usually was. He said that he'd asked Harold to grab a few brews with him on a handful of occasions, but that Harold would always shrug off the offers or act like he had too many other things going on. Abel described Harold as somewhat of a ghost; a shadow of a man that really only exists in the background and in the mind. The whole time he spoke, I couldn't help but stare at the ruggedness of that man's beard. I mean, really? If he finds a wife, I wonder how she will put up with such a mountainous bird's nest of a face.

Come to think of it, I don't know how my wife puts up with my own faults these days. The guilt I feel for putting Thomas and Annie beneath my work has been tremendous lately. I have the opportunity to make it up to them next weekend, though. It *is* Christmas, after all. Annie went down to the general store yesterday and picked up a good amount of toys that Thomas had asked for. Still, I feel like I have not spent sufficient time with them in months. This year, I left a stack of bills on the dresser-top with an accompanying note that it be used for Christmas shopping. By the time I get home these days, I eat a late dinner with the family and it's only a pair of hours before we are all tucked into bed. I suppose I do get to talk to them for a bit in the mornings; but it isn't nearly enough. I keep reassuring myself that I will find time for my family after the holidays are done with; it's really the only thought that keeps me going. As long as there are no further unforeseen expenses, we should be able to get by on my regular work hours until next holiday season.

I've been debating back and forth with myself on whether or not to get Harold a gift for the holidays. I could get him a nice basket of bold teas and candles; or perhaps a more ear-pleasing instrumental piece for the new phonograph would be suitable. My willingness to purchase him a gift all depends on his attitude. I've made my effort at apologizing and am now leaving the outcome up to him. I don't mean to sound childish, as Harold so politely described me, but I'm simply exhausted. The days crawl on, but seem to shorten with each new sunset.

I am lying in bed next to Annie now; it's barely past ten o'clock at night. It seems all I do anymore is wake, work, and sleep. At least tomorrow is Sunday. After church, I may take Thomas and Annie out for a nice meal with the bit of money I made today. Ferrero's has a new Italian course that Annie has been begging to sample. Come to think of it, she asked me about it weeks ago. I do hope that they are still offering the course. Ferrero's has a bit of something for everyone; their staff a pleasing, friendly incentive.

As I lay here next to my wife, I can't help but notice how beautiful she looks illuminated under the candlelight. I am a lucky man; lucky enough to have a woman who has kept up with her appearance even after being joined in marriage. She works hard to look decent for me. If only I were a better husband, I'd spend more time grooming myself properly rather than worrying about finances all of the time. I know that she appreciates the dedication and the work I put in, but I see my own neglect in her eyes; hear it in the cracks of her voice. With every meal, there is a bit of disappointment baked into the dish. Annie should be able to talk to me about anything; and I feel like we are strictly business these days. My God, our relationship is becoming much like Harold's and mine.

Admittedly, there isn't much I can do at the present moment. Many of my family issues will have to wait until after the holidays or I will surely find myself in an inescapable guillotine of debt. It's been . . . I can't even begin to remember the last time we were intimate together. There have been a few forced instances since my mother's illness, but I couldn't put a date or time on them. By *forced* I don't mean that I put myself upon Annie; simply that we looked at each other up and down and decided we were due to be intimate. Perhaps we've simply lost the molding that holds our relationship together. Thomas is the most important thing to her; and ensuring that they both have a decent way of life is what is most meaningful to me. Maybe I can learn something from Harold after all. I thought this journal was a ridiculous idea at first, but now I see it as quite a useful tool.

I can use my writings as a method of venting, and it won't judge me for my mistakes or imperfections. This paper won't spin around on me and throw insults into my face; nor will it tell me to be a better man or to pay more attention to my family. It simply listens; absorbing every thought I put into its body. As I write this, it slowly dawns on me how useful of a friend Harold is to me. He is sort of like this journal, though he can give me actual useful feedback. I suppose I act as the very same to him; when I'm not ridiculing him of course. God, I guess the heavy workload has really gotten to me lately. I've been a terrible advisor to him. Maybe I will invite him to lunch with the family tomorrow; extend another hand and see if he grabs it. I know he won't act foolish in front of Thomas.

But why would he not show up to work at the press? What I've said or done couldn't have possibly upset him that much. And I have never known Harold to be a music connoisseur. Why would he sporadically invest in such expensive equipment? Unless he's using the phonograph machine to keep himself awake, that is. All of this pressure between us is juvenile and downright unnecessary. When I see all of this foolishness written down on paper, it speaks volumes to me. I need Harold and he needs me.

I must sound like an awful mess in this log. I suppose that's because I truthfully am a mess. I feel as if I am knee-deep in a swamp, mud cluttered between my toes. I'm trying to move in the right direction, but my finances and friendships are holding me to a much more cautious pace. Here I am rambling on and on about random problems and concerns in my life, when I have a wonderful wife and a brilliant, healthy son to be thankful for. I've got nothing to groan about. Harold is the one that needs real help. I've decided to invite him out to eat with my family tomorrow. I'll leave early in the morning and jog over to his house. If he won't answer, I'll simply leave a note with the time and place to meet. I won't give up on him, because I know he would never give up on me.

*10:10pm*

    Harold is proving to be a 'tough nut to crack', as my father would say. I still remember it like it was just the other day; my father would come through the front door at a quarter after six every night. An ebony briefcase swinging in his left hand, he'd rest his cane in the tin can next to the door and call through the house, "Something seems to be missing!" And he wouldn't leave the door until my mother and I would come and greet him. He would embrace me each night, and he wouldn't even think of talking about his day until he'd heard how ours had been. God, I miss him. He's been gone for more than six years now. I've been wondering a lot lately as to how I steered so far away from his morals; what made him a real man.

    I'm there for my family, but I'm always first to complain about a rude customer at the tea shop. Annie and Thomas always seem to come second to my own problems. I don't do it intentionally; God knows that I don't. I suppose it's the lifestyle I've been living, the same one I'm sure these pages are tired of hearing about. But my father was a great man. He caught the putrid lung disease back in late 1896. He lived past what the doctor's said he would, but I still lost him too soon. If he were here now, he'd know how to help Harold.

I am glad, at least, that Harold had the pleasure of meeting my father before he passed. Harold moved here in 1897, just a short year before my father left us. In fact, he was with us the first time that Harold and I met. My father, of course, is the founder of Tappling Teas. I was still working under his wing at the time, even though I was near twenty-four years old. I had been working at the shop since I was old enough to count petty change and fake a smile. I loved it. I would stop by after school twice a week and help my father close the store down each evening. He would let me keep a few coins for myself so that I'd learn the value of money at a young age. Not like I could really help it, but shows how much good that lesson did. He would always say to me, "Son, no matter how important money seems to you right now; remember that people are more valuable. If you trust in people and build strong relationships, then the money naturally finds you in a genuine way."

I remember the day that I met Harold clearly. It was a rather frigid October afternoon, the wind bustling through freshly-turned amber and citrine leaves. I watched as weightless petals drifted towards a browning ground. My brief vision of decaying beauty was shaken as a bell rang and my eyes left the window pane. The tea shop was packed with customers. I barely kept pace at the register as my father boiled fresh pots of water in the back. The line of eager customers wrapped tightly around the display table. Deep in the line, a woman bundled in snow-white cotton scarves sighed loudly, causing me to look up and see the most peculiar man opening the door. He took one step inside and ran his head right into the side of the damn doorframe. I remember because he tried to brush his forehead off like it hadn't actually happened. It made me chuckle, reminding me to slow down a bit and make sure I was still providing my customers with a smile.

As customers came and went, I watched as young Harold, around twenty years old at the time, crept awkwardly slow around the store. He would peer inside a basket of tea, look around nonchalantly, and stick his face almost entirely inside of the basket to get a good smell of the herbs. I watched as he did this over and over again with every single type of tea we had out for a display. For a split second, I thought he might be trying to steal from us; but I soon realized he was nothing more than a curious lad. There was just something about his mannerisms that kept me laughing during the busiest of times. He must have stayed in the shop for near forty-five minutes before he finally picked up a handful of teabags. Even though his hands were full, he waited off to the side of the display table until every other customer had left the shop.

"Hello," I said to him, kindly motioning him up to the counter. He seemed surprised at the sound of my voice. "Oh!" He jumped slightly. "Hello. I . . . I just need to grab myself a few of these. Very nice day, isn't it?" He was blatantly nervous; almost like he'd never dealt with another human-being before. My father brought a fresh pot of tea out from the back and set it on the countertop. I can remember the spice of the cinnamon blend rising with the steam and tickling my nose. "And that," Harold pointed at the pot. "I'd like a cup of that too. Please." As I was calculating the price for all of the tea he was purchasing, which by the way I hadn't seen anyone buy this much tea in my entire lifetime, I couldn't help but ask him; "Are you alright?" I questioned. He jumped again. "What do you mean?" he asked. I finished adding up his total as he reached for his wallet. "You just seem a little . . . confused." I said. "Well I should be," he said promptly. "It's only my third day here." "I figured as much," I said. "American?"

I knew the answer before he even responded. Of course he was American. He looked and talked like one. He walked and breathed like one. It didn't hurt that I'd spotted a wad of American bills in his wallet either. "American," he said, as if my guess had pleased him. "Why move all the way here?" I asked, taking his only few European bills into my hand. He shrugged as I counted them. "I suppose I just like the atmosphere better," he said. And that's all there really was to it. "Well let me know if you need help finding anything around town," I said, handing him his change. "I've been here all my life." He looked at the coins in his hand. I could tell he had no idea if I'd given him the right amount or not. "Thanks," he said, grabbing his bag from the counter and turning to leave. "My name is John," I said. He didn't return the greeting; he merely waved with the back of his hand and walked out the door.

"Interesting chap," my father said, placing his hand on my shoulder. "Just a bit," I responded. His grip was strong. "He sure enjoyed the scents of all our teas though." I chuckled, filling my father in on Harold's peculiar behavior. As I write this, I find it distressing that Harold no longer enjoys experimenting with different teas and flavor additives. I mean, the man buys unscented candles for God's sake. I can't possibly imagine how boring that must be. You light the candle, and there's just . . . there's just no satisfaction to it! With respect, he has been buying black tea from me a few times a week for years now. I suppose he has grown comfortable with all that is familiar; the routine, grinding clockwork of life if you will. Now, he is afraid to mix anything up; almost like I am, now that I think about it. Alas, I digress.

Back to that day - I can remember walking around the store adjusting baskets and tidying up. The next big rush loomed overhead, and it wasn't long before it hit. Back behind the counter I went, and back into the preparation room my father walked. My next customer was Margie, the very same girl I'd try introducing Harold to countless times in the near future. She brought her washed, empty cup up to the counter. "Hey John," she said. Her voice was smooth, sliding into me like gently-aged bourbon tickling the pit of my stomach. I always told myself that if I hadn't married Annie, Margie would have been my main infatuation. That would have never happened of course, as Thomas was almost a year old by this point. Annie and I had gotten married when I was only twenty-two. "Did someone leave you a tip?" she said, handing me a black leather wallet.

There was nothing fake about Margie. From her natural fingernails to her glistening blonde and curly hair, she was a genuinely stunning woman. I took the wallet from her outstretched hand and set it off to the side. Margie's perfect pale lips parted, and my mouth opened to speak. "How are you and Annie?" she said. I bit my tongue.

Margie and I chatted for a few moments, about generic politics and family life. As we shared laughs, we both remembered the other customers standing in line behind her. "I'll let you go," she said sweetly. With a smile, she picked up her tea and turned for the door. I didn't care that she hadn't paid for it. As more customers filtered in and out, I couldn't help but keep my mind on Margie. The store emptied soon enough, and I was back to watching autumn decay outside the store window. My father stepped out from the back after awhile. "Did someone leave that?" he said, pointing at the wallet I had set off to the side. "Yeah," I said. "Not sure who though." My father looked at me, almost as if he were disappointed. "Well, look and find out. Then go and give it to him." He said. I stared at him for a moment. The stone in his eyes was always sincere; that of a genuinely caring man. "You want me to go and give it to him?" I asked again. He continued to stare at me with the same stern face. "I know, I know," I said. "People first; then money."

I opened the wallet and immediately noticed the overflow of American bills. I couldn't help but feel a bit overjoyed. I'd relished in the company of that young gent when he'd been here. He was quite . . . interesting to me in a nicely-intended way. "Any information?" My father asked, suddenly appearing behind me, his hand pressing firmly against my shoulder once more. His voice was hot on my neck. I flipped through an assortment of cards before finally finding a crumpled piece of paper with a scribbled address on it. "This could be his address," I said, showing my father the paper. He took it from me, reading it quickly before looking out the window. "That's less than fifteen minutes away from here," he said. "Wouldn't hurt to take it there and see if that's the owner."

And so I put my coat on and headed towards the house with the crinkled address in my hands. Truthfully, I was happy to experience October from anywhere but a window pane. I passed several dressed houses littered with toothless jack-o-lanterns. A plain, virgin pumpkin used to stand for the celebration of harvest, so I figured these mutilated gourds must be a symbol of the death of that harvest. People around town would leave them out in their front yards until Thanksgiving, or even later sometimes. Our family never celebrated Halloween. My father always saw it as "The Devil's Holiday," celebrated only by those who devoted their lives to Satan. Even as a child I knew that my father was exaggerating this old fable he'd created on his own. Halloween is, and will always be, just an innocent holiday for us to all dress up and pretend to be something we're not. I may not have taken the best advice from my father at times, but I was especially careful not to take this piece.

I carved pumpkins with Thomas the first year he could hold a sculpting knife. As a matter of fact, this year was the first ever we hadn't carved pumpkins together in his young life. I bought the pumpkins from the market, and I really intended to sit with him and Annie and carve them; but I guess Annie gave up on me too. As I left for the tea shop one day, I noticed they'd begun to rot on the front stoop. By the time I had come home, I found that Annie and Thomas had given them each faces without me. Yet another mistake I made this year.

Once I arrived at the address, I immediately noticed the peculiar decorations that robed the house. A plushy scarecrow was nailed to a wooden cross near the mailbox. A frown had been slit across its face, where white stuffing vomited from the holes. More than a dozen jack-o-lanterns, already lit for the night, lined the walkway to the front door. It was the strangest array of festivities I'd ever seen; enough to both impress and confuse my twenty-three year old self. "This has to be his house," I remember thinking to myself with a guilty grin.

I approached the lightly dolled-up shack, admiring each separate grin on the jack-o-lantern's faces. As I got closer to the front door, each facial carving looked more frightening than the one that lied before it. I reached the stoop, pausing for a moment to admire the final jack-o-lantern. The gourd's eyes looked towards its forehead, where a rusty hatchet sat deep in its cranium. Scars littered the nose-less creature's cheeks of blood-orange. The mouth looked as if someone's fist had plowed right through it. A naturally strung spider web ran from the vegetable's stem to the rooftop of the house. It looked fitting; almost as if it were a decoration itself. Just as I reached my hand out to knock, the door flung open. There stood the peculiar man from the tea shop, almost as if he'd been waiting for me;

watching from a nearby window. "Johnny!" he cried with both shock and pleasure.

"John," I corrected him, reaching into my coat pocket for the wallet. "Right," the man said. "Like I said - Johnny!"No one had called me Johnny since I grew out of nicknames more than a decade ago. My father would call me by the name every now and then, but only when I'd done something wrong. "What are you doing here?" he said, balancing his thin board of a body against the door frame. I removed my hand from my coat pocket, extending his wallet out to him. "You left your wallet at the tea shop," I said. He took the billfold from my hand, opening it quickly and examining its guts. "Didn't steal any money from me, did ya?" he said with a sarcastic smile similar to that of the jack-o-lanterns behind me. "N . . . no . . ." I began. The gent gave me a good chuck on the shoulder, closing his wallet and returning it to its home in his back pocket. "I'm just messing with you," he said. "A bit of good old American humor, right?" We paused with the silence. Finally, he shifted his arm to unblock the doorway. "Would you like to come in?" he asked.

I looked behind my shoulder, nonchalantly nodding to the butchered scarecrow. "I really shouldn't," I said, returning my attention to the doorway. "I have to get back to the shop." The chap looked at me up and down, as if he was sizing me up. "So you came all this way to give me my wallet back?" he asked. "I shrugged slightly, feeling the warm air inside my coat escape out its bottom; a colder air took its place. "Yes, I suppose so," I responded. "Now that's how you do business!" He said with a heartfelt smile. "I know you need to get back to work, but you keep that address you took out of my wallet and keep it safe. You're welcome back here any time." "Thanks," I said, stretching out my hand. The man shook it promptly, before I even had the chance to fully extend it. "Harold," he said. "My name is Harold."

I turned away from the house, and I remember getting the oddest feeling that Harold and I would one day become close friends. Since that day, he began stopping by Tappling Teas on a regular basis. He was always asking for the most interesting flavors that we had in stock; begging for blends with more and more floral notes to be exact. Of course, this all comes before I began creating my own blends and receiving shipments from Japan. Back in the day, we always sold out of our self-grown blends in a matter of hours; something that my father was extremely proud of. He babied each plant as they triumphantly grew in the garden out back. I still make an effort these days, but I suppose I've never put as much time or love into the plants as my father did. Since he's passed away, I typically only plant a fraction of what the earth used to produce for us. When my father died, I swear a bit of that garden died with him. Even in the years that I've sewn more,

I could never get more than half of what I planted to be of any use.

I suppose that I've let the quality of our products dwindle throughout the years. I'm guilty of using imperfect tea leaves to fill up empty spaces. Some of the leaves are a dying mustard yellow color; others are far beyond dead and drenched in dreary grey. I blame it on my hectic lifestyle once more. I truly do care about my father's legacy and the quality he upheld; it's just hard for my supply to match demand at times. While I can only imagine how disappointed my father would be in me, I saw real disappointment in the eyes of his past daily customers. "It doesn't taste like what your father used to brew up," they'd say. Most of them gave me a couple of chances to redeem myself, but they were let down every time. Eventually, the old-time regulars stopped coming.  At one point, they were all true friends of my father who swore that our tea was some sort of uplifting elixir. I'm not sure where they go for their tea these days. I guess therein lies the true reason I began my partnership with Anthony.

Anthony, as I've mentioned before, is my resource who imports exceptional teas from Japan. The most ridiculous but delectable brews come from his trades. Many are steeped with various types of tree bark for added flavor. *He* is the one who actually approached me, believe it or not. A few months ago he walked into my near-empty shop and offered his services. I couldn't turn him down, really. What choice did I have? Since he's been getting me new products, I've seen a significant bump in sales and activity. I still haven't had the chance to redeem myself to one of those old-timer bastards, though. None of them have come around in years. Half of them are probably dead.

It seems that Anthony read my mind about the sleep-aid pills I was going to ask him for. He delivered my shipment last Thursday and I found a prescription bottle at the bottom of the crate. Along with the pills, I received three refills on my most popular teas, two new foreign batches to brew and sample, as well as a few extra boxes of coffee packets for Harold. I remember telling Anthony about my 'acquaintance with sleep problems' when I requested the instant coffee from him the first time. He didn't quite understand how caffeine would help with sleep deprivation, so I was forced to explain how my nameless friend would rather stay up throughout the nights than wrestle with sleep. I'm rather glad he included the pills; I can slip them to Harold beneath the table at lunch tomorrow. I don't know if he'll take them or not, but the least I can do is offer them to him. I'm sure he'll be desperate enough one night to take them.

As for myself, I too have been finding it difficult to sleep in my own bed. I know my issues are largely due to my conscience kicking me for neglecting Annie and Thomas lately, but my worry for Harold is playing a huge factor in it as well. I am already more than an hour past my usual doze time.

All of this reflection on my father, my past, and my failures doesn't help either. I'd best keep a rational eye on myself or I may be ordering a few of those coffee packets for my own use! I know I shouldn't joke about Harold's condition, no matter how light the humor is. Maybe all he needs is a bit of comfort like I do? Perhaps he believes these guilty feelings are able to present themselves to him in a physical form? Regardless, this only proves my initial point that the man requires more sleep. Before I develop any unhealthy habits such as Harold has, I am going to blow out the light and take a stab at sleep. My mind feels as if it is stuck in a full-out sprint; only I'm stepping on broken glass every step of the way.

*1:15 am*

I've just swallowed three of the sleeping pills I had initially reserved for Harold. I don't know how else to sleep tonight. Hell, I don't know if medication is capable of soothing the beast of this paranoia.

About two hours ago, just as I was fading off to sleep, a light knock came on the door downstairs. At first I thought that I'd merely heard the wind, but a persistently louder second knock shattered that thought. With a groan, my feet hit the shivering floor. Drowsy hands knocked away still-forming clusters of eye sand. Annie flipped over to face the wall; she hadn't heard the knocking. I tucked my feet into my slippers and shuffled to the hallway. The staircase felt brittle beneath my feet; a hollow carcass to the unkindly cold air. A kerosene lantern shone dimly in the dining quarters. As the washy light blurred my vision, a third knock came at the door. Whoever this chap at my doorstep was, he'd better have a damn good reason for being so bloody impatient at this hour. I flung the door open with my own impatience, expecting to see one of Thomas's school friends standing before me. Although it was late, his mates had been known to come around after ten o'clock on Saturdays. I told them each and every time that Thomas was in bed, but they'd keep coming back time after time again.

I fear that stories of Thomas's classmates will have to wait. My mind clouds with distractions as I attempt to write. It was not one of Thomas's classmates that stood before me, but rather, it was Harold waiting on my doorstep. He stood in a filthy pair of once-white pajamas, his figure adorning the year's first snow twirling behind him. His head was unnervingly hatless, his hair littered with the dandruff of fresh snowfall. With no jacket or trusty umbrella by his side, the man that stood before me was not the Harold that I'd come to know. Drenched in the weight of the blizzard, Harold shivered furiously without sound. As I moved to say his name, his hands rose and a water-stained envelope was thrust into my hands. Its contents were heavy, imitating a thick deck of playing cards. The envelope was worn and showed years of age. Still, Harold did not speak. Hands in the pockets of his pajama bottoms, he remained fixated on the powdered doormat. His hair was an oil spill drowning in an arctic sea. Unmoving, he waited for me to open the envelope that I had been fingering in my hands.

I parted the envelopes lips and pulled its contents into my hand. I was now holding several dozen pictures of a young girl. She was unfamiliar to me, and not quite old enough to be titled a woman. If I were made to guess her age, I'd wager she was maybe sixteen or seventeen? Her hair sat straight at shoulder-length, naturally brown with light sparkles of amber throughout. She was no doubt a pretty girl, though her beauty was stained due to the poor condition of the photographs. A few of the photos were completely ruined by water damage, and many others were faded beyond the point of clarity. They must have been taken before the release of the Browning camera model.

The pictures turned slowly in my hands. The girl wore a floral-print dress in several of the photographs. In one photo in-particular, she held the bottom of the dress up, as if welcoming the wind underneath of it. There was another in which she grabbed at the crotch of the dress, a bashful look forever pasted on her face. The redness of her cheeks was uncannily distinguishable, even through the worn black and white film. At last, I arrived at the last few pictures in the stack. Sitting next to the girl on a park bench was Harold; a much younger Harold. He sat with his arm around her, donning an unwrinkled sweater vest and a pair of black slacks.

"Her name was Hazel Matthews," Harold said, his head lifting from the ground at last. My attention shifted from the photographs to the open door. Harold's mouth hung open, an unfinished sentence lingering on his tongue. Bloodshot eyes, both tired and teary, stared straight into me as the truth finally left him. "And I killed her in 1897."

*Chapter Six – Faithless*
*From the Journal of: Harold Elway*
*December 19ᵗʰ, 1905*

I told him. I bloody told him. Oh, Christ.

What in the hell am I expected to do now? Where am I supposed to run to from here? Oh shit; bloody, bloody *shit*. I knew I couldn't keep my whorish mouth shut forever. Jesus, help me. Jesus, forgive me. God has undoubtedly forsaken me for damning him, but *Goddammit* I messed up. I can't calm down; can't let my guard down from here on out. I grow tired of pacing back and forth across the room, much like the monotonous pendulum of a grandfather clock. What if Johnny tattles my unsung secret? No, no he won't tell. He can't tell. If he does tell . . . I'll . . . I'll . . . oh, hell . . .

Jesus Christ, if you can read this, please forgive me. It isn't like you're oblivious to what I've done, but I beg you to hear my thousandth apology; to numb yourself to the sin I've committed. I'll bow down to you from this day on; slit my wrists and sacrifice my blood to you. I shall drink and eat to your discretion; live every moment for *you*. Christ, please; I call for your forgiveness. I may not have been the most holy of men lately, or even in my entire lifetime for that matter, but know not where else to turn except your feet. I have committed one of the deadliest of sins; worse than gluttony – dire of lust and greed. I know that hell keeps its kindle for me, but I ask that you speak to the devil, let him too know of my apologies.

I'll go to church every Sunday. I'll start going to church every Sunday. I'll pray for every prosperous meal and worship every piece of dried, crusted bread. I'll spit out the wine of your blood with honor into the gold-plated bowl. What more, I'll even spread your teachings across London. I'll . . . I'll help build a church; help build a school. I'll do anything at all; anything to dry this spilt news up. *I* kept the secret; *you* kept the secret for so long - So Goddamn long. And now I've gone and released the deepest skeleton in my closet.

Okay. Okay, okay. Johnny trusts you. I mean me. Johnny trusts *me*; Johnny knows *me*. He wouldn't skin me alive and leave my bones for the buzzards of the law. There's no way he'd tattle to one of his hired doctor friends about this, right? Or maybe he would. Who cares? They don't even know my name. They'd better not know my name. What if he told the bloody Japs? No, no; that's silly. Why would he tell the Japs? He *could* tell the Japs, though.

Listen to me. I sound as if craziness already defines me. But what if I am crazy? No, I'm not crazy. Crazy people act incredibly . . . crazy; and I'm not acting crazy.  Alright, alright – This is all going to work itself out. No one is going to find this journal until I'm long gone. I'll be dead; six feet in the ground, and then what are they going to do? Hang the bones of a dead man? Johnny promised me his silence last night. Even if he does blab, he can't prove that I ever said anything. I'll deny it all. Oh but *God*. No . . . No, I can't hide from God. He already knows what I've done. He will forgive me. He *must* forgive me. I've prayed, haven't I? Muttered my fair share of apologies and paid into faith?

. . .

I cannot fool the wrinkles in this paper. I will not be saved. Shit, I don't even know if God is real anymore. I've been a non-believer verging on agnosticism for years. But please, do not think ill of me or call me damned just yet.  Don't think I'm such a terrible person for doubting the Heavenly Father that so many put their empty faith into. I simply think that if a higher being existed, he or she would have somehow intervened in my path by now.

I used to blame God for the crime I committed. I used to stare into the mirror and say "God made me kill that little girl; God made me do it." And I'd look harder into the mirror and say, "God made her want my body. God caused the drool to dribble from her chin to my chest. God coaxed her towards me, and she submitted; she obeyed." Never have I been more wrong. Slowly, painfully: I stole the faith from that girl and placed it in myself.

I moved to London eight years ago in an attempt to escape the horrid crime I'd committed. I tried to push the murder out of my memory for a few months; but the guilt persisted. Every waking moment, I heard her screaming in either pain or pleasure; there was no longer distinction between the two. She was a beautiful, nasty girl. Cute as a cherry blossom, her roots were grounded deeply in the curiosity of filth. I was her first; her only true love. Leading her to the bedroom wasn't easy for me, though. It took months to get her comfortable enough to stand bare before my eyes. Once she had me for the first time, she became an addict. She came back to me night after night, begging under the American stars for me to bed her. I was a young, testosterone-fueled man back then. There was no wrong in what we did. We were in an oath-sworn relationship, where couples make love without question.

At nineteen years old, it began as an innocent game for me. I'd never been much of a ladies' man. Attractive enough? Sure, I'd like to think I was; but I typically kept to myself. I'd been out of school for more than a year before I met Hazel. My sister had sent me to pick up her order of flowers down at the Petal Grove Florist - Two dozen tulips. I had never fetched an order for my sister before, thus I arrived clueless as to where to begin my search. I'd never set foot in any sort of floral shop before; why would I? Lost, confused, and slightly pissed, I am stuck blindly peering through a sea of lilies and daffodils attempting to find tulips with the name 'Elway' on them. Just as annoyance finds me, there is a light tap on my shoulder that near makes my heart jump into my windpipe.

I turn around to see a blossom more beautiful than any flower in the entire nursery. Hazel stood before me, a white apron sitting atop her grass-green long-sleeved shirt. She was elegantly covered with dirt. "Elway?" She asked, smiling and revealing a set of glistening pearl teeth. "Elway," I said, captivated by the shimmer of sapphire in her eyes instead. "My sister sent me."

"I figured," she said, motioning me to follow her to the front counter. I didn't even know this girl's name yet and I was already tripping over my own feet. I'd soon learn that she had just turned sixteen. I couldn't help but stare as her hips swayed back and forth, back and forth. She moved with I liked to call 'sexual class'.  It wasn't as if she was begging for me or anyone else to gawk at her, but she naturally carried herself in an attractive manner. She swung through the wooden gate behind the cashier's counter and continued to the sunroom. In a trance, I held the gate open with a push of my hand and began following her into the back. She hadn't noticed that I had followed, and began singing a bit of a tune.

"La lala, laaa . . ." She hummed, her voice cleansing my ears like a purifying blast of spring-water. I watched as she grabbed the trays of flowers from the table to her right. "Oh!" She said with a turn, cutting her melody short. "You weren't supposed to . . ." I suddenly realized what I had done. "Oh," I clapped, embracing the awkwardness. "Sorry, I . . ." But she interrupted me. "No," she said with sweetness. "It's alright. You looked a little lost out there; not like I should expect you to know where you're going." We exchanged smiles.

From that day forward, I picked up every order for my sister, Claire? No . . . Carrie . . . *shit.* What is her bloody name? I shall refer to her as Claire. Claire was heavily into gardening. Our back yard was always lush with fresh produce and hypnotic flowers. One summer, she planted sunflowers right outside my bedroom window. I'd wake up every morning to the sight of a dozen glistening suns sparkling through the glass. Though the area's weather wasn't ideal for flowers like this, they'd always find their moments to shine.

The third time I picked up a floral order, I finally held the courage to ask Hazel for a night out on the town. She didn't hesitate. "Yes!" She squeaked, like a cute little mouse with a neatly tied bow in her hair. I was no longer a virgin thanks to a girl in the past years of my life, but my lust for Hazel felt like something special. I wasn't just out to bed her until boredom struck. I saw her face everywhere;

anywhere I went. When she finally agreed to celebrate our relationship physically, it was nothing short of entrancing. As I mentioned, she turned into quite the addict after that. So you see? We weren't just partners. We were lovers. God, I loved her.

And that's where God and I found our differences. After the *incident,* I packed up my belongings and moved to London in a matter of weeks. I found an advertisement for the very house I live in now in a newspaper I stole from a gentleman on the train-ride over. Right next to the advertisement was a 'help wanted' snippet for the printing press I still work at today. I've heard people say before that starting clean is hard to do. Maybe that's true for one's conscience, but I had a new life set up in London before I even arrived.

I tried tirelessly to push the memory of what I'd done to the back of my brain. Months of the calendar deteriorated until I realized that this notion was more than impossible. I'd hear those screams; feel those nails slide down the drapes of my spine. But back then, I knew that the guilt was all in my head. And I'd blame God, I'd say, "God, please forgive me for hurting that girl. I didn't want to do it. She made me do it. No, she was innocent. You made me do it, God. You live within me and it was your home within me that did it. Why have you forsaken me, God?" And another month withered away; and then another and another until the anniversary of Hazel's death was behind me. I saw winter murder and baptize London three times until it finally struck me. "God didn't make me kill that little girl. I killed her. I Killed Hazel."

And from that point on, I began asking God for forgiveness. "I'm sorry I blamed you, Lord; I didn't mean for my guilt to come across like that. I take responsibility for what I did and I ask for your forgiveness." Night after night, month after month, I went on praying without so much as a speckle of light to show that God had heard me. I wanted him to reach his hand down and say, "Harold, it's not your fault, son. You didn't do this with purpose. I forgive you. Anger is in our nature. You gave her judgment just as I do every day," but *no*. God never answered me. He had forgotten me.

In the final earnest prayer I ever said, I whispered, "God: If you can hear me - kill me where I stand." He did not, evidently. It took a bit of time, but this lack of a holy response slowly killed my faith. God wasn't talking to me, and he sure as hell didn't kill Hazel. I did. And then I began to see things in a more individualistic sense. I was; I am, responsible for my past, present, and future. I can control tomorrow just as much as I can control today. God would not grant me a new life: No, I would grant it to myself. And so I secretly renounced my faith. God no longer had a part in my life.

So why do I still speak to God at times? Why do I still use the Lord's name, whether it be in fright or vain? I suppose it is because a tiny ounce of faith still bubbles in blackest part of my heart. I can't be sure if there is an afterlife or a God, but to be safe; I never convince myself to officially declare that there is or isn't. I grew up in a Christian family and I admit the guilt of betrayal can still sting. What would my father think; my mother and sister? I suppose it doesn't matter now. I've already let them down. I never told them I was leaving. I just . . . left. And I haven't written or spoken to them since.

I pray to protect myself; I still talk to Jesus as if he has his ears on the railroad tracks. Hell, maybe he does; so who am I to judge or scoff? God, imaginary or not, knows the true extent of my faith. I cannot fool him with false prayers or contrived words. God is no fool; he can hear my thoughts just as he hears my silent prayers.

When humans meet disaster, God is their only answer. Even if they have not attended church in a decade, the second their mother becomes ill is the very second they put on their best suit and walk into the house of the Lord. People are so disgustingly fake these days. I watch hypocrisy grow and it angers me; but I am no different. I only think that I am. If I were any better, I wouldn't be afraid to broadcast my religious views.  I just know that if there is a God, he isn't going to save you; especially if you've ignored him for the better part of your life.

Oh but Hazel; sweet, sweet, Hazel. That night she came to me . . . I'm. Just. I'm. I'm not sozzled enough to talk about that night yet. I'm sipping on an endless glass of whiskey as I write this. Perhaps later the alcohol will convince me to bare it all, but for now I will recount the past few nights.

Earlier in the week I wrote of experimenting with the drug Salvia divinorum. I thought that a light cup of tea would help me sleep, but it seemed to have strikingly disappointing effects. Instead of giving myself to Hazel again, I removed the contents of the bag and smoked them in an old pipe my father gave me. I've already written of the experiences that followed, but that night I had a vision. Well, more of a message I should say.

In the dream the night that Johnny *slept* over, it was as if I was a spectator inside my own brain. There sat a dead, greyed lump on one side and a burning cyan maze on the other. This time around, however, instead of seeing inside of my brain it was as if I could *hear* inside of it. It was as if my true self was talking to me; ordering and advising me on what to do. It knew everything about my sad, sad life. It knew of the haunts I'd been experiencing, the sleep issues I'd been having, but most importantly; it knew where I'd hid the photographs. Once I accepted that it was my own hands and not God or anyone else that had killed Hazel, it was easier for me to push those memories to the back of my brain. Soon enough, I thought of the murder as a cardboard dream itself. It didn't feel real, like it hadn't actually happened. I was able to live my life as an innocent man, free of guilt for many ignorant months. Until now, it's as if I'd even forgot my own childhood. Of course I remembered my mother and father, but it's as if they had lived here in London and were only a street away. I would kick myself for never visiting them, especially on the weekends.

But that voice I heard in my dream . . . *it* knew. It warned me that we were in danger; that I needed to tear the nails from the stairwell and look at the girl I had killed. I needed to remember. I had suppressed my memories so deep inside that I lived my life based off of what I knew since the day I forgot. The salvia must have weakened me; tapped into parts of my brain that haven't been accessed in years. Hmpfh. I guess Johnny and the doctor's weren't as wrong as I thought after all. My mind was making up new images to hide the old ones. What is this feeling? I feel like I'm having an epiphany, but it doesn't feel quite genuine yet.

The morning after the dream, I woke in a puddle of my own sweat. My eyes opened to see my completely naked body; my clothes had been torn away and kicked to the basement of the bed. I remember the sense of being swallowed in my own sweat just before bedtime, but I was thawed and freezing in the morning. The drug's effects had worn off completely. I came down the staircase, the afternoon light shining through the window pane. It had already passed noon, but the feeling of obligation did not pester me. I felt no bond to my job at the press; no guilt or remorse for sleeping in past my shift's starting point. I drifted into the kitchen, seeing the newly constructed, slightly shorter tower of dishes that Johnny and I had cleared only a night before. I don't eat much. I'm not even sure how the pile got that high so quickly. I put on some water and prepared a cup of black tea.

It must have been three hours that I stared at that staircase. I hovered around it, kicking it gently with my foot before retreating to the ground floor in childish fear. I drank cup after cup of Johnny's rotten tea; a black blend that I'd bought more than a year prior. I soon switched over to coffee, desperate for something to shake this feeling out of me. My body began to tremble; my bones rattling and clambering against each other. A bit of coffee spilled from the shaking and splattered onto my bare foot. I remember feeling as if it should burn me, but there was no scolding. It felt cold, rather, almost like the liquid had already cooled and was being bothered by a gust of wind.

I couldn't bring myself to write that day, or for the next few days for that matter. The only obligation on my mind was that envelope sitting under the fourth step from the ground floor; the one I'd packed and nailed away the day I moved into this bastard house.  It sat there more than eight years, waiting for me; knowing I'd eventually come. I'm sure that part of me acknowledged the envelopes presence, but as soon as I would begin to remember, I would think about the weather or some other safeguard.

An entire day went by and I could do no more than stare blankly at the plank of wood. Night came and went seamlessly with no disturbances. I opened the front door around two in the morning and sat outside on the stoop until another boring sunrise. It wasn't until the next afternoon, just after I'd decided against walking to work again, that I knew I had to remind myself of what was in that envelope. I grabbed an old hammer from the bottom cabinet of the pantry; more than likely the same hammer I'd used to nail the step down eight years ago. Its teeth were rusted; it's head a dull, beaten, balding man. I was ravenous for the package now; like a vulture to a lion's carcass. Instinct told me to beat the wood with the head of the hammer; smash holes into its surface to reach my treasure quicker. Luckily, rationality was on my side at the time; too bad it only held me for a moment.

I attempted to pry the first nail up by the back-end of the hammer, but this proved itself impossible. I had beaten the nails so far down into the wood that they had fused with one another. The head of the nails had sunk past the body of the wood from years of foot traffic. I moved to a different nail; same story. My heartbeat grew impatient in my chest. Suddenly, I *had* to reach that envelope at all costs. I took a good look across the board. I'd tried so hard to keep everyone out of this step for good. I didn't want anyone getting to it; even myself. It didn't take long for the frustration to shoot through my veins in high volume, and I resorted back to instinct.

I gripped the hammer tight as a blade and raised my hand in the air as high as it could reach. *BANG;* but the board did not break. Again, I raised the mighty elder hammer and *BANG;* down it came upon the step. There was a light crack this time. I weakened it with a few shortened bursts. They felt like light drummers' taps compared to the strength I'd been using. It probably did little good in the long run; I think that's the point that I began to get nervous. I raised the hammer again, and *BANG; CRACK.* The board splintered apart, revealing a small hole in its left side. I flipped the hammer around and swung the teeth of the blunt weapon into the hole. I grasped the handle with both hands, and I pried, pried, pried until *SNAP;* the center of the step cracked in defeat. I gazed into the hole, throwing the hammer to the bottom of the staircase with a *clunk.* There sat the once white envelope, still looking as full as I remembered it in a film of damp dirt.

I can't be sure how much time I spent looking at the photographs. There were maybe two-dozen of them, all taken during the same summer. The summer we fell in the love; the summer I took her life. They brought back insidious memories; an outweighed mixture of the good and the bad. I sat at the dining table, ripping at my cheeks with uncut fingernails. Moments later, I was holding my ribs and laughing in delight. I came to the only family picture we'd ever taken together. It was her entire family and I.

Hazel's mother welcomed me into their family with artless arms. She was a school teacher, focusing primarily on United States history for lower grade levels. She'd sometimes forget that she wasn't in class and speak to us *kids* like we were students of hers. She'd laugh the forced mistake off every time, though, and so would we. Her brother liked me just as much. He was slightly younger than her; maybe by four or five years; I can't remember exactly. His name was David. Their family fit the stereotypical white American family. Hazel was astonishingly beautiful and talented in the arts. Her job at the florist fit her gender and bustling personality. David was still too young to work when I knew him, but he participated in just about every after-school sport you could imagine. He never walked in the door until at least seven, sometimes eight o'clock at night.

I remember one evening in which David covered for us when Hazel was supposed to be home before eight. David had a late football practice after school and Hazel and I had lost track of time down at the Glennbrooke park. We'd been out all day, finding simple enjoyment in each other's company by holding hands on a lone park bench. It was the same day we took so many of those pictures that lie in the envelope. Daylight was of no importance, and time had slipped away from our minds. David's school was only a few blocks away and we happened to run into him while we were walking back to the Matthews house. David trusted me with his sister. He knew I'd never hurt her. I never thought I would either. Regardless, he told us to stick with him until we got home. I remember making conversation about the new camera I'd just purchased. David was amazed that I'd take the time and money to send the device back to the factory when it needed new film. I didn't care. I saw it as a way of holding onto the past; an idea that is obviously not friendly with me any longer.

When we arrived at the Matthew's house, we opened the door to find Hazel's father, Richard, waiting for us in the living quarters. By the time we had set foot in the house, he had lowered his newspaper and set his pipe in the nearby ashtray. "Harold," he said to me, suddenly crossing his arms. "Did I not say eight?" I moved to talk, "You sai . . ." but David interrupted me. "They were watching me practice," he said, removing his coat and hanging it on the nearby rack. He didn't as much as look at his father; obviously a professional at this sort of thing. I can only imagine what he got away with in his later teenage years. Mr. Matthews looked at his son for a moment, and then to Hazel and I. His eyes moved from to our center, where we'd forgotten that we still had our hands clenched together. "Nnnnn . . ." he croaked in a false clearing of his throat. "Oh," I said suddenly, unlocking my fingers from Hazel's. "Sorry Mr. Matthews." I said. He smiled lightly. "Say goodnight, Harold." He said, picking up his newspaper once more. I kissed Hazel gently on the cheek and left for the evening.

Mr. Matthews didn't hate me by any means. He was just an overprotective father; something that every father was to his daughter during those times. He needed to be - the streets were full of freaks and rats that were out to hurt any good-looking women that roamed them after dark. I accepted this natural and obligatory feeling of dislike between Mr. Matthews and I. On the side, we had laughed and shared stories before. I didn't want Hazel to think her father and I had gotten too close, however, as I feared it might scare her away from me. See, even though we loved each other and called our relationship perfect, no seventeen year old girl and twenty year old boy want to think about the seriousness of their relationship while they're still growing up. Only sometimes; they are forced to.

After I had looked through the photographs what seemed like a hundred times, I simply sat. There was nothing to occupy myself with except for my own thoughts. I slept for four hours that night, and once again was free from any form of haunting. The next morning, I lost it. For the first time in years I could actually see through my younger eyes. I saw the night that I killed her. I saw the look in her eyes; tasted the sweetness of her lips. I was sprawled out on the floor; it must have been nearly noon by this point. I could feel her hair flowing through my fingertips; always so soft. I recall being near tears, and then *BANG, BANG, BANG;* a knock on the front door. In the middle of daylight, it found me. *She.* Found me.

And then came the footsteps from the stairwell. One by one they croaked and whimpered. I closed my eyes and drew in a deep pocket of breath. But then the footsteps paused. They sounded close now, like they were nearing the bottom step. Then came a squeaking *crack,* followed by another footstep. These noises weren't inside my head. No, they had to be real. She had just hopped the broken step and landed on the third stair from the ground floor. I knew exactly where she was now.

Or so I thought, until *BANG, BANG, BANG;* from the kitchen window now. And then I remembered, "The phonograph!" I said aloud. I'd already forgotten about it. I had strolled out two nights before to pick it up from the music shop. I can't remember its name; I'd never been there before. I hurried in and grabbed a single record from the shelf. I'm not even sure what the vinyl was, but it later turned out to sound absolutely horrible. I figured the noise would help drown out the haunts and I hadn't had a chance to use it before now.

I rushed to the corner of the room, where I had already set up the machine. I tore the record from its package, ripping the sleeve entirely as I tossed it against the wall. I slammed the thick, black disk down onto the machine and pressed the needle down; hard. I was greeted with an unwelcomed *ripping* sound; almost like that of tearing a hundred pairs of trousers at once. And then the most obnoxious spew of horns and instruments started to play. The horridness of the music almost distracted me from the fact that Hazel, or at least some part of her, was in the room with me.

The music blared; a hundred trumpets screaming murder into the living quarters. But then I heard it again; just as loud as it had been a minute ago - the creaking of two more wooden panels, and then a heavier clunk as she reached the bottom step. I looked over to the stairwell. And there she was: Hazel; spinning as a blurry haze of glowing particles. I hadn't been mistaken before. It was *her* standing at my door the night Johnny stayed over. She had taken her physical form in a fuzzy masquerade of fog, imitating ghostly wasps thirsting to find their leader. Each cell of her body rotated in a sickening cyclone, the motion alone enough to strike up the urge to vomit. "I'm sorry . . ." I called to her. Her head turned to the left like a confused puppy. "I'm sorry!" I screeched now. She was unmoving.

At the front door this time, came the banging of fists. "No," I said lowly. "How can she be knocking at the door if she is standing right in front of me?" Who was on the other side? But then again, how could she have been walking down the stairwell and clanging on the outside walls in the nights prior? I moved towards the door as her mouth shot open.

The familiar spiders crawled out from beneath her tongue. Shielding my eyes, I could do no more than cower. I waited for the monsters to consume my body, devour me from the inside out, or at the very least feast on the hair atop my head. Instead, I felt nothing more than a brisk wind.

I was on my knees now. As I brought my head out from my chest, I gazed at the new emptiness of the stairwell. "Hazel?" I whispered lightly. There was no response. I watched as my own breath fought for warmth in the atmosphere. "Hazel?" I called again, leaning my head forwards. Afternoon light failed to shine in through the perfectly open kitchen window. The horn instruments, which had sporadically disappeared from my hearing for a moment, came back into unwanted remembrance. "Hazel?" I said a bit louder this time. *BANG, BANG, BANG.*

The clamber shot through me like an injection of snake venom. "I've said my apologies!" I screeched, stumbling to my feet. I picked up a nearby chair and hurled it at the kitchen in dumb frustration. It clipped the edge of the door frame, falling short of its goal and breaking one of its four legs. "I told you long ago to leave me be! I remember, Goddammit; I remember!"

The sound of the music sickened me; like I was a passenger on a twisted carnival ride as the room spun around me. I fell backwards, slamming my head punishingly against the floor. I heard the slight scraping of metallic tin before a lonely, thunderous *BANG* rang through the house. The record skipped, and I knew that the spirit had gone.

I ran to the kitchen sink, hands over my wildly pulsating throat. Days of cold coffee and stale tea worked their way through my esophagus. The taste of earthy espresso collided with sour honey and less than zesty lemon. The metal basin within reach, I was too late to find that there was no room for my waste. My stomach didn't have the patience. Leaf-brown liquid convulsed from my mouth with ease, bile spraying across the pillar of dishes and spattering like freckles onto my clothing and skin. My head remained trapped on the carousel; the ride not eager to slow.

Fifteen minutes passed, my bottom glued to the kitchen floor as the spinning calmed. My mouth was sticky. The licking of my inside-cheek felt as if my tongue had run over a slimy mound of miniscule warts. I could not drink anything to alleviate the taste. Even water came regurgitating back up onto the floor. I remained still even after the spinning had stopped.

I suppose this was the defining moment that I realized the seriousness of my condition; a lukewarm epiphany of sorts. I was a man nearing his thirties - a killer; no wife, no child. I abandoned everything I used to call my childhood. My mother, my father, my loving sister; I'd left them all in undeserved wonderment for *this*. I could not imagine how pitiful

I looked sitting on the kitchen floor in the middle of daylight, wearing sleepwear covered in scared-straight vomit. I looked like a fool. I *am* a fool.

I changed into my daywear, washing my pajamas in the nearly frozen outside spout. I spent the next three hours doing all of the household chores I'd neglected the past few months. The dishes were wiped free of their grime, the lamp-shades were freed of their blankets of dust, the knocked over trash bin was finally put upright. I don't own many things, but the small amount of possessions I do own make my home appear cluttered.

And then? Then . . . Then I just sat. I did not move, I did not think, I did not count my breaths or rub at the corners of my mouth. There was no drink by my side or cigar between my lips; no excuses in my shirt pocket or apologies beneath my breath. Through a frosting window pane, I watched the coldest day of winter grow colder. And then came the darkness. I did not light a candle, or fuel the lantern in the corner. The record player did not spin that night. London stayed hungry for my sanity.

As the night aged, I saw vibrant images of Hazel; her brown, amber hair resting above her shoulders. She smiled as she brushed the strains with her ring-less left hand. Her name felt suited for the oak in her hair. My mind had finally submitted to remembrance, but I could not see any other day but her last.

She was wearing that vibrant purple dress, the one spotted with floral pattern. I used to joke with her, saying she ought to wear that dress to the floral shop. If she did, other men would *pick* her. She'd roll the marbles in her eyes, and I'd reach my arm around her shoulder and tilt them back the right away. We were to play a game of chess with her brother David. We held small tournaments every few weeks or so, simply for pleasure. David usually won; he was the best at every sport, physical or mental.

When I arrived at Hazel's house that night, she was waiting for me outside on the stairs of the stoop. Her hands squeezed at her kneecaps as she secretly counted the cracks of the sidewalk. "Are we going in?" was the first thing I can recall saying to her. I was already upset about the night before - she had left me alone and waiting at the park. We were to meet at dusk and enjoy a peaceful walk before the day ended, but she never showed. Hazel was not bothered from her gaze.

"I said, 'are we going in?'" I demanded with a bit of a spark. She did not move. Something was wrong. The house gleamed down at me as I began counting the cracks of the sidewalk with her, pulling a peppermint hard candy out of my pocket. The silence was thicker than the humidity of the summer air. "Will you take a walk with me?" she asked as I popped the mint into my mouth. "But what about . . . ?" I began, but she cut me short, rising to her feet. "They aren't in the mood for games tonight." The cracks in the sidewalk seemed to separate further. Was this the beginning of a breakup? Is this how it all began? I'd been through a handful of relationships before, but nothing that mattered to me as much as this. She grabbed me by the hand, and we walked.

"Where are we going?" I asked. "Just for a walk," she said, her grip loosening with every step. Our fingers chafed sloppily together like a broken lock and key. I grabbed her hand with a tight squeeze as we turned the corner from her street. "Ouch!" She yelped, pulling her hand from mine like it was some form of animal trap. "What is wrong with you?!" I screamed. We stood in front of a stranger's house now. Hazel collapsed into a heap of self-inflicted tears. "You!" She screeched." You!"

As I sat at the dining table alone last night and reflected on the past, I could taste the peppermint-heavy scoff I made more than eight years ago. The memory gagged me. "Me?" I stammered, throwing my hands to the wind. "What did I do? I haven't done anything!" "No!" She screeched through the cascade that had fallen to the corners of her mouth. "I didn't mean . . . it's . . . it's *not* you. It's . . ." Her eyes were heavy with regret. "Harold," she whimpered. "We have a problem."

"A problem?" I said, more boisterous now. She readied her hands in a prayer. "Please," she said softly. "You have to listen." She looked at me as if expecting a response. She told me to listen; so I did just that. "My father . . ." she began. A few crickets rubbed for their mates in a far-off field. "My father . . ." A bat fluttered from one tree to another. "Your father *what?*" I said with crossed arms. She interrupted the flow of salty fluids from her left eye. "My father is going to kill you." Footsteps clapped behind us, but I turned to see only darkness.

*No,* I thought to myself, backing away from her softly. *Noooo, no, no; it isn't possible.* My brain tried to comfort me. "Harold," she said, reaching those peach hands out to me. "No!" I said aloud this time. "You can't be. It can't be true. You're . . . lying. You're . . . I . . ." Intelligent thoughts were buried by a flustered blizzard of ash in my head. I saw the escaped tears in the corners of her lips, and I felt the urge to wipe them; but I couldn't. I wiped at my own mouth instead, though there was nothing there. "I'm having our child, Harold."

I wanted to keep calm; I should have stayed calm. "No!" I screamed, pushing her by the shoulders onto the grass below. I saw a flicker in the window of the wooden house before us. A black figure appeared and the curtain parted from the window pane. I didn't care. "You're lying!" I said, pointing with my index finger as she held the ground. "I wouldn't lie!" She whined. "I visited the doctor this morning. The tests were positive, Harold. I had two done just to be sure." My hands ran through my then slightly longer hair. It felt sticky in the summer heat. "Your father knows?" I asked. She was sitting on the ground with her knees crossed now. "No," she said. "Not yet."

"You can't tell him. *We* can't tell him, Hazel!" My panic was growing fast. Her father *would* murder me. Hell, my own father would murder me. Both of our parents were strictly united with God. They believed in consummating love the night of marriage. Any sort of sexual act before the night of matrimony was considered damnable. I guess it's good I don't believe in that brainwashing nonsense any more.

The door of the house opened and a young gentleman stepped his head out. "Hey!" he yelled from the now-dark house. "Do we have a problem here?" he said. "I've got a revolver in my hand. Now you're gonna' leave that pretty girl alone or I'll come out there and send its chamber spinnin'.""No, there's no problem," I called back to the figure. "Then I suggest you get far away from her," he boasted, stepping out of the front door and shutting it behind him. He hadn't been bluffing. The silver shell of the weapon glistened under mischievous sparkling moonlight. It would have been beautiful if its eyes weren't set on me.

"Hazel," I called. She sat still in the grime of the grass. Her eyes would not welcome me. "Hazel, let's go." I said to her. "I'll meet you back at your house." She didn't respond. "Goddammit, kid!" The stranger roared again. "You got a hearing problem?!" He stepped out from the box of his stoop and onto the grass. This southern cowboy wasn't messing around with me. "I'm leaving," I said. "I'm going now, see?" I put my hands up like I was a victim of a hold-up. In some light, I *was* being robbed; robbed of any chance to understand or make sense of the situation. I backed away slowly from the house. The man approached me faster; and then I ran. Like a frightened skunk, I ran; leaving the rotten stench of my cowardice behind. As I turned the corner to Hazel's street, I caught a glimpse of the man consoling my girl as he helped her to her feet.

I slowed to a jog just after the turn, and then to a paced, methodical walk. When I arrived at Hazel's house, I sat just off to the side of the porch so that her father could not see me through the window. All I needed was for him to look outside and spot me. He'd come out and demand to know where his daughter was, and I wouldn't be able to tell him.

An hour passed. Hazel should have been back long before now. I felt the onyx eyes of her father peering through the curtains behind me, but I had enough sense to stay out of sight. I cannot remember how much longer I waited, but I eventually rose in impatience and walked back to the end of the street. Peering around the corner, I saw only lampposts. I treaded carefully to the house we had been in front of more than an hour ago. The lamp above me flickered with the moon. What was I supposed to do? I couldn't raise a child in this world at twenty years old; not to mention the fact that the kid's mother was

underage at seventeen. I barely had the funds to keep
Hazel happy and entertained. Somehow, I knew that
none of that would matter soon enough.

The street was empty; adorned only by rusted
garbage cans and the trash that had escaped them.
The streetlight bulbs were weak, useless against the
surrounding nightfall. I could not find my shadow;
perhaps even he was afraid of the bubbling
unpredictability inside. I didn't know where to go or
who to talk to. Hazel; I had to talk to Hazel, of
course. I thought if I apologized to the man who'd
protected Hazel from my rampage, he'd be able to
tell me where she went. There was a flickering light
in the upper left window. My shirt stuck to my
stomach in a glue-like sweat. The wind was chilling
to it now. I approached the front door, and then . . .
then . . . Goddammit.

I don't remember.

I saw it playing in my head over and over just a
few days ago; but since last night I can't recall what
happened after that moment. I see the light upstairs
in the man's cloaked window, and then the light
above my mind flickers, burns, and simmers. I've
had a bit too much to drink tonight, but I feel that it
has helped me cope with the decision that I made
yesterday. My memory appears to be taking the form
of a hairless lab rat. It feels lost and abused,
mistreated even. Countless bends and churns result

in a lack of progress; a disappointing look at blank walls of sharp vacancy. Just as the maze seems impassable, my little rat finds a bit of cheese; pieces of my memory. But these molded, swiss-like fragments contain countless holes and tunnels that are too small to crawl through. I am left only partially informed with each finding; choking as I am forced to eat the spotted hollowness of remembrance. Yet, the rat pushes onwards. No doubt it will hit a thousand dead ends before finding its priceless, filled Gouda.

Speaking of last night, I felt that had no other choice other than to turn to Johnny. My head sat lopsided with the heavy weight of failure. I thought that confessing my deepest sin would help me remember; help calm the wicked, restless soul of my once sugar-sweet Hazel. The forcing of my brain to remember Hazel caused a tremendous guilt-trip; one that I am not sure if I will return from. Perhaps all my former-love wants is for me to reminisce on her; to acknowledge that we had something magnificent that we both played a part in ruining.

No. I am wrong. I am remembering it wrong. *She* ruined it. She ruined *everything* for us. Her hair did not glisten as brightly as I have been tricked into believing. Those eyes were as black and twisted as the unearthed roots of a long-dead hickory. Those teeth were stained with my tainted blood. She held open her mouth and my heart went *dripping, dripping, dripping.*

She would *snatch* up my arteries and chaw them, interlace them, deflate them; until I could not suffer any longer. She caused her own death. My hands were dangling puppets; she was my suicidal manipulator. So unstable was her selfish, greedy mind. But *why?* I can't remember *Why?!* The house, the light, the house, the light, the house, the light . . . This fluctuating anger gets me nowhere. Last night, as the city basked in twilight, I flipped through more of those medical notes that Johnny had retrieved for me. Among the heap of mimicking words was a note that I had not noticed before; one signed by a 'Dr. Naragavitz,' I found it sticking to the back of a different note, bound by a dab of glue. I'm not sure how the glue had gotten there. Maybe it had spilt, or maybe Johnny didn't want me to find it but felt guilty withholding it from me. Unlike the others, it did not simply say "Too little sleep, appointment needed for full diagnosis." But rather, it was a most peculiar note. It said, "Corruption through repression. Alternative options to medication; see if interested." The address of the office had been torn from the glue, but in the bottom right-hand corner was the handwritten number '52'.

And so I thought for some time but could not come up with an answer. Whoever Naragavitz was, it seemed like he almost didn't want me to find him. Too bad for him; I wanted to meet him. I *needed* to meet him. He was the only doctor who hadn't thrown the guilt of sleep deprivation into my face.

An imbecile with a bogus degree is my definition for 'doctor'. The frustration of not being able to find the address only added to the poisonous stew that was already brewing inside of me. I cannot stand wallowing in my own decomposing saneness any longer. This damned house is a trap that she's got me in. I didn't want the haunts to start last night, and thus I decided I wouldn't even give them a chance. Hazel would never forgive me, even though her death was her own fault anyways. Ungrateful little bitch.

I ran out of my poor man's mansion; I'm almost certain I left the front door invitingly open. When I arrived home this morning, the phonograph was gone. Whoever took it didn't seem to bother much else thankfully; not that there's much they could take anyways. They did swipe the jar of kerosene Johnny had left for me, though; damn shame, really. That oily gold is expensive these days. The lid of my humidor had been left open as well, but I was unsure if anything had been taken.

As I dashed through the filth of my half-clean pajamas, the stench of petrified vomit lifted from the fabric. Watery pink stains now adorned the sleeve cuffs and button-linings. The snowfall was the first London had seen this winter; surprising for the month's position, really. Normally, I'd be astounded; flabbergasted even, at how beautiful I'd forgotten the cotton fluff was from the year prior. Instead, the Godly dandruff was imposing; uninvited. Its chilling brush on my neck felt intrusive, like it was attempting to permeate my willing skin. I was pressed get out of the blizzard before it ate me alive. I stopped abruptly, my slippers skidding against a thin membrane of ice. *Where was I?* I looked around at the city I'd created my new life in. It was all suddenly so strange to me; a foreign land that I could not call home. My heart thudded louder, trying vigorously to pump warm blood through my freezing body. *The clock tower*: I saw it now, sitting in the chest of Central Square. Tappling Teas was on the corner, and Johnny's house wasn't far from there.

The clock tower looked astronomically lanky in the winter twilight. Its contorted hands had the appearance of rusty syringes. I felt like a patient; bound by a straightjacket and chains, just waiting for the *tick, tick, tick,* of the needles to point their blame at me. The needles would send their venomous yet precious liquid cargo soaring through my veins until the poison ate my blackened heart into nothingness. She appeared to me then.

The churning cyan particles distinguished themselves easily from the diluted whiteness of snowfall. She spiraled through the air, rising from an unknown source. My eyes fixated in a forced trance. I watched as she drifted to the top of the clock tower. In the quilted distance, she made her unstable physical form visible to me again. Though she was far off, there was no doubting that it was Hazel. I called her name into the bothered night. My own voice echoed around me, as if I were surrounded by walls of ringing aluminum. "Hazel!" I called again. She was not bothered by my grievance. Her body stood erect; stiffly tall atop the tower as she gazed into the smothered skyline before her. She was a lost, painted owl.

"Hazel!" I called her name again. There was still no response. *Tick, tick, tick,* and the tower struck eleven with a *gong*. My body was freed from its mysterious bind as a tornado of snowfall stirred from the ground and threw itself into my unsuspecting face. The coolness slipped into my shirt collar. I danced alone in the moonlight, shaking the feathery dust from my nightwear. When I looked back to the clock tower, Hazel had left me.

Something trivial struck me at this point. "Johnny," I said aloud. Johnny was the only poor sap who had offered to help me. I had to find out if he knew where he'd gotten that doctor's note from. Hazel's breath would not let my attention wander. Her torment was no longer confined to the loneliness of the house. She had followed me out into the night. Wherever I went from now on, she would be there with me. It is almost as if she is . . . inside of me, lying dormant until my sanity is weak enough to let her take control. None of it made any sense. I had to admit; Johnny's advice was much needed. And so I filled that need.

I told him everything; the entire story up until I could remember it. He kept asking *how*. *How* did I kill her? *How* could I bring myself to do it? *How* could I leave my entire family behind? And the whole time I could only shake my head, angering the floorboards by saying "I don't know. I don't bloody know."

Johnny didn't have much to say last night. He promised before returning to bed that he would keep my secret. I don't think he slept much, though. I heard footsteps upstairs on several occasions. I'm not sure if they were his or Hazel's; my brain was so burnt that that there was no clear distinction. I slept on the loveseat in Johnny's living room for about two hours. The rest of the time, I sat awake looking through books on his bookshelf for any clues of '52'. When I had asked Johnny about the note, he didn't seem to know what I was talking about. "I never saw a Dr. Naragavitz," he said to me. But then *how* did the note get on my table? *How* did it get mixed into the pile with the other notes? Now it was I who was asking, *how?*

The Tappling family rose late the next morning, even later than usual for a Sunday. Annie came down the stairs to find me sitting on the loveseat with a cup of tea around 8:00am. She was still in the comfort of her night robe. "Oh!" She jumped at the sight of me. "Harold, I . . . I . . ." "Johnny didn't tell you I was here?" I asked. "No," she responded with astonishment. "I'm a tight sleeper, I suppose. I knew Johnny had gotten up from bed last night, but I fell right back asleep." My thumb rubbed at the ceramic lip of the mug. "Sorry," I said earnestly. "It's alright," she mumbled as she made sure her chest was covered by the pearly off-white robe. "I'll run and get dressed and make you some breakfast," She moved to the stairs as I called to her. "No, no. It's alright. I can wait until lunch. We're going to Ferrero's, aren't we?" She stopped at the peak of the staircase. "We are?" She asked with a puzzled turn of the head. I didn't mean to ruin Johnny's surprise, I really didn't. He had asked me to go with them the night before, but he never told me that it was a surprise.

Regardless, we went. Annie acted surprised when Johnny stopped in front of the restaurant. The snow had stopped from the night before, and all that remained were litters of footprints. We ate lunch together; I paid my own way, of course. I had a wonderful time catching up with Thomas. The little guy always seemed to look up to me. I was friendly to him, but it perplexed me that he found me so interesting. I wouldn't call my showcased life interesting in any light. He told me about his extra-curricular activities at school. On Mondays he would stay after school for an additional hour-long study group. On Tuesdays and Wednesdays he would play football with a group of friends in the school field. As he was telling me this, I was blinded by the mound of delicious pasta on the plate in front of me. I slurped an exceptionally long noodle into my mouth, setting my fork back into the sea of alfredo sauce. I felt a cold splotch on my left lip and reached for my napkin. "You remind me a lot of David," I said with a full mouth.

I stopped chewing. I wish I'd choked on my own words just moments before. "Who's David?" Thomas asked, taking a bite of heavily seasoned ground-up sausage. The noodles slowly slid down my throat as I searched for an answer. I looked over to see Johnny darting me a frantic glare. "Who's David?" Thomas asked again. My mouth felt dry, parched; like I was trying to digest a teaspoon of cinnamon. I held up my index finger to him as I took a slow, well-executed drink of water. "David is the Cooper boy," Johnny said. "Of course, he's all grown up now. He comes into the tea shop every once in a while to catch up; just an old friend, Thomas." Thomas shrugged, copying me and taking a drink of water for himself. Johnny was a smart guy. He always knew the right thing to say.

I left the family with my gratitude outside of the restaurant. I gave Thomas a gentle rub on the head. His hair was getting long now. Annie winked at me, and I smiled. Johnny hadn't suspected that Annie knew about the dinner at all. I shook Johnny's hand. "Tomorrow?" He asked me. "Tomorrow," I said. "I'll come see you before work tomorrow." As the Tappling family and I parted ways, I couldn't help but feel uncomfortably vulnerable. Johnny had proved his loyalty to me, but something inside warned me to keep my distance. It would forever be possible that he could tell someone that I was a murderer. What if he told Annie? Thomas would be so disappointed in me.

Paranoia struck harder as the walk home lengthened. I began watching the markings on mailboxes as I walked by. *1834, 1836, 1838.* What was even more disturbing was that my once-forgotten past was now making appearances in my every day conversation. David? Really? How had I compared Johnny's son to someone I hadn't seen in almost a decade? *1872, 1874.* I felt a strange compulsiveness to read every mailbox as I passed them by. How could I be sure Johnny wouldn't rat me out? If I *did* remember how the rest of that night played out, should I tell him? *Could* I tell him? How had Hazel followed me into Central Square last night? *1888, 1890 . . .* and then I came to a smaller mailbox; one that had been knocked to the ground and been buried lightly in snow. There was no house in front of it. There was only a tiny alcove with a set of stairs leading down to a metal door. I bent down and brushed the colorless dust from the metal. *52.*

It didn't make any sense. The number didn't match any of the other addresses; I checked doubly. Sitting right between *1890* and *1892* was this tiny stairwell that lead to the flat face of a door. I tried turning the knob, but it was locked, of course. I'd forgotten that it was Sunday for a brisk moment. "Dr. Naragavitz," was printed discretely just above the door handle. It wasn't heavily displayed that this was a doctor's office; or that the place even existed in the first place. Taking notes of my surroundings; the street name, the location, I counted 3,327 steps between the office and my house. Not terribly far. *52 West Minster St.*, I wrote on the torn note, completing the once naked address.

I cannot focus any more tonight. Alcohol collides with guilt, worry, fearfulness, and mistrust. I am quitting my job at the printing press tomorrow. Directly afterwards; I am walking to 52 West Minster Street. Hopefully Dr. Naragavitz takes walk-in appointments; not like I'll give him the option of saying no.

Hazel controlled me once before; I won't allow her to do that again. I began my second life years ago; what's to stop me from starting a third?

*Chapter Seven – Virgin Patient*
*From the Journal of: Dr. Yovan Naragavitz*
*December 20th, 1905*

My name is Dr. Yovan Naragavitz. I am a licensed practitioner in modern medicine and surgical procedures. Today is the twentieth of December, 1905. Christmas is just a few days off, and I do not typically take new patients at this time. Today, however, I met a man whom I believe is perfect for the experiments I have been researching.

I am not a well-known doctor in London. Patients come to me and demand pill after pill, diagnosis after diagnosis; but I do not give in to these begging rats. People seem to have a hard time understanding that illness cannot always be cured or defined. Sometimes, a case is unexplainable and known only by the hidden thoughts in our very brains. Like me, this new patient originated from America. Poor guy must have gotten tired of the bustling American life just as I did. I've been settled here in London for only a few months now.

I am not your typical doctor. You cannot pay me off for a prescription or recommendation for an absence from work. I care about the inner mind of my patients. After all, what is a human being? When I look into the mirror, I am Yovan Naragavitz. But what I see staring back; is that the real me? And how do I define myself? People can look at me and say, "That's Yovan," but how do they know? I am only the name that my parents gave me. My name is only the thing that I call my appearance. My body is not really myself. My skin simply holds the structure of my body together; a house for the blood cells and organs that keep me alive and functioning. And can I not alter my physical appearance if I choose to? I could drop a pound tomorrow or choose to gain one. So am I my heart? My liver; my lungs? No, I must be my brain. But what part of the brain am I? My brain is not simply a single thing with a single thought that defines me as Yovan. It is the most complex organ in my body; capable of carrying out thought and action. It tells my arms which way to move; my feet when to walk. It is my most interesting organ, but it is not me. So what is a human then?

A human is not a single thing; it is a highly complex structure composed of many parts and organs working together to create the appearance of a single thing. I am defined by the hobbies I enjoy; the choices that a certain section of my brain tells me to make that day. At times I'll give a poor beggar a handful of coins. Other days, I feel like robbing his rusty tin can for my own personal benefit. We are walking, bustling, natural machines; and we are capable of anything. Just as we call a lamp post a lamp post, it is not a single thing. It is many things collected into a single structure that we have named. I often ask my patients to look into a mirror and ask themselves; *who am I?* The answer can never be defined or permanent. They will always say, "I enjoy devoting time to animals," or, "My favorite color is blue." It is all of these things combined that defines a person. We decide who we can trust in; who our friends our based on the similarities we have in these hobbies and choices.

I asked my patient today, "Who are you?" He looked into the mirror and said, "I am Harold Elway. And I am in dire need of your help." I found this most interesting. He did not dabble into matters of what style clothing he prefers or what his favorite activities are. I feel as if he is perfect for my experiment. If it is successful, I will be the most sought-after doctor of the times.

Upon arriving at my office this morning, I found this chap waiting for me outside the door. I'm not sure how he even found the place in the midst of all the snow. It ceased for a bit yesterday afternoon, but picked up heavily before nightfall. The first thing I noticed was this man's hung-over and still-inebriated state. Several times he excused himself to dry-heave into an empty bucket. He wanted privacy in all of this; but I insisted on watching. You never know what you will discover just by watching a person's actions.

I invited Harold into my office. It isn't a pretty place. The atmosphere is dull, ill-lit and full of tossed hospital beds with dirtied sheets. My surgical instruments are littered about here and there. I clean them after use, of course, but I can never seem to get them back into the bag. Cobwebs litter the corners, and fresh webs run across the ceiling stone. I don't even know the exact size of my office. If I had to guess, I'd say fourteen feet by ten feet? In my defense, I am a busy, well-respected doctor. I don't have time to clean or tidy up. I take in patients and spend my spare time researching medicine. I guess you could say I have this childish dream of being famous for something. All my life I have wanted to do something so significant, that I receive some sort of award for it.

Harold and I sat in front of each other. I do not use a desk to separate myself from my patients like most other doctors. I use an old clipboard on my knee to take notes. He first asked me if a man named Johnny came to ask about his situation a few days ago. I couldn't help but chuckle. I don't always get the names of all of my patients; and I certainly didn't catch one of a non-paying messenger boy. "Doesn't ring a bell with me," I said to him. "I *am* interested, however, in what your reasons are for coming here." The patient looked at me with a defeated groan. "I do not know where else to turn," he replied. "I've done some awful things in my lifetime, and they are quickly catching up with me." I scribbled a few notes down in my pad to console him. They were only long, black streaks with no significance. His case didn't appear to be anything new to me initially.

"I haven't slept on a normal schedule in months," he said, rubbing the corner of his mouth. I knew the nervous tick; he wasn't the only one who I'd seen use it. There was something he wasn't telling me. "I keep myself up at night with anything I can find," he continued. "Coffee, tea, anything with caffeine; I'll drink to disillusion myself even further from reality, thinking that it will help. It never does. I smoke cigars to occupy my hands. I fear that if I don't, I'll tear out my own brain." It was then that I began to pay attention. "And would that be so crazy?" I asked him. Harold looked at me with puzzled arrogance. "What?" he asked me. I tapped my pen against the paper. "To tear out one's own brain? It is your brain that's doing this to you; you realize this, yes?" I could tell that he felt bothered by the directness of my approach. "I understand that it's part of it," he said, avoiding eye contact. "But I feel that there are greater forces at work here."

"What sort of forces?" I asked him. I was interested now. "You are bound by confidentiality?" he asked me. I lowered the clipboard with a scoff. "Take a look around you," I said. "Does it look like anyone even knows this place exists? My foundations are built on helping people just like you,

Mr. Elway. Your name, history, actions; everything you do or say here is confidential between you, me, and this notepad. I provide hope to people who don't know where else to turn. You are not merely a patient to me, but a friend as well. I care about helping you." His muscles relaxed a bit, fitting the mold of the chair better. "But to help you, I need to know everything. What you are describing is a deep psychological disorder. Without all of the facts, we could risk misdiagnosis. This would be a waste of time for us both, and a huge step in the wrong direction for you. You came to me for help, Mr. Elway. You must be willing to sacrifice your secrecy in order to obtain that."

There was a brief instance of silence, and then a cool gust of air as I felt the stress between us rush away. "I murdered someone," he said. "Long ago; more than eight years ago, I murdered someone." His confession did not catch me off guard; I'd helped killers before. "A lover?" I asked. "Yes!" he said surprised, like I was some sort of psychic mind reader. Lovers were the most common victims. "And what happened?" I asked. "I don't remember it all. It's been dormant in me for so long. It's like I hid it from myself; like I wouldn't allow myself to remember." "So you had repressed the memory of her?" I asked. He nodded back. "Interesting," I took a few additional notes. "Why did you find it necessary to take her life?" I asked. Harold stared back with a blank expression. "I can't remember it all," he said. This wasn't uncommon for someone in Harold's situation.

"I remember that night; she told me that she was pregnant. We were young; very young. I was only twenty and she was three years younger than me. Our parents were both very religious and neither of us had the patience or finances to raise a child. She told me, and I . . . I lost it. I erupted on her in front of a stranger's house. I pushed her down in a frenzy, but then the man inside the home stepped out. He threatened me with a revolver; kept pressuring me until I ran away. I waited outside her home for more than an hour." Harold paused for a moment, rubbing his mouth again. "So I went back looking for her. I went back to the stranger's house. He was a younger man, I remember. I stood in front of the house and decided to knock on the door. I wanted to apologize and see if he had seen her . . . Hazel . . . was her name by the way. There was a light on in the upstairs of the home. I went to knock on the door, and then that's where I lose my memory." "It's excellent you remember even that much," I said, attempting to keep him calm. The more at ease he felt, the easier it would be for him to remember. Whenever we struggle to remember a specific thing, we never actually remember it until long after we stop thinking about it. The same is true when trying to remember someone's name. If you are approaching a man you've met once or twice in your lifetime, you won't remember his name until four hours later when you're sitting at home and it's too late to be of any use.

"Our first priority is to remember the rest of that night." I said to him. "But we aren't going to force it out of you. It's going to slip from your lips into a puddle of drool onto the floor." I rose from the chair and walked over to a nearby bookshelf. I sensed the felt of the back sleepwear eye mask I've been using for years. "What the hell is that thing?" Harold asked me. "It only blocks out the light," I said. "Through relaxation you will find the answers. Here." I tossed him the eye mask. "Put it on."

He looked a bit skeptical at first, rubbing his thumb across the mask's body before pulling the string across the back of his head. "So I just sit here?" he asked, pulling the blindfold over his eyes. "Oh!" I said, plucking a record from the bookshelf and spinning to face him. "No, I apologize. Please lay in the bed just over to your right." Harold remained seated in the chair for a moment. "But I can't see," he said with a shrug of his hands. "Let's see how well you can focus with that thing strapped to your head," I said. "It will be a good measure of how adept you are with your other four senses." "I don't really see how this will help me." Harold remarked, rising from the chair. "Don't worry, Harold." I chimed in. "Everything that I do is for good reason." Shuffling across the room, I set the record onto the phonograph. It was a smooth collection of ambient sounds and noises that I had picked up at a yard sale.

This was my first time using the phonograph as well; I'd recently picked it up after a recommendation from a friend of mine. I'd been researching the results of relaxation therapy for quite some time. I'd coaxed many hidden thoughts out of my patients before, but the addition of swooning tidal waves and chirping birds was supposed to help move the process along. I set the needle down and the calming sound of wind began to blow through the bleak basement I called my office. I looked back at Harold just in time to see him kick the legs of another chair. He wasn't even walking in the right direction. I told him it was to his right, didn't I? "Harold!" I said. "Where are you going?" "This isn't very relaxing, you know that?" he said, a bit agitated. "I can't find the right way to go. You said the right. Does that mean *your* right or *my* right?" I crossed my arms with a tasteful smirk. "Shouldn't it be assumed that it is *your* right?" I had poor expectations for this fool's performance.

Eventually, we got the poor bastard to the nearest hospital bed. I couldn't quite remember if I'd washed the sheets on that one. "Now put your legs up," I said, fixing Harold's palms face up towards the ceiling. There was a pin-sized blood stain near his left hand. Nope. Definitely hadn't washed that one. "Now, Harold," I began. "Take me back to that night. Tell me . . ." "Why are there chirping seagulls?" he said. "Shhhhh," I hushed him, trying to control my grin. I knew he couldn't see me, but he was right.

This ambient record sounded a bit silly. "In all seriousness," I croaked, pulling up a chair to sit next to the patient. "If you expect this treatment to work, you'll have to buy into it. Now tell me about that night."

It was difficult for him to begin. At first, it seemed that Mr. Elway could barely recall the events he had recited to me mere moments ago. The record switched over to the calming noise of pattering rainfall. "It was hot that night," the patient said at last. He started from the beginning. I had already heard the story before, but I was hoping that he would reach its struggle point and seamlessly soothe into the forgotten ending. "I reached the front door," he said at last." There was a heavy suspension. The illusive rainfall continued to pour. "But then I stopped," he said. My chest sank. My God, the therapy had actually worked.

"What if this guy wasn't willing to listen to my story?" Harold said. "There was nothing holding him back from pulling that trigger and sending a bullet through my ribcage at the very sight of me. I waited at the door, as if it were going to open for me at any moment. And then I heard that all too familiar laughter. Hazel's laughter. It creaked from the parted upstairs window. I could pick that giggle out of a crowd of a thousand. This chuckle wasn't forced; it was one of genuine pleasure." Harold's speech flowed fluently now. It felt as if I was an observer standing behind him that night.

"I stepped back and peered into the window. Still blocked by the curtain, I could hardly make out the form of dancing shadows. My mind was frosted with wonderment. What was Hazel doing in this guy's house? I mean what the *hell* was Hazel doing in this guy's house?!" The patient's fists were clenched now, exposing every bubbling vein and petrified hair. "The shadows disappeared and I heard that laugh again. It wasn't just a laugh, though. No, it was followed by a flock of pleasurable moans. How soon would they nest in mistrust? Had they already nested?"

"I tried jiggling the front door handle, but it was locked; something quite uncommon. People trusted each other more back then than they do now. It's sad, really; such trust lost in a mere eight years. Stepping around to the back yard, I remember hearing the *crack* of a fallen branch as my shoe snapped it in two. Had they heard? I was too dizzy with heightening wrath to bother myself with the answer. The yard was spoiled with apple trees and shaded cherry blossoms. This kid was well-off; a nice home that appeared to be all his. More than likely it was a hand-me down. Maybe his parents had passed on and left it to him; I don't know. I just knew he wouldn't be alive much longer to enjoy it."

"Almost as if God, who I still believed in at that time, had laid it out for me; there was a wall lined with lattice running up to an open window. *Too perfect,* I remember thinking to myself. God was inviting me inside. He knew that I had been wronged; he knew that I was due vengeance. Bits of leaves were woven throughout the gaps in the wooden fence, but they were nothing I couldn't reach between. I threw my hands up, grabbing at two gaps in the lattice. My right hand ached as it felt the bite of a thorn. I hiked my feet upwards, sliding them into higher gaps. I began to climb with one purpose: To kill."

"I hadn't thought of hurting Hazel at this point. We still had talking to do. No; I wanted to kill whoever this guy was violating my ripened girl. She was so ruined by me, but she was mine; still mine. That behemoth probably didn't even know she was carrying my child. I had horrible thoughts. I'd grab a kitchen knife and cut the appendage off this freak; shove it down his own throat. He'd choke on his own demise; he'd swallow what he ruined my Hazel with. And Hazel? Ohhh . . . Hazel. I didn't know what I was going to do to her quite yet."

"I climbed higher, higher, faster, faster. I didn't bother looking downwards. I felt superhuman, like I was some unknown breed of animal stalking its prey. I reached the top window and thrust it upwards, almost losing my balance and falling to a dusty death. Silence wasn't an option any more. I heard her again; moaning, groaning, screaming, and writhing in ecstasy. She never moaned like that for me. I had crawled inside now. Finding myself in an empty bedroom, I figured he must have been the only one living in the home. I hoped this to be the case with the way he was making my girl's screams shatter through the thinness of the walls. They were in the next room over; a hallway and a cracked door the only obstacles between us. They hadn't heard me enter the house.  I searched the room for anything I could use. I'd hoped to find the revolver I was threatened with only hours ago, but I settled on a gold-plated letter opener on the dresser drawer. This spoiled bastard must have been using this room as his own personal study. Perhaps he should've kept with his discipline this night. There's one lesson he forgot to read: Never mess with Arthur Elway's girl."

I raised an eyebrow, but let the patient continue his story regardless. I didn't want to risk losing connection to the story. He was enthralled in a replication of his old life now; one where his name apparently used to be Arthur. I drew a line at the top of the form where I had listed Harold's name. *Arthur* I wrote beneath it. Typically, people tended to change their last names as well. Then again, Harold was quite a peculiar fellow to begin with. I'd never met a man with such a scrambled conscience.

"The letter-opener was sharp at the tip; perfect for misusage. It had no teeth, but bared a shimmering cast of perfection. I set foot into the hallway. The lust filling the house was nearly enough to smoke me out. My hand grabbed at the side of the door. I cracked it open, creating a slightly larger gap. Hazel. Oh my God, it really was Hazel. She was

beneath him, suffocating under the sweat of a body I
could never acquire. The man was more defined than
I; chiseled as a Grecian statue with the stamina of a
racing horse. Our love never looked like that. I was
never up to it; she was never into it. There was a dim
candle burning, making the disgusting sweat of my
betrayal sparkle with tease. I could hear him
inserting himself into her; the sound of moisture,
wetness, ruin. She moaned, he screamed, I died
inside."

"I wanted to charge into the room; slit the
bastard's throat. And then? Then I wanted to stab
Hazel. Thrust this innocent instrument into her gut
and watch her bleed for me. She'd spill the reasons
*why* and I'd have my last chance at speaking to her.
She wasn't very far along in her pregnancy; she
couldn't have been. She wasn't showing but a slight
bump now, but I wanted to kill that child. I didn't
want it. I no longer considered it mine. It was my
seed sewn in a witch's body. But I couldn't do it; not
because I couldn't convince myself, but because I
saw the shimmer of the revolver on the night stand.
It was almost as if they were expecting me to find
them. A hundred questions grabbed my brain in a
fist. Had they met before? Was this the first time
she'd cheated on me? Was our love not as defined as
I'd thought? Had I been too controlling? Too
demanding? And then I swore I heard the voice of
God. 'No,' he said to me. It was a clear message. God
had left the window open; built the lattice leading up

to it. He had sent his angels to deliver the letter-opener to me. He had led me to her; led me to this. And this is why I despise him to this day. I earnestly believed he could speak to me."

There was a break in Harold's speech. He was sweating now; drunk with hatred for the past. "Bucket," he said. His change of tone made me shift my seated cross-legged position. "Bucket?" I asked with bare confusion. "Forget it!" He shrieked, ripping the eye mask from his face and tossing it to the side. He ran to the other end of the room, stumbling over bags and chairs from the sudden blindness of light. He reached for the bucket and proceeded to dry-heave into it once more. A bit of tar-like liquid dripped from his mouth and into the metal. "I'm sick, doctor," the patient said to me, spitting into the bucket. "I'm sick."

"Can you go on?" I asked Harold, remaining hopeful. The room reeked of acidic liquor. "It's gone," he said to me, shaking his hands like he was trying to rid them of memory. "It's left me. All I see now is that scene of them touching; grinding." I rose from my seat. "You've made excellent progress today, Harold. Or should I call you Arthur?" The patient's hands stopped shaking. Without warning he lunged at me, grabbing me by the shirt color and knocking my clipboard to the ground. His face rippled with sweat; the scent of body odor prominent. "Don't you *ever, EVER,* call me Arthur again. Do you hear me?" His wrists trembled against my body. He was scared; afraid that I knew the entirety of his secret. I reassured him that the information was confidential with me. "I apologize," he said at last. "I'm not myself lately." "How do you define yourself?" I asked him with a quick response. He sighed, bowing his head in some sort of respect or defeat. "I don't know any more." He said. "I just don't know."

"We still have ten minutes in our session, Harold," I said as he reached for his coat from the rack. "Right," he said, resting it back onto the knob. "I suppose that's what I'm paying you for, isn't it?" he joked for comfort. We sat facing each other once more. "Tell me, Harold," I said. "Have you experienced any out of the ordinary dreams lately?" His eyes lit up, as if I'd yet again accomplished some sort of physic feat. "Yes!" he said. "Yes, twice now!" Can you describe them to me?" I asked, leaning inwards. Harold's eyes darted back and forth as if he were in the deepest sanctum of sleep. "I can," he replied. "I see them in my head as we speak." "My most recent dream was induced by an experiment," Harold began. "An experiment?" I repeated. "What kind of experiment?" Harold scratched at the back of his neck, grinding the left side of his teeth together. "I sort of . . . smoked something," he mumbled. "A bit of Japanese tea." I had never heard of anyone doing this before. He had my interest peaked. "So you took the tea out of the bag and smoked it in a pipe?" I asked, baffled. I didn't mean for my face to become so contorted, but I fear that it did. "That's correct," he replied. I sat unmoving. Exactly what kind of idiot was I dealing with here? "Just any old tea?" I spat out, tapping my pen against the board. "Not exactly," Harold replied. "It was a blend that included Salvia Divinorum," My eyes widened. "Ohhhh." I hummed. "That explains a lot, then." Harold nodded. The experiment was something that he obviously wasn't proud of. He told me how he'd tried to steep two bags in the same cup, but experienced very little effect from the drug. He then told me of the itching spiders and taunting figures he thought he had seen. The whole thing sounded like a terrible nightmare to me.

"But one night I had a strange dream," he continued. "It was as if my memory of Hazel emerged in my sleep. Something inside of me warned me to remember; it said that if I didn't listen to it, then we could both die. It was like a second voice; something that was part of me that didn't exactly feel like me." "Your subconscious," I said, looking for his agreement.

"Oh God," Harold croaked. "Not you too. That's what every other doctor has written about me. I suppose you're going to tell me all I need is more sleep too?" "No, no." I said reaching my hand out to pat him gently on the knee. He shuttered slightly at my touch. "That's not it at all, Mr. Elway. Sure, more sleep would undoubtedly help you; but it is not the cause of your problems. These haunts you've told me

of, they will not simply go away because you stick to a normal schedule. Hazel is . . . inside of you. She's been lying dormant in you for so long; her anger has been building inside of you for so long. She has infected you, Harold. Just like gangrene of the foot, she has infected you. She's in your head, forcing you to face her because she feels betrayed and forgotten."
"And what does she know about betrayal?!" Harold launched up from his chair and drew his face close to mine. His spit chilled my lip. "What does she know?! She betrayed me! She slept with that . . . that monstrous God of a kid!" I'd had enough of Harold's disillusionment. Sometimes, a doctor needs to give his patient a spoonful of truth. "And why did she?!" I screamed, rising and pushing Harold at the shoulder blades. "Stand back from me Harold! *This* is why Hazel betrayed you! *This* is why she slept with that kid! You never comforted her! You were always blaming, blaming, blaming. She told you about the child and you lost your senses. Look at yourself! You've been in my face three times within the hour tonight! It doesn't surprise me to learn that you're a killer, Harold. I knew that you were infected the moment you walked in the door!"

I stared into the eyes of a stunned beast. It was as if the man had never been scolded in his lifetime. "You are *sick,* Harold! Thinking about her isn't going to make her go away. She's inside of you, leeching from your brain like an enlarged flea. *That* is why your dreams are so important. They exist inside of you. Whatever that voice is telling you, you don't know if it can be trusted. The only way to know if those thoughts are yours or Hazels is to . . ."

"To what?!" Harold screeched back. I could not tell him yet. No, he wasn't ready: Soon; but not yet. "The truth is: I don't know." I responded, releasing my guard. Harold did the same. "I think we're done here," he said, striding for the coat rack once more. A whisk of dust followed in the wind behind him. "Our time is up." I picked up the clipboard, setting it back down on my desk across the way. "Indeed it is," I remarked. It wasn't as if we were fighting like children, rather we were both merely frustrated at Harold's attitude. I caught the smell of grease as he whisked his coat over his white-collared shirt. "You work in the factories?" I asked. He tugged at his collars with a snap, as if he were making a significant statement. "Used to," he said. "I quit this morning." I kinked my neck to the left, feeling an audible *crack*. "I see," I said. "May I ask why you quit your job?" Harold looked at the floor before chuckling a bit. "Next time," he said. "Where did you work?" I asked. The door was open, December breath seeping into my already chilled office. "I used to work at the press down on 14th," he said with disdain. "Oh, so you know Abel?" I asked.

Harold inhaled the arctic air, pausing before exhaling it into my dampening office. "Yeah, I know Abel," he said to me. "He's a nice fellow. He stopped me on my way out of the press today. We are meeting for drinks later tonight. How do you know of him?" He waited for an answer, the cold phalanges of winter grasping at the still-open door. "He's an old friend," I said. "And we are bound by confidentiality, yes?" Harold asked abruptly. "Absolutely," I said with a grin. "Now close my God damn door." Harold chuckled and left me with a tip of his hat.

I feel the relationship between the patient and myself growing rapidly. Harold's case is proving to be one of usefulness and peculiarity. I've been a doctor for more than fourteen years, studying for twenty-two. They spit on me for advancing science in my old country. I was outcast for my procedures in forgotten America. That won't happen here in London. No, they won't be mocking me here. They'll be begging me to perform on them; pleading for me to fill my calendar with their dying bodies. With every *cough* they'll scream, "Operate! Operate!" and I'll draw my dirtied scalpel from the drawer beneath my shelf of trophies. I'll tightly grip the acne of the stainless steel handle, lowering the blade closer to the patient's bodies; closing the gap between metal and flesh. They'll *beg* for my talent and I'll *jab, slit, cut!* And the bodies will pour open! Hopeless corpses writhing in rotten guts . . . I can save them all. I *will* save them all.

Maybe there will be a parade for me? Yes, I'd like to think of one on Christmas day! All the mice walking in a line with crimson banners and rivers of flags! *'Naragavitz! Naragavitz!'* they'll chant; my name echoing off of every city brick. Their voices will collide and be heard from the heavens. God will be disappointed in his very own son! With years of the compulsive praising of Jesus behind them, they'll worship my brilliance! God will reach out to me then; ask me to be his true offspring. And he will grant me an eternal life of fortune and success!

But that is all in due time; the world owes it to me. Harold is a nice fellow, and I cannot promise that this trickery will come without guilt. But where else does he have to turn in all honesty? With my expertise, he'll grow from unsung idiot to revolutionary hero! That poor little girl is trapped in his head. He's relying on me to set her free; to set *him* free! Failure has not even crossed my mind. Abel was right about this place. America is not the land of opportunity. London is alive with my genius!

I must ask Abel for another loan. Money has been a bit hard to come by since I moved here. Abel has been generous enough to lend me money every month or two to keep my research going. He believes in my success; finally a man that believes in my work! He knows that the money will come back to him one day. I'm sure he's partly helping me so that I will take care of him financially in the future, but what is the harm in that? His resources are allowing me to live my dream! All I need now is a few vials of anesthesia for my work to go into action; *that*, and Harold's consent. I'm almost there. Even after a single day, I can feel his hopelessness confiding in me. He gave up long ago. My aspirations are only beginning.

*Chapter Eight – Needle Rainfall*
*From the Journal of: Harold Elway*
*December 21st, 1905*

Hazel visited me after my meeting with Abel last night. Like an ever-boiling pot, she burns me more each visit. There were the familiar haunts, and the now-regular appearance of sparkling dust. "I'm sorry, love!" I called to her. She closed her ears again. "I'd play our favorite tune if I still had the phonograph!" I pleaded. She stood with her head aimed down at the stairwell, hopeless. I could watch her only for a moment. Her head twisted at me in disgust, a gnarly curl in her upper lip. It was obvious to me now. Hazel would never forgive me. My only choice was to remove her from my memory.

She lives inside of me; Dr. Naragavitz has made me understand this. I think I'd almost rather be haunted by her footsteps each night than stare at her blank expression. Whenever she looks into my eyes, I feel sheer emptiness; like she is sucking what remains of my soul from my body. Sometimes, it's as if she isn't even there; like I'm screaming at the wall behind her imaginary figure. The doctor's notes have made me question . . . *is* she really there? I know that she exists within me, but am I the only one that can see her? If Johnny were here, could he see her too? No, that can't be true. She exists within my own mind. But is she something physical that I can touch? She'll never allow it . . .

While Hazel still holds her grasp over me, Dr. Naragavitz gave me a breath of new hope today. It was only our second session, and he has already provided me with an answer for the haunts. While the treatment is risky, I promised him a definite answer. It sounds quite ridiculous; but perhaps too ridiculous to go wrong.

We began our session by talking about Abel. My heavily-bearded coworker and I went out for a few beers last night. I know I've said that I'm not much of a beer drinker, but I'm easily convinced when social anxiety is hitting me hardest. I never used to have a problem befriending others, but I suppose I owe it all to that summer night in 1897.

Abel was saddened by the grapevine news that I was leaving the press. He stopped me as I was walking out the door yesterday morning, and he is actually the one who arranged our meeting. When I think about it, I suppose that we have grown somewhat close in the past few months. Though he is younger than I, we seem to relate very well. He bought the first round last night and we began carrying on about life at the press. There are certain parts of the work that I'll miss, but I will have to rely on my savings for the next few months until I can find another job. "What made you want to leave?" Abel asked me, his voice husky and rugged. His question made me stop mid-sip. "I suppose I've just had enough of factory work," I responded. "I feel like I am at a part in my life where I need to follow what's truly important to me. Every new day that I spend there, I feel more and more like a mere part of the machines themselves."

It was all a colossal lie, but I did not trust Abel with my past just yet. I couldn't bring myself to tell him about Hazel, about my life in America, or even about my own family. "I grew up in a religious family," he said. There was an awkward pause between our glasses. "But I don't follow it too closely anymore." I felt relieved, comfortable enough to order us another round of beers. "I've been struggling with the big man a bit myself lately." I said.

We spent the next half-hour or so talking about religion. While Abel certainly isn't a non-believer, it certainly sounds like he's on that path that I took. "I feel as if there just isn't any way of proving that God exists," he said with another sip. His speech had begun to slur drinks ago. "I mean, how *can* you tell?" he asked. "Precisely!" I responded. "He's never answered a prayer of mine, and I'll be damned if he starts now." In the end, we ultimately decided that we are both perhaps a bit agnostic. We cannot truly be sure that God exists, and if he does; how can we be made aware?

I rather enjoyed my conversation with Abel. I would never say this aloud, but his disposition is far more interesting than that dry, beaten sandbag Johnny calls a personality. Don't get me wrong, Johnny is certainly a dear friend; I simply feel that we are drifting apart lately. I don't know if it is because I told him my deepest secret, or perhaps I am being a bit selfish and egotistical in our conversations. I sound like a panicked pre-teen girl in this writing. I'm a twenty-eight year old man. I should be concerned with my own problems; not making acquaintances.

Abel spoke of his life before the printing press. He was a hard working boy; grew up in London and has stayed faithful to his land. "My father was a carpenter," he said. "He tried to get me into the business, but I never saw the value in it." We were beyond drunk now. "My mother stayed at home. There just wasn't any opportunity for her outside of the house. It saddens me, really." Abel stared down into his glass, examining his frothy piss of a reflection. "I miss my mother," he said at last. "I miss her every day." I waited for him to continue, but he never did.

"Did she leave you?" I asked, breaking the silence. "She . . ." he stirred his newly filled glass with the dirt of his index finger. "She committed suicide a few years ago. My father . . . he couldn't move along in London without her. He gave up his work as a carpenter and moved across the seas. He offered me the chance to follow him, but I couldn't bring myself to abandon London like that. It's such a beautiful land. It's where I grew up, where I learned to live and love; my home." Abel's personal lament triggered a few feelings about my own past. I thought of my own mother, a house wife just like his. I could see her beautiful blonde hair in the fog of my mind; I could smell her sweet, daisy perfume. I nearly remembered her name. "I know what it's like to lose a love," I said at last. He looked at me with a twisted eyebrow, expecting me to continue. I didn't.

"Stay in touch," Abel said as we parted ways outside the bar window. "I've got your address. I'll stop by soon. How about another beer in a few days?" I felt the warmth of friendship inside my chest. "Sounds great," I said. "Oh, and Abel?" He turned to face me. "You really ought to shave. You look a bit ridiculous." He laughed through drunken hiccups, nearly visible bubbles of ethanol slipping from his lips. "I'll get right on it, friend," he chuckled cheerfully. I admit that it is rather nice having a friend that I can simply relax with. I can tell that Abel is indeed a deep, critical thinker such as I. He does not cower from the unknown or the unexplained. He and I are going to have quite a few in-depth discussions one day.

I walked home from the bar a drunken mess. The malted spit on my lip was acidic to my tongue. I remember swinging around a few lamp posts, as if I were auditioning for some kind of cheerful dance number. When I arrived home, it took me near ten tries to fit my key into the lock. I should have stayed out the entirety of the night. When I opened the door, I immediately saw Hazel standing before me.

In my drunkenness, I was unafraid; weary of her mystical horseshit. "Awww, who cares?" I said, slamming the door behind me and waving my hand at her. "What makes you so special?" I learned a valuable lesson last night. No matter how drunk you are, don't anger your ex-lover; especially if you just happen to be her killer. Within the hour, she had tapped into every nerve in my body. Thus began the night described at the beginning of my entry.

When I woke up from my few hours of sleep the next morning, I immediately realized that I was nearly late for my appointment with Dr. Naragavitz. I felt a bit awkward hobbling to his office with yet another shameful hangover. But who am I kidding? He isn't judging me. He's a doctor for Christ's sake. His job is to help chronic drinkers and hypochondriacs such as me.

"Sorry! Sorry!" I said, swinging into his office a few strikes past late. "No worries, Harold," he said, a deceitfully calm expression on his face. "Are you prepared to begin?" I kicked off my shoes and rushed to the bed I had been lying in the day before. "No need for the oceans and birds just yet," I boasted. "I remember."

"You do?" the doctor asked, shuffling to his desk like a shell-less hermit crab. He retrieved his clipboard from the table; the sound of a dragging chair leg was nothing short of obnoxious. "Not all of it," I said, placing my hands in a crossed pattern. "Keep that phonograph handy." Dr. Naragavitz leaned in, waiting for my story to begin. "Whoa there doctor," I said with an outstretched hand. "You're a little too close for my liking here." He adjusted his legs nervously. "Sorry," he said. "You seem rather calm about all of this." My eyebrows lowered. He was right. Why was I so calm? Was I still a bit drunk from the night before?

Before I had the chance to resume my story, the doctor's side-note about my attitude did quite a number on my posture. The collar of my shirt suddenly felt constricting. I unbuttoned the top latch, releasing the rotten odor of unbathed chest hair. Why did he have to say something about my behavior? Couldn't he have just let me tell the story at my own pace? I mean, shouldn't a doctor know better than that? Lucky for the both of us, the story remained fresh in my mind. As the memories began chucking from my throat, the hurt struck me right between the eyes.

"I was watching them through the doorway," I said with a salty gulp. "My mind was full of hornets; begging for my hand to cut both betrayers with the letter opener it held. So many narcissistic thoughts pummeled my brain, I . . . I didn't have time to recognize them all. I was quickly drowning in the thickness of groan-filled air. He was on top of her, satisfying her like I never could. The smell of sex is so disgusting when you're not involved. I knew that I had to move quickly. If either one of them noticed that the door was ajar, it would give my presence away immediately. An oily painting of a pasture horse watched them from the other side of the room. The invented blade felt weightless in my hand. I braced myself, preparing to launch through the door and jab the weapon into the back of that chiseled bastard's neck. I wanted to see him writhe in pain before I took his life. I wanted to watch his autobiography play in his eyes."

"My teeth tasted of chalk dust. My disgust fluttered at the door frame. Just as I began to push my way into the room, I was stopped by the sickening sight before me. The filthy skunk had finished his business inside of Hazel. I couldn't believe how careless she had been; not like it really mattered. I saw the sweat drip from his forehead down onto Hazel's slick, naked stomach. I recognized that look in his eyes. He had used her; just like I'd used a half a dozen girls before I met Hazel. This was nothing special for him. It was merely a hungry night. He perhaps did not know that Hazel was pregnant; he probably didn't even know that we were together. He didn't deserve to die for this."

"I slipped back into the hallway. As steam twirled from the bedroom, I tipped quietly back into the study I had come from. The desk itself was naked without the letter opener. With a deep breath, I let rationality enter me. I couldn't kill Hazel with this thing. There would be blood across the drapes; a room drowning in evidence that all pointed back to me. No, I had to do this a different way. I set the letter opener back onto its resting place. The kid was laughing from the other room now; I could tell he was already finished with her. He'd throw her outside like a misbehaved dog in mere moments. It was there that I would wait for her."

"I climbed back down the cedar lattice, my skin bothered once more by its jutting thorns. A few feet from the ground, I let go and fell to the grass below. I remember the sound of squashed mud between the tracks of my work boots. My jeans were stained with a pint of grungy water. I remember thinking; had I left footprints in the office? What about the hallway? It didn't matter, really. I hadn't done any harm. The guy hadn't even seen my face; there was no way he could connect the prints back to me. I returned to the front of the house. The air had cooled now, providing a welcomed chill to the summer night."

"I stood just beyond the street corner. When she turned it, I would be waiting for her; waiting for an explanation. I had been right in my predictions. It wasn't but five minutes before I heard the door slam and saw that filthy whore standing outside in disbelief. He had merely been her confidant. Not an ounce of shame hung over me as she began walking towards me, her home just around the corner. I waited . . . waited . . . waited . . . her sobs could be heard closer now. And I waited . . . waited. . . I felt the rush of anger building inside of me again. *Not here*, I thought. And then she turned the corner.

Her face was raped with tears. "Arthur!" She screeched, jumping backwards with the intent of fleeing. "Hazel, wait!" I called. There was sincerity in my voice. "I need to talk to you. I'm prepared to talk about our situation." There was an imaginary wall of brick between us. Her face was awestruck, filthy. "But . . ." she began. "I know what you did tonight." I said, remaining still. I held my hands up, almost as if she had stolen the revolver from the kid and had it aimed at me. "It's okay," I said. "I understand. I just want to talk." There was another pause. "Take a walk with me?" I asked, pleading. She nodded calmly, extending her hand. I took it in obscure intent. What a dumb whore.

"You slept with him?" I asked. Our shoes were quiet against the gravel road. "Yes," she said, stirring up more tears. "Shhhh . . ." I hushed, caressing her hand in a circular, sexual motion. "I understand," I said. "He listened to me," Hazel began. Her voice was whiny; obnoxious. "He held me tightly; something you haven't done in a long time." I felt her excuses translating into anger. I stopped the buildup before it had a chance to escalate and

explode. "And you confided in him," I said
decisively. I watched as she shook her head up and
down. "And he used you?" Her head again moved
vertically. "He didn't care about us; about our
relationship? So he knew that you were pregnant?"
She tasted her lip. "Yes," she said solemnly. "Yes,
and he consoled me . . . and. . . and it just lead to the
bedroom. Arthur, I'm so sorry!" She shrieked. "I
know," I said calmly. "I understand." I didn't. And
that bitch wasn't sorry enough.

"What do we do?" She asked. I shrugged
lightly, feeling the new crispness of the summer
night. "We move on," I said, falsely defeated. I had
been leading her to Glennbrooke Park through the
course of our walk, the one we frequented every
week; the same one we took those photos in. "But I
betrayed you; I betrayed our love." She whispered in
shame. "No," I nearly interrupted her. "I betrayed
*you*. I didn't listen to you. I should have handled this
more like an adult; not like an idiotic child." Her
hand wrapped tighter around mine with the
statement. We had arrived at the park, alone.

"Can we sit on our favorite bench?" she asked
me." "Of course," I replied sweetly. We walked over
to the bench in heavy silence. A year of memories
flashed before me. I saw the day we took those
photos; I saw the night we made love behind the
bench. It disgusted me. We sat then, still tied by our
hands. Her familiar floral print dress had grown
boring in my eyes. This was no longer love. This was

pure hatred. There was no excuse for what that wench had done to me. "I love you, Arthur Elway." She said, wrapping her arms around my neck. I fished my pockets for my last remaining peppermint. "I love you too, Hazel Matthews." I said, disrobing the hard candy and setting it gently on my tongue. I refused to return her embrace.

She released me from the hold, smiling through smeared eyeliner. I tossed the candy wrapper to the park floor. "Arthur! Don't litter in our special spot!" she said in a nagging yet joking tone. I couldn't believe her imbecility. She was already trying to joke with me? Like I'd already forgotten she whored herself out to a complete stranger? My upper lip twitched as she bent down and picked up the wrapper. "I'd miss that smile of yours if you left me," she said, shoving the wrapper into the pocket of her dress. "You don't need to worry," I said, running my fingers through her hair. "*I'm* not going anywhere." The moon was a crescent that night; cracked, destroyed. It beamed down upon us, as if giving me a sign of understanding and approval. "Hazel," I said, my fingers still in her hair. "Yes?" She looked up at me with beading, questionable eyes. "Kiss me?" I asked in sugared prayer. She closed her eyes and moved in for the kiss, her lips slightly parted. I stuck out my tongue and tore the fading peppermint from its plate. "Hazel," I whispered mere centimeters from her mouth. She licked her lips, tasting my peppermint breath. "Yes, Arthur?" she asked seductively. My mouth could not hold its jack-o-lantern grin. "Burn in Hell." I spat.

Hazel's eyes and mouth shot open in awe, providing just enough room for me to shove that peppermint candy into her begging throat. She squealed in terrorized confusion, trying desperately to clamber to her feet. My hand pressed tightly against her lips, covering her mouth and denying it oxygen. I felt her upper jaw attempting to topple my palm, her teeth grazing my skin. I stood. Now it was my turn to take control of her. I towered over her body, using my arms to press her against the back of the park bench. I could hear the peppermint clinking against her teeth, fearful for escape. The air from her nostrils felt warm against my knuckles. "You did this to yourself!" I screamed. Her feet kicked against age-old dirt, hitting my legs a number of times. "Stop fighting me!" I screeched, pressing her head harder against the backbone of the bench. I felt her teeth again try and graze my skin. "Goddammit, Hazel!" I cried. I had had enough.

I grabbed her cheeks with my nails and palm, pulling her head towards me. "Do you love me now?!" my voice shot through the manmade wilderness. "How could you be so careless?!" I shoved my arm forwards, slamming the back of her head against the park bench. Her eyes widened with hurt; pools of dreary red and black being drained. "Do you love my body more than his?!" My wrath continued as I again thrashed her head against the wooden loveseat. Her struggle weakened. The air passing through her nose was hardly enough to keep her conscious. I felt the goose pimples in her skin flourish. She appeared tired, weak; but I couldn't stop. I was filled with hormonal rage. I beat her head against the ridges of the bench again and again.

*BANG, BANG, BANG.*

"You filthy whore!" I screeched, sliding my fingers down through her gaping mouth. I grabbed at her bottom jaw, feeling her canine teeth weakly nibble at my fingers. "This loose mouth of yours has caused quite a bit of trouble." I howled. Her tongue licked against my fingers; the peppermint sliding from her cavity, to the bench, and then to the dirt. I slammed her senseless brain against the bench once more. My fingers became drenched with slime as they crawled deeper into her throat. "How will you speak if I rip out your voice?" I threatened. I heard the cool, rushing water of the river just over the hill. "No," I said with a snarl. "No. I'll be damned if you get the best of me."

She was hardly conscious still; her body limp but still squirming in my arms. I drug her to the befouled dirt floor; her pale legs but a reddened row of hills and mountains. I picked her up by the armpits. They were sweaty and reeked of the night's arousal. Her head wobbled lightly as I drug her up to the top of the hill. I'd let the river deal with her. I watched my adrenaline-filled muscles bulge from my t-shirt. I was drenched in her sweat now. Reaching the top of the mound, I threw her back against the body of an oak tree. "Don't move," I threatened with an outstretched finger; as if she could. I peered down into the ravine. The river must have been a hundred feet below us. Its water flow was heavy from summer rain; its torso jutting with sharpened rocks. My heart thudded against its homely ribcage. I turned to find that Hazel was completely unconscious now. That's when it hit me.

"Jesus Christ!" I wailed, my heart filling with remorse. The rage inside had rapidly dispersed. I saw what I had done through reality's eyes. The wasp-like vision I'd been seeing through had vanished. I hadn't wanted to hurt Hazel; I really hadn't. I remember running over to her. *Was she dead?* No, she was still breathing. She was weakly unconscious. I tugged at her shoulders, bringing her body forward. Blood strung like a line of drying clothes from her hair to the tree trunk. Its sight forced a gasp as I released her shoulders and sent her head back into the tree bark. I had moved from anger, to rage, to depression, to fear in a matter of moments. My hands felt the side of my face before rubbing at the corner of my lips. I looked around me at the ever-shrouding darkness. Loneliness was a taunting gift.

I walked around Hazel, seeing the disaster that was the back of her head. The tree trunk was covered in the stickiness of clotting blood. It smelled and looked like an overly-sweetened pomegranate. There was a hemorrhaging hole that covered near half of her skull; a gunky, pink tragedy poking through in protrusion. She'd bleed out before I'd be able to help her. I rose to my feet, my hands again clawing at my cheeks. Profanity came in a storm of tears. There was the thunder of screams; the lightning of remembrance. I had killed my love. I had killed Hazel Matthews.

Or had I?

"You won't be the end of me," I threatened her nearly lifeless corpse again. The rushing water below openly awaited her body. I had no other choice. Arthur Elway hadn't killed Hazel Matthews. Nature had. I grabbed her from the front this time, again by the armpits. I carried her to the edge of the park's cliff. I longed for a free hand to run through her hair once more. "I love you, Hazel," I said softly. Almost as if giving her up voluntarily, her underarms slipped from my hands in a grease of perspiration. I watched as her body fell to the river below, nearly in a blur of slow motion. Her dress blew up in the wind, and I remembered what had brought us to this.

I could not watch as her corpse neared the rocks. I turned away, shutting my eyes in wrinkles of anticipation. I swear I could hear every bone in her body break as they hit the rocks below; their brittleness was no match for the daggers of stone. She was dead; I knew as quickly as I heard the grisly splash on the water. Float away, love. Float away.

It was a painful few moments before I could bring myself to look over the ravine again. I don't know what I feared more; seeing her lifeless body in the riverbed, or missing the chance to see it one last time. When I brought myself to look, she was gone. The river had already carried her away in faithful summer rain. The night was quiet now; all was quiet.

The memory of her murder was hypnotic, and I woke in Dr. Naragavitz's office as if I had been having a wet, lucid dream. I hadn't even noticed the sound of seagulls and ocean waves playing in the background. "When did you start that music?" I asked, groggily wiping at my eyes. "A while ago," Naragavitz said. "Where did you go after that?" Neither his pen nor his head lifted from his clipboard. "All I wanted to do was go home," I said, sitting straight up in the bed now with my legs draped over its side. "And so did you?" Naragavitz questioned. I shook the dizziness in my head. "Not at first," I said. "I didn't know where to go."

The doctor poured me a glass of water from a pitcher on his desk. Its temperature was less than lukewarm. Still, I was parched; emotionally drained. "I went to the Matthews house," I said. "I thought that if I showed up there looking for Hazel, her father wouldn't suspect that I knew a thing. It was late by this time; past midnight by a few ticks. When I rounded the corner to the Matthews house, I could see that the oil burner in the living room was still shining brightly. I moved for the door, but stopped myself suddenly. I couldn't show up looking like this. My hair was curled in summer sweat. My pants were filthy with mud, sitting tightly under a soaking wet t-shirt. The shirt too was covered in grime, with adorning blood stains on the upper chest. The sudden realization that I was wearing Hazel's blood was too much for me to bear. I sprinted towards my home, a fresh plan in mind. I ripped the shirt off of my damp body, clenching it in a fist as I ran. I had a plan now, and very little time to carry it out."

"I arrived home, and I admit it was difficult not to stay. I snuck quietly in the front door. My family had gone to bed long ago. Full of fright and shock, my room felt smaller than usual as I stepped inside. It was cluttered with a mess of clothes and papers. I picked up the nearest shirt I could find and threw it over my head, the smell of death still dominant. From my bed post, I took my best jacket; a black suit coat I wore only on special evenings. Wearing this would build my alibi with the Matthews. Creaking back down the stairs, I noticed the bloody t-shirt still in my hands. If it hadn't been summer, I'd simply start a fire in the fireplace and burn it up."

As I talked to the doctor, I found it difficult to remember the rest of the evening. The details were getting less and less clear as time went on. "I rinsed the shirt in the basement sink," I said. "It was still drenched with stains, though. My father kept a collection of old cut up rags, sheets, and t-shirts in a cardboard box on the basement shelf. They were all covered in mysterious stains; some from paint, some from dirt. My father would use them when working around the house. My mother would use the cleaner pieces as dusting rags. I didn't have time to think of another option. I grabbed the nearest pair of scissors and cut the shirt into hand-sized squares. The box was already overflowing with rags. No one would notice if I stashed the separated shirt at the bottom of the pile. I waited until the next bonfire a few weeks after that. An old friend had a couple of guys over for a get together. I stashed the shirt patches in my pocket, and when no one was watching I threw them into the bursting coals."

Back to that night; I dashed back to the Matthews house with care. I carried a small wooden bucket of soapy dishwater and the scrub brush my mother used to clean the kitchen floor. When I arrived, the light at the window was still burning. I stashed the cleaning supplies under a neighbors bush. Mr. Matthews face pasted to the window as I crossed it. Before I could reach the first step of the stoop, the door swung open with his rage. "Where the *hell* is my daughter?" he demanded. I stood a trivial boy, gazing up at his God-like figure. Not only was the man four inches taller than me, but I looked like his helpless disciple at the bottom of the stairs. He quivered with a mimicking lip. It's as if he was waiting for me to bow down on my knees. "That's why I'm here," I said. My voice weighed heavier than usual.

"What do you mean, 'that's why you're here'?" He croaked, deepening his voice to undermine my own. "She didn't show up for our date," I said. "She didn't?" Mr. Matthews asked, his attitude shifting from one level of concerned father to another. "Well, then you must have done something to upset her kid," he said with a more relaxed stance. "She looked upset when she walked out of here tonight. So you must know where she is then, right?" I shrugged, my hands fluffing my suit jacket into his awareness. "I thought I heard you both talking out here shortly after she left," he said defensively. "Mr. Matthews," I said innocently, "Whoever she was talking to, it wasn't me."

Mr. Matthews liked me. He thought I was a good kid; suitable for his daughter. It didn't take much to convince him that I was telling what he believed to be the truth. "Should I wait here with you?" I asked him. "No, no," he shook his head, placing his hand on my shoulder. "You go home. You can come by tomorrow and see her. I'm going to wait another half-hour and then I'm going out looking." I nodded with a covered lip. "Are you sure?" I asked, "I'm worried about her. It isn't like her to stand me up like this." Mr. Matthews stared emptily into the night. "You're right, kid," he said. "This isn't like her at all."

Mr. Matthews had already gone back inside by the time I reached the neighbor's yard. I bent down, casually picking up the bucket and brush without stopping. America was deep in its own summer sweat. As I walked past the house I'd broken into not long ago, I saw that the light in upstairs window had gone out. My girl must have worn the kid out quite a bit. It didn't surprise me; he wasn't the only who had grown tired of her. Did I feel guilty at the time? Sure. But now all of this extra work was proving to be a bother.

I was a walking dead man; mentally drained and frightened for my future. I arrived back at the park, arms burning from carrying the heavy pale. Nature was still; save for the smell of death drifting throughout the air. The park bench had a few splotches on its back bone, with the exception of a heavy paint streak on its upper lip. The blood had dried rapidly in the humidity of the night. I thrust the brush down into the water, which by now was hardly outdoor temperature. The water slipped up my wrist, preparing a chill from the air as I withdrew my arm. The smaller splotches were easy to clean away. I was able to scrub them in so they looked as if they belonged in the original woodwork. It didn't look so bad. Now the bench had a bit of cherry in its wood.

The streak of the lip had run downwards and dripped onto the seat a bit. I doused the brush, scrubbing the splotch again and again. It had done a decent job cleaning the mess, but it wasn't perfect. Compulsively, I scrubbed harder until my forearms bulged with soreness. Still not perfect enough, but it would have to do. The patch could pass for another brushed up piece of wood. After all, they'd find Hazel's body far down the river. They wouldn't have a clue where to begin searching for her point of entry into the water.

Looking down at my feet, I mashed the remnants of the peppermint into the dirt. The fragments of candy would dissolve fully before they'd ever be found. There was light dew on the lime-grass that kept the bits of blood vitalized. This made it easier for the marks to drip into the dirt; into the forgotten. What could I do? I couldn't scrub each blade of grass.

I came to the edge of the ravine. The ground looked clear, but then again the moonlight had been blocked by a few jutting trees. The only real mess was on the skin of the old oak tree. I scrubbed bristles against bark; but like the bench, it had already been stained. I rested the brush beside the bucket, putting my hands on my hip to size up the tree. I was a stronger man than this overweight elder. Drying my hands against the filth of my jeans, I lashed out at the oak. I tore its protective skin from its fragile body; put cracks in its shell like an old, worthless tortoise. I didn't stop until whitewashed carmine was all that stared back. My boots kicked at the ground, knocking the pieces into a pile near the edge. With hopes that the river would wash away the skin, I swept them over the cliff.

The bucket was the last of the evidence. I peered into its body, seeing my own sad reflection in the water of Hazel's cloudy blood. It was the last I saw of her life. I swung the bucket by its handle, sending its contents waving into the abyss. The river sounded quieter than it had mere hours ago; much quieter. Scrubbing the bristles of the brush into the earth, I swapped the marks of red for stains of brown. I had finished. I carried the bucket around my arm in a sling. My relief was short-lived.

The crude sound of a snapping twig interrupted my success. Someone else was in the park with me now. Their footsteps ran against the dirt like an inbound train. Then came the tune of rubber against plastic as I saw the figure climb the steps of the child's play area. It was a tall shadow with flowing form, its coat rippling against the wind. Whoever it was, they hadn't seen me yet. I stood alone in the center of the grass field; nowhere for me to go. Running would cause too much noise. I decided it would be best to let the figure search the play area as I attempted to sneak out of its vision. I resumed walking at a normal pace, raising my knees higher to prevent the rustling of grass.

The figure rattled through the chain curtains of the swing set now. The moonlight failed to hide anything that night, including my body. I was nearly to the street when I heard it scream. "Hey!" The voice, a man's, shot like thunder through the sky. I did not turn around. "Hey you!" he called again. My mind ached. Should I run? No, what if he could outrun me? Why cause suspicion if I don't have to? "You deaf?! Come here!" The man called again. He was fast approaching me now. I panicked, dumping the bucket into the grass. "Can I *help* you?" I said with intended attitude; my feet prepared to dash. As the man grew closer, I squinted into the darkness and took a few steps forward myself. "What are you doing out here this late? You know what happened to . . ." I interrupted him as we came face to face. "Mr. Matthews?" I said.

"Arthur?" Mr. Matthews asked, relaxing his stern stance with me for the second time that night. "What are you doing here? I thought I told you to go home." I shook his hand. The calluses could have torn holes in my skin. "I couldn't," I said, gulping heavily. "I don't know where she is . . . I . . . I . . ." I began to mumble on the brink of a breakdown. Mr. Matthews grabbed my shoulders. "It's alright, Arthur," he said. "It's alright. I know you're worried too. That's why I'm here. Hazel always talks about coming here with you. I thought she might be here." He could read my concern through the tenseness in my shoulders. He sighed deeply, the smell of coffee heavy on his breath. "I guess we were both wrong."

As he released his hold on me, I felt the trickle of falling rain on my forehead. Thunder rolled in the distance. Back then, I might have even thought that the incoming storm was a sign; Hazel's tears from Heaven. I know how foolish that sounds now. Either way, the teardrops were my savior. They'd wash away the blood in the grass; drench the park bench in an all-night downpour. The rain would fuel the river; wash the bark clean and send Hazel's body even further down the creek. I had no idea where her corpse was now. It would prove a bad omen to search for it, only serving to fingerprint me closer to the crime. "Let's get you home," Mr. Matthews said, motioning for me to follow. He hadn't noticed the bucket near his feet.

Mr. Matthews walked me to my house, sporadically calling out Hazel's name as if she were a lost household pet. By the tenth shout I felt like screaming, 'She's bloody dead already!' to shut him up. We arrived at my home just as the storm fully appeared overhead. "Please stay inside the rest of the night, Arthur," Mr. Matthews said as I opened the front door. "And you?" I asked, grinding my shoes against the porch cement. "I'm going to keep looking," he said. I offered him the umbrella near my feet, and he took it with a solemn grin. He nodded at me, as if he already knew they'd find her dead the next morning.

The wind picked up into a fierce slaughter of needling rain that night. The ground was a blanket of tree branches by the time morning rolled around. Thus, I had my first sleepless night. I went back to the park the next morning. The bucket had been washed away by the storm.

There was a look in Dr. Naragavitz's eyes that I did not like. It was a sickening slurp of a grin, almost like the story I told him had been erotic. "And after that?" he said, beating his pen against the paper. "What are you writing anyways?" I asked, trying to peer over the clipboard. "And then what happened?" Naragavitz said again, ignoring my request.

"I was questioned by the police. I was interviewed by the Matthews family. Even my own family had a set of questions for me. I stayed in town for more than a month. The Matthews family never suspected me; not even for a second. I was by their side nearly every night, praying to a God that I was beginning to have doubts with. The day of Hazel's funeral was one of the hardest days in my life. I loved that girl . . . I *still* love that girl. I remember Mrs. Matthews handing me a handkerchief; looking into my eyes and feeling that my tears were authentic. It was a black rag of dishcloth material, good at hiding tears."

"A week went by after that. Each day was harder than the last. I'm not quite sure what got to me first: the fear of being found or the constant yearning memories of her. I couldn't walk down the street without seeing a memory replay in my head. Each footstep echoed her name. You know, I never went back to the park after that day. I was *never* the same after that night."

"And so you left?" Dr. Naragavitz asked, finally paying attention to me and not his clipboard. "And so I left." I mimicked politely. "I couldn't say goodbye to my family. It was too difficult. I hadn't been the best son lately. My father and I had grown apart in the passing years. I was still my mother's baby, and I knew it would hurt her too bad to tell her that I was leaving. I was afraid that I would tell her and she would convince me not to go. London was my only option. And I . . . I . . . well; I suppose that's it then, isn't it?" Dr. Naragavitz stared back, setting his paperwork off to the side. "I suppose it is," he said.

I sat up in the hospital bed. "So would you say that Hazel lives inside of you?" Naragavitz asked. "That she has a special place in you in which she resides?" I brushed the oily grime in my hair. "Yes," I said. "Without a doubt. It's as if she controls part of me without my approval; like I see my true self only part of the time." My fingers were sticky. "I feel like she scrapes the insides of my skull, like she is begging for me to remember her. But when I think about her, it is never enough to satisfy her. She continues her crying, screaming, and cackling. She won't let me rest." The doctor rose to his feet, placing his hands behind his back as he paced around the room. "And that dream you had," he said. "The one where your brain was blue and grey - how did you feel about that?" I rubbed my fingers against my forehead. They were slick with perspiration. "Like I was sick," I said. "Like half of me was already dead; controlled by Hazel."

The doctor rubbed at his stubble of a beard. "So you would say that the grey half feels dead?" I rubbed at the back of my neck now. "Yes," I replied. "Like that half's dead and there's a bridge in the center to the other side. It's only a matter of time before she crosses it and the right side becomes infected with her memory too. I fear at that time that I will lose control completely. If Hazel doesn't kill me; I'll have killed myself by that point." Naragavitz played with his stubble a moment longer.

"Interesting," he said. "So it's the left side that's dead then?" I shook my head. "I don't know if it is dead or not." I replied. "But it is surely poisoned with her control." The doctor rubbed his hands together. I could almost feel the warmth of the friction. "Like a tumor?" he asked. I nodded. "Hmmm," he bit his lower lip. "You know we can remove tumors now, Harold. People become sick, infected, disoriented. We cut them open, remove the diseased organ, and they are back to their normal selves. The brain is as much an organ as a kidney or lung, you know." My hands moved to the corners of my lips. I was nervous now; but he was right.

The doctor turned to face me. "You are willing to do anything to be rid of her, correct?" I could no longer make eye contact. "Yes," I said sternly. "And you want to be normal again, yes?" He came closer to me. "Yes," I said, sweating harder. "And that's why you came to me, right?!" He spit at me. "To get better? To no longer live in fear?! To live! To breathe?!" The freshness of his breath was in my face now. "Yes!" I erupted from my seat, fed up with the torment. He stared back at my heavily panting body. "Good," he whispered, more relaxed now. "Because I have an answer for you."

"They've been practicing it secretly for quite a few years now," The doctor said, again pacing the room. "It hasn't had much success; but that is due to the carelessness of the doctor. Myself, I have seen the procedure done three times. I have watched each doctor make mistakes and I now know how to carry out the procedure perfectly. Only twenty percent of the patients thus far have survived, but the ones that did lived free of guilt and worry. They are free, Harold, free as birds basking in the rising sun. You could be amongst those birds. Do you want to chirp with them? Or would rather squawk in remembrance?"

"With you, I can guarantee your success rate at more than double what it has been in the past. I will be the only one conducting the procedure. There will be no one to make mistakes." We stood in front of each other, man to man. "It's called a lobotomy," he said. "I can remove that rotten half of your brain, leaving your mind cleansed and refreshed. Hazel won't be able to infect you any further. I will remove the left half of the brain, thus removing her venom. You will wake from the procedure as a new man.

You will no longer confuse Arthur with Harold, and vice-versa. You will able to sleep again. You will be able to live again. You will be able to love again. But only if you let me help you."

I could not find any words, only dry skin on the side of my mouth. My fingers were stained with rolls of black dots. What he was saying seemed insane, but somehow made irrational sense. We have two lungs that we don't need; two kidneys while one serves as a spare. Why should the brain be different than any other organ? We have only one heart. But why would our brains be divided in two if they could not be separated? I rose from the hospital bed. "Harold?" Dr. Naragavitz said. I sensed the nervousness in his stance. "Harold?" he asked again.

The door seemed far off as I walked with a blurry gaze. My mind was numb, boxing decisions back and forth. Did I really have any other option? I couldn't live with Hazel any longer. But what if the procedure was unsuccessful? Would I be better off dead? "Harold!" The doctor screamed as I threw my coat over my shoulders. "I don't know how much time we have." I fit the top hat firmly onto my head, feeling it warm both sides of my skull equally. I opened the door to rotting winter. I stepped out, shattering newly fallen snowfall. "Schedule the procedure," I said. The doctor's smile was the last thing I saw before the door broke us apart.

*Chapter Nine – Submission*
*From the Journal of: Johnny Tappling*
*December 23rd, 1905*

Now it is I that fear for my own sanity. These past few days have been unbearable. I do not know what God thinks I have done to deserve all of this. Perhaps he is angry with me for keeping Harold's secret. The lord and I both know that what Harold has done is unforgivable. The Burden stopped by yesterday to tell me the rest of his story. On several occasions he tried to put me behind his eyes; to put me into his past. I could not do it - no matter how hard I tried. I'm no killer. I am Johnny Tappling: failing tea salesman and neglectful husband.

God, where to even begin? I am worried about Harold. I am worried about Thomas. I am worried about Annie. I am worried about myself. Things have turned sour ever since Harold let me into his past. At first I wanted to help the man, but now I just want him out of my life. I care about him, but he has brought this family nothing but immense pain. It began two evenings ago when Harold stepped into Tappling Teas.

We have only spoken twice since he told me about Hazel. I was near falling asleep on the countertop during the afternoon down time. I was expecting Thomas to walk in when I heard the door chime, but was rather surprised to see Harold standing there instead. "Johnny," he said to me with pride in his voice. "I finally listened to your nagging advice. I saw a doctor." "That's great, Harold!" I said, moving to shake his hand. "Doctor Steinman, I bet?" Harold shook his head in rejection. "No," he replied. "He's not a mainstream doctor." "Hmmph," I snorted, "His name isn't Dr. Jekyll, is it?" Harold laughed, letting go of my hand. "You're a funny guy, Johnny." He said. "His name is Dr. Naragavitz. You know the one I asked you about earlier in the week? I found his information amongst the pile of papers you gave me, but you didn't seem to recall getting in touch with him?" I could not move. "Hello?" Harold asked, waving his hand across my pale-stricken face. "Johnny. Hello? How about a pat on the back or something?" I'd been waiting all this time for Harold to see a doctor; months and months of waiting. Now that he's finally gone, he sees Dr. Naragavitz?"

"Harold," I said sternly, crossing eyes with him." You have to stay away from Naragavitz. I know I told you to see a doctor, but you have to *promise* me that you'll stay away from Dr. Naragavitz," Harold looked back as an injured fawn.

"Stay away?" he questioned. "Stay away? I finally listen to you after all these months, and now you want me to ignore your own advice?" I stepped forward. "No, Harold. Listen." My voice was dire. "I want you to get help from a doctor; just not Dr. Naragavitz."

When Harold first told me about the mysterious note he'd found, I thought for a brief moment that I must have merely forgotten about that particular doctor visit. The more I thought, the more this memory lapse bothered me. I had never even heard of a Dr. Naragavitz in my life. The name sounded foreign. He couldn't have been from London; not even America.

"Harold," I said. "I figured if anyone knew who Naragavitz was, it would be Anthony. You remember Anthony, right? The gent who gets the teas from Japan; the same guy who smuggles the coffee packets in for you?" Harold didn't move. His face flourished with rosy redness. "Naragavitz is originally from Russia. He practiced medicine in his home country before moving to America after reading of the 'land of opportunity'. He isn't right in the head, Harold. The guy's completely insane."

"Insane?!" Harold scoffed. "He's the sanest person I've ever met. His diagnosis makes logical sense. There's no whitewashed jargon or incoherent jumbling of diagnoses. He knew exactly what treatment I needed from the very second I walked in his door. In fact, he knew what I needed *before* I even

set foot in his office!" The room reeked of imbecility.
"And what is that you need, Harold?" I shot back.
"Surgery? He wants to cut you open and you're
going to let him, aren't you?" Harold stared blankly
at my forehead. "So what if I am?" he asked. "None
of your suggestions have helped. You failed to help
me as a friend, and now you can't even support my
decision to seek treatment!"

"He's going to ruin you, Harold!" I was forcing
him to look me in the eyes now. "Anthony told me
everything. His medical license has been revoked for
over a year. He's wanted by the American
authorities." Harold scoffed. "Well then he's just like
me," he said. "He's got a past to run from just like I
do. That makes him a bad person, does it? He
understands what I'm running from. How could you
ever understand? You live your cushiony life with
your perfect family; your beautiful wife and
exemplary son. You don't know a thing about true
torture." I could only laugh. "And that's a bad
thing?" I said. "Now you're angry at me for having a
family; for being somewhat successful? Let me tell
you, Harold: My family life is far from perfect. Annie
and I haven't made love in months. I only see
Thomas briefly before he heads off to bed. I don't
even know the last time Annie and I had time alone.
You don't . . ." Just then the door opened and
Thomas walked in.

I'd forgotten today was the day he was coming
to help me after school. I was a disaster; an

emotional, blistering wreck. Harold's forehead glistened with sweat and anger. His hair had parted in greasy points. "Hi, Harold!" Thomas came jogging through the shop and stepped up to the counter. His presence was ill-timed; his voice a scratchy annoyance. "Buying some tea? What's going on?" Harold turned to face my son. "Why are you all sweaty?" he asked, tugging at the dismal brown scarf around his own neck. "Did you run here?" Harold scratched his uncut nails against the countertop. "No," Harold said. "Harold was just leaving," I interrupted. I didn't need him filling Thomas's head with his insanity.

"Thomas," I said, my own nails now scratching at the wood. "You're here to help, right?" He nodded back. The look on his face told me he'd noticed the redness in my own cheeks. "Here," I said, handing him a half-empty flask of black dragon tea. "Do me a favor and make a new batch of tea; your choice. Any flavor you want." His face lit up with obnoxious joy. "Sure!" He said, grabbing the cold flask from my hands. "But it's still pretty full. I . . ." "Thomas!" I belted, banging my palm against the table. A bit of dust exploded in the sting. "Please just fill it up." I tasted resentment as he disappeared into the back. Harold would not look at me. "As I was saying," I said in undertone. "My family isn't perfect. And that's *your* fault."

What I saw staring back was a man of understanding; a man who knew that he'd only burdened me with his friendship. Harold knew that his past had leaked into my future. It wasn't right for him to weigh me down with his tainted saddle. He had been using me much like a horse. He thought that I was stronger than him; someone that was reliable and had a way of getting things for him. But he knew now that he had kicked me one too many times. I suppose I knew it all along too, but the fact hadn't hit me hard until now. Harold adjusted his hat and nodded with a smolder. The threshold of friendship and self-respect had finally been opened. He walked out into the afternoon, his umbrella still resting on my table.

Harold's problems have cost me time and money that I never even had for my own family. He has tapped out my once innocent conscious and replaced it with worry. My gaze on the umbrella was shattered by the sound of clanging steel. "Thomas?!" I called, leaving my post and walking into the back room. "Dammit, Thomas!" The vacuum flask laid in pieces on the floor. The lid had cracked; the pump completely snapped in half. Thomas stood with his arms by his side, his pants soaked in steaming tea. His navy flannel jacket was stained in splashed waves. "Sorry, Dad, I . . ." He began to say. My frustration didn't give him the chance to finish.

"God, Thomas! All you had to do was dump out the old stuff and fill it with hot water. I thought you'd be able to handle that, but I guess that I was wrong." Now my own son wouldn't even look at me.

I knew I was being harsh, but the words continued to flow. I told him how disappointed I was in him, that I had noticed his slipping grades. I even went as low as to threaten the certainty of his Christmas presents. "Man up! Man up!" I said to him. "Now clean this up!" As he looked up to me, there were kindling coals of onyx in his young eyes. He didn't need to say anything. His look told me where I could shove my request. "Thomas, I . . ." I moved to rub his shoulder. He brushed past me and ran out into the sales floor. I heard the front door slam.

I caught my reflection in the mirror above the sink. I saw myself for what I would eventually become. Alone. Harold's burden had cost me everything. I'd spent my hard earned coins trying to find him a diagnosis. The time I put into helping him had robbed my family of a husband and a father. Harold's friendship had always been something that I valued. But this word-of-mouth guilt is too much, even for two men. Hmpfh. I suppose three men if I'm including that psychotic doctor.

For the first time since learning of Harold's crime, I saw him more as a killer than a friend. I thought about losing Thomas. My own son is just as much of a child as Hazel was. Harold killed someone's child. No family should ever have to watch their own child be lowered into the dirt. It's not the way it's meant to be; it's not the way God intended. I stood in the emptying room, the disaster of the broken flask around me as a nightmare played in my head. I could see Thomas now, standing outside my bedroom door at midnight. He was banging on my door, pleading for me to let him in. I wouldn't. I heard the creaking of footsteps coming up the stairwell; saw Thomas spin around to face the shadows. And then there was Harold, grabbing at Thomas's mouth to smother his screams. His fingers were denting Thomas's tiny, still-developing Adam's apple. He pressed harder, harder, deeper, stronger; until I saw my son's throat collapse.

Harold would never touch my family. He would never see them again; I wouldn't give him the chance. Harold Elway is no longer a friend of mine. He is a helpless murderer. I have let him ruin me; I've been too weak to see it until now. Perhaps I could still catch Thomas if I hurried. I ran out into the sales floor, crashing through the front door. The street was full of startled strangers. My son was nowhere to be seen. I'd make it up to Thomas later tonight. I'd settle everything then.

When I stepped back into the shop, I saw that Harold's umbrella was no longer leaning against the center table. My first thought was that he'd snuck back in and grabbed it. As I went to grab a wash rag, it hit me that I had only heard the door shut once. "Thomas!" I yelled, dropping the rag and running out the front door once more. He must have seen the umbrella and grabbed it on his way out. He knew where Harold lived too. I used to let Thomas walk with him some days when I had to work late. The very thought of that sickens me now. I couldn't let Harold near my son. What if he hurt him? What if he told him about his past? He wouldn't do that, would he? God, who knows what he'll do anymore? He's bloody insane.

The door crashed behind me in a fatherly panic. Thomas had been running when he left here, but he couldn't have gotten far. I didn't bother locking the shop. Work wasn't my priority anymore. Family was.

I don't know how many shoulders I brushed into. I shouldn't have been as afraid as I was. Deep down, I knew that Harold would never hurt my family. But then again, he hadn't been himself lately. I didn't even know who the real Harold Elway was. Thomas wasn't around the first corner. I tore around the second bend, brain bustling. As I passed Thomas's school, I wondered what my words had triggered in Harold's own brain. It wasn't like him to leave an argument without the last word. I began wishing he would have just dumped tea over my head again. This time, it's as if I poured the cup of filth over my own son. How could I have been so negligent? He wasn't around the third turn either.

December felt warm against my coatless body. Poor Thomas, he probably thought he was going to get shafted on presents again this year. I had let my anger for Harold lash out and grab hold of Thomas. My empty stomach carried me faster through the streets. The ground was still lightly covered in snowfall. My feet struggled against the ice, but I wasn't about to let that keep me from ensuring Thomas's safety. I nearly wiped out around the fourth corner, but caught my balance before forcing myself to a complete stop. Down the street in front of me was a brown scarf flapping up from the brick.

"Thomas!" I screamed, again dashing in his direction. Kneeling over him was that screwy bastard: Harold. "Goddammit!" I screeched, now in a full-tackle position. "I'll kill you, Harold! I'll bloody kill you!" As I neared the pair, my former friend stood and stretched his arms out in front of him. He waved to slow me down, but my one-sided mind wouldn't let me. I plowed straight into his gut, sending him flying to the ground. He crippled under the adrenaline of my weight, putting his forearms in front of his face as I desperately beat him into the brick.

"Dad!" I heard, as my arms shot harder. "Dad!" My fists clenched tighter. I tore Harold's arms away by the wrists and spit into his gaping mouth. "Dad!" I heard again, blunting Harold's resistance. I felt a light pull on my shoulder as I turned to see Thomas holding onto my shirt. "Stop!" He said, "Stop! He didn't do anything! What's wrong with you?!" His voice cracked heavily, the words seeping into me. I realized that he was right. Harold wasn't fighting back; he was merely trying to protect himself. Still in a daze, I quickly removed myself from Harold and shot to my feet. I felt the adrenaline rush from my body, leaving me faint. "My God!" I said, rushing to hold Thomas in my arms. "Your face!" I cried. "What happened to your face?!"

Thomas's left eye bled like a rotten raspberry. His cheeks had been cut and riddled with scratches. The blue in his jacket was stained with muddied snow. "Thomas, what happened?!" I yelled. Harold sat up slowly behind me, stretching to retrieve his top hat that I had knocked away. "Some kids at school jumped me," he said, pushing himself away from my embrace. "They've been giving me some trouble. They saw me walk by the school and chased after me. I know I shouldn't have been going this way, but Harold forgot his umbrella at your store. All I was doing was trying to get it back to him." For the first time, I saw a man in my son. "Why did you attack Harold?" He had every right to judge me.

"I thought he was hurting you," I spat. "I thought he . . . uh . . . ." "Hurting me?" Thomas interrupted. "Why would Harold hurt me? He's the one who chased the kids away. He was at the end of the street when they jumped me. I yelled for him and he came running to help me." Harold stood behind us now, brushing the street sludge from his suit. "Sorry they took your umbrella, Harold." Thomas said. "I tried." Harold shook his head innocently. "It's alright, Thomas. I can always get another. That was very nice of you to try and bring it to me." Thomas ran and embraced Harold. "Thanks for helping me," he said. My knee still against the cold street, I finally rose and began wiping the dirt from my own clothes. "Who attacked you, Thomas?" I asked. He coughed, expelling a cloud of frosty breath into the air. "No one," he said. "You don't have time to hear it." Thomas took off in a run towards home. I could feel Harold's condescending glare. "You thought I'd hurt your son?" he asked, disgusted. I sighed deeply as I watched him turn and walk away. There I was again. Alone.

What have I become? Am I already a bitter, old man in his young thirties? I have shattered the trust of my dearest friend. I am not someone my son looks up to and respects. My wife? God, my wife doesn't even know who I am. *I* don't know who I am any more. That look that Thomas gave me; I've never been more ashamed in my life. It's bad enough when your own father gives it to you, but when it comes from your own son? Someone who is supposed to be less mature and experienced than you? He may as well have shoved a dagger through my rotten heart.

When I came home tonight, Thomas would not speak to me. Annie tells me that she understands the stress I've been under, but I know she is lying out of politeness. It's only a matter of time before she gives me the same stare that Thomas did. The pearl earrings I just wrapped her for Christmas will be meaningless. Objects don't make me a man.

We were able to get Thomas nearly everything on his Christmas list this year. Although they all cost quite a bit of money, I now feel that they still aren't enough. Perhaps all my family needs for the holidays is a better man in their lives. Harold just wants to find a friend in me again. However, his presence around my family is still discomforting. He loves my son; but he loved that girl at one point too. That devil inside of Harold; how can I be sure it doesn't still live within him? We are only human, I admit. Our natural instincts tell us to do whatever it takes to survive. Harold, young and misguided, did what he thought it took for him to feel justice.

Justice, unfortunately, has been a bit sour itself these past few years. It doesn't seem to matter which country you call home; each case you hear sounds more absurd than the last. I surely wouldn't call Harold's actions justified; but in the world we find ourselves in today, there are much worse criminals. Serial killers and mass murderers; chronic rapists who deflower countless lives. In the end, the life they end up ruining the most is always their own. Harold is a petty criminal in that regard, though he still feels the scorpion's tale of consequence.

Still, there is no space for him in my life at this time. He is highly unstable and I think that we should keep our friendship at somewhat of a standstill. Harold must understand that before I can help him, I must learn to be a better family man; to find time to balance my work life with personal and family time. This is a lesson I should have learned years ago from *my* father. Now *I* look like the child. I just want to make things right with Harold before I write him off for awhile. I suppose I will try and patch things up briefly with him before taking some time for myself.

Alas, I could continue feeling sorry for myself and fill this journal with countless random recordings, but that would get me nowhere. My only option is to look forward from this point. I have no choice but to try and repair my family once more, both financially and structurally. Annie would not allow me to continue pestering Thomas to speak with me. She said that it would be best to let the boy settle down for a day and try and talk with him tomorrow. There is no school in honor of Christmas Eve, so hopefully I will have a chance to speak with him at breakfast. I was scheduled to work a half-day at Tappling Teas tomorrow to deal with the desperate times, but today's events have struck a change of heart in me. When I die, I will be measured for the qualities I possessed; not for how much money was in my pocket.

As for Dr. Naragavitz, I suppose it is Harold's right to seek treatment wherever he desires. Perhaps it will keep him occupied while I am working out my personal issues. I do not know what kind of surgery the doctor wants to perform on him, but maybe I was too quick to jump at Naragavitz. All I remember is what I heard from Anthony a few days ago. When I asked about the sleeping pills, he joked that he had gotten the pills from the crazy doctor. He acted shocked that I did not know who Naragavitz was.

Anthony sometimes forgets that we don't all have the luxury of traveling as much as he does. He was supposed to bring back an American newspaper article for me to read, but I suppose he never got around to it. I am expecting a delivery the day after Christmas; perhaps I will ask him about it then.

Up until now, I could not decide what to get Harold for the holidays. Now the answer is as clear as day. Perhaps I will even throw in a box of chocolates from Maggie's Delectable's and a few candles from The Wax Parlor. I can only hope that he will accept my apologetic gift with a kind heart. I want him to know that we remain friends and that he can continue to trust me.

The night is growing old now, and I can't help but be kept awake by the day's withering events. The winter nights are so quiet compared to the summer croaks of horny crickets. Perhaps the loneliness of winter tests the true strength of a man's psyche. It is truly man's toughest mental battle against Mother Nature. Twisters come and go; floods drown our shops and homes; but nothing tests your endurance like the brittleness of the joyous seasons.

After breakfast tomorrow, I am going to go out and finish the remainder of my Christmas shopping. I believe that I will stop at Harold's Christmas morning in hopes of making things right for the holidays. All I can do right now is try and mend what is broken. I pray that I can reach Harold myself before the doctor does; or at the very least find out what kind of operation Harold is considering. If I do not write for a few days, I wish a Happy Holidays to my family. It can only get better from here onwards.

*Chapter Ten – An Early Gift*
*From the Journal of: Dr. Yovan Naragavitz*
*December 24th, 1905*

The brain is a magnificent thing, capable of fathoming endless possibilities. Admiration, satisfaction, manipulation, glorification . . . I could ramble on and on in my own rhetoric. But every now and then our mind becomes ill, just like the rest of our body. At times our mind feels a little foggy - a quick nap might fix it; sometimes a few days are necessary instead. But what if the brain can't seem to fix itself; if it is forever poisoned or damaged?

I would say a lobotomy is much like any sort of amputation. If one gets frostbite or a touch of gangrene, the only plausible option is to remove the infected area. If a man loses an arm, he has another to work with. If he should lose an eye, he has another to see him through the day. The same is true for a kidney. In fact, some organs are completely unnecessary. I have been doing extensive research on the uselessness of the appendix lately. If the brain were any different than these organs, than why would God have split it in two for us? The simple bickering of the left and right brain is a mere myth in today's fast-developing medical world. The two work together, yes; but they do not need each other. Their reliance on their other half is what we are still experimenting with as medical technology moves forward.

I have spent years researching the procedure I am about to perform on patient number forty-seven: Harold Elway. I have watched doctors fail, try again, and fail again. I have seen classmates of mine butchered in the streets for their reckless procedures. An old teacher of mine was jailed not more than a year ago for failing to successfully carry out a lobotomy. I watched that procedure. I know where he went wrong. And I know how to avoid such novice mistakes.

There is a lot riding on the success of this procedure. I have already outlined my plans for a trophy case in my home. Yesterday, I put a down payment on an empty office building near Central Square. After hearing of my inevitable achievements with Harold, the fools of the world will flock to my feet. They will join hands and sing for me to heal them - and for a nominal fee; I will be able to. I will be their hero; their savior. I will cure any nauseating illness they whine of. I will shine my medals with the clothes off their backs. *I* will be *God.*

Abel pulled through with the last bit of money that I needed for the anesthesia. He even fronted me money for the payment on the office building. He has been a wonderful friend to me. Unlike the rest of society, Abel is a smart man who has his rare dull moments. He often wants to know the names of my patients; what their illnesses are and if there is anything he can do to assist me. While my practices are a bit unwelcomed, I stick to my agreement of confidentiality. I have assured Abel time and time again that his finances are going towards the very best use of my skills. He was persistent with this last loan, though. I had no choice but to agree and let him assist me.

He is nothing more than a struggling factory worker. His interest in the medical field is wasted. He doesn't have the brains to make himself into a doctor. He constantly throws this mumbled nonsense into my ears about what he read in the latest medical textbook. Luckily, Harold's procedure is one that we both agree to be important to the future of surgery. Am I using him in that way? I did promise he would see his fair share of my future wealth. I'm not being unfair, am I? Ech. Who really cares?

One day I dream of owning a mansion all to myself. No bothersome wife or crying children to distract me from my work. There will be only beautiful silence while the neighbors adore me. I would never bog myself down with pets either. A dog is just as needy as a woman; a cat is just as helpless as one too. They exist with only needs for me to serve them. Without human intervention, pets are nearly helpless. Even the ones without homes feed off of the garbage that humans throw away. Without pets, some people get lonely. It's a good thing I'm not like most other people.

The putrid thoughts of family or marriage have never poisoned my mind. Relationships only get in the way of the individuals deepest desires. Countless women have their aspirations murdered the moment they pop out a child. A thousand men have lost their masculinity and boyhood ambitions to a bottle and a blanket. Some argue that their partners 'keep them in check,' or 'remind them of what is truly important.' Horseshit. The truth lies in what I have already explained; that what makes us who we are is a combination of our firing neurons and thoughts. We are a collection of our experiences and a branching tree limb of feelings. We act out in a way that is different from what we call normal, but since we indeed acted that way, then that feeling or action is undeniably part of who we are. In Harold's case, a part of what defines him is deathly ill.

Harold and I are not too different from each other. His desire for family life has been lost in the dust for years now. I surely don't think that such wasted lust can be recovered at this point. He killed any hope he had of finding a wife when he killed Hazel. Johnny's boy, Thomas, fills any void that he might be feeling from the lack of having his own child. Something inside of Harold made him do what he did for a reason, and now it seems to have finally gotten the best of him.

It is because Harold and I are so similar that we both have decided to advance the date of the surgery. It seems that both our priorities are on the outcome of the procedure. Because we have no connection to a family of any sort, the holiday isn't much of a holiday to either one of us. None of these other fabricated vacation days mean anything either. Holidays are for enjoying with families. Those without families grow to loathe them more with each passing year. I never really thought that I was missing out on much.

I had originally approached Harold with a surgery date of December 29th, but an event involving Johnny the other day had him practically clawing at my door. He came to my office just before closing time last night. He's lucky he caught me, actually. I usually head home early when I don't have any patients on the agenda; which I rarely do. Ironically, the only reason I was still at the office was because I was going over the jumbled transcripts of our previous sessions.

It was just after four in the afternoon, and Harold came bursting into my office in a sweat. "Harold!" I called out, springing from my seat. He rushed towards my desk and swiped my glass of water from its surface. Panting heavily, he gulped the entire glass. I could tell immediately he was suffering from a panic attack. "What's going on?" I asked. He slammed the glass back onto the table, briefly securing it before it shattered from the impact. Patients often cannot measure their own strength when under significant stress, worry, or anger. I crossed my hands, biting the underside of my tongue with a lump in my cheek.

"Sorry," Harold said, now pacing back and forth in front of my desk frantically. He walked tall with a heavy slouch in his upper back. His steps were strong, with the exception of a limp in his right leg. "Sorry, sorry, sorry . . ." he repeated over and over again. "It's alright," I said, motioning him to sit in the nearest bed. "She told me to kill him," he said, ignoring my request. I grabbed my clipboard, flipping to the last page of notes that I had taken. "Kill who?" I asked. "Who told you? Hazel?"

Harold stared back with a blank slate. Of course it was Hazel who had told him. "Kill who?" I repeated again. "That's why you're here, Harold. I can't help you unless you give me information." His steps continued at a rapid pace. "Thomas!" He screeched, grabbing at the back of the closest chair. A mist of spit spewed from the name. "Thomas! Johnny's boy!" *Jesus!* I nearly yelped at the sound of the boy's name. My professionalism was strong enough to keep my wits intact. "And . . . You didn't follow through with this decree, right?" I questioned. He darted back in squints. "Of course I didn't *bloody* touch him!" he screeched. His fingernails dug harder into the back of the chair, so much so that I thought he might splinter it.

I let the patient wallow in self-awkwardness for a moment. "She told me I should have let him die," I coughed faintly at Harold's voice. "So not to kill him?" I asked. "But to let him die?" The patient nodded his head. "What did she mean by let him die?" I said, writing. Harold straddled around the chair he had been clinging to and finally sat down, hissing as he grabbed at his leg. Without further hesitation, he began telling me of the day he had experienced so far. Apparently his friend Johnny had written him off ever since they last spoke. In my own opinion, it sounds like that Johnny fellow has a few mental problems of his own. "Do you think he'll tell your secret?" I asked. Harold could not answer me.

Shortly after Harold stormed out of the tea shop, young Thomas apparently discovered that Harold had left his umbrella leaning against the table. Considering the boy has grown quite fond of Harold, he thought he'd be doing him a great favor by returning it to him. "I was walking down Orchard Street," Harold added. "I heard someone chirp my name, and I turned around to see Thomas waving my umbrella in the air. I had left the tea shop fuming with anger, and I admit it brightened my mood to see that the boy had followed me all that way just to return my umbrella. I'd say we were a good seventy yards from each other. Just as I rose my finger to acknowledge him, three boys jumped out of the alley way from his left. They were bigger than Thomas, but I could not make out how old they appeared to be." "So he was jumped then?" I added. Harold nodded. Sometimes reassurance and repetition help a patient recall a story better. Details thus far had been a bit scarce.

"The biggest boy," Harold said. "He knocked Thomas to the ground. He was the first to start beating him square in the face. The other two boys, just a tad smaller, got on both sides of him and began kicking him in the ribs. I could almost feel that poor boy's pain as they sunk themselves into him. I sprinted faster than I have in a decade. They didn't have much time to beat up Thomas, but I still felt like I could have gotten to him faster. They fled when I came within a few yards or so. One of the younger kids, whom I then saw was wearing a handkerchief around his face, grabbed my umbrella from the street and drug it along with him. As I reached Thomas, the kids disappeared back into the alley, hollering profanity and other unintelligible curses. They must have thought they were some real rough cowboys or something of the nature."

"I kneeled down over Thomas. Fresh blood tore seams beneath his eyelids. He tried to sit up, but I coaxed him back downwards. I wanted to get a good bit of that blood cleaned up before it ran down his face. I took the handkerchief out of my suit pocket and wiped beneath his eyelids. Thomas cringed a bit of course, emitting a viper-like hissing sound as I dabbed at his cheek bones. He was a strong boy, though; obviously bitter in his pride and careful not to shed a tear. I moved my hands down to his sides, tenderly pressing against his ribs. He gave a light twitch, but my touch didn't seem to bother him much. I figured he'd just be a bit sore; nothing broken."

"The wounds on his face were still fresh, oozing with lineage. He told me that his father had yelled at him, and proceeded to tell me of the detest he had for his dad's absence in his life lately. As he spoke, I realized that he was a lot like his father whether he liked it or not. I could see Johnny in his eyes; all the things he loved in one eye, and all the things he hated in the other. 'He seems to be bothered with something lately,' Thomas said. 'It isn't just work or money.' I couldn't help but feel guilty. They were my problems that were weighing Johnny down."

"That's when I asked if he knew who had attacked him. He said it was three boys who had been bothering him at school. Before now, they'd only shoved him or cursed at him. One day they snagged one of his school books and tore it up into pieces. Thomas said he hadn't done anything to harm them, but that the boys simply picked on him because they were older. I believe he said they were two grades above him. That's when I heard a shout from further up the street."

"It was Johnny. He came dashing towards me. That's the fastest I've ever seen that man run. I put my arms out to try and stop him, but I saw the delirium in his eyes just before he hit me. He straddled my body, putting all of his strength into weighing me down. He then began to beat me, and I could only guard my face to protect myself. It was apparent that he thought *I* was the one who'd beaten up Thomas. Perhaps if he'd spent a second of his time listening to his son, he'd know that he had been having problems in the schoolyard."

I let Harold continue his speech without interruption. He seemed enthralled in his own story now, like it was some sort of unfathomable fairy tale with vital life lessons intertwined. I couldn't help but roll my thumbs a bit. I'd heard similar stories from patients before. They dodge the real reason for their visit until they have nowhere left to go but straight through it.

"Johnny is a two-faced bastard." Harold said, regaining my attention. "But Harold," I said, leaning forward. "Aren't we all a bit two-faced? When you hurt Hazel, wasn't that just your other face? We are all made up of complex emotions and unpredictable behaviors. Johnny is simply bogged down with your burden. *You* are simply handicapped by your burden. It isn't fair for you to blame him for his erratic behavior. We have all been in that position before. The thing that makes you different is that you have remnants of another person living in one half of your brain. Hazel has moved in against your own will throughout all of these years. Sometimes these feelings that you experience *aren't* really you. They come from the part of you that Hazel has infected. The difference is that *you* are sick, Harold." The patient looked towards the floor, rubbing his forehead. "I suppose that explains what happened next." he said.

Harold looked proudly into the corner of the room as he continued. "There's a ravenous demon inside of me. He came out to play that summer night. Regrets, regrets; I've tinkered with regrets. But the sheer thrill of being in control of a person's life; choosing whether they live or die . . ." His hands wrapped around an imaginary neck. "There's nothing like that thrill. All it took to infect me was a single feeding. Now Hazel has my life in her palm. She must be feeling such euphoria, confident that she has a good chance of winning this battle. I had my chance to release the demon, and I was too weak to control it. Though it lead me to nothing but mistakes, God Damn it felt good."

Harold was sick with misguided delight. "I left Johnny standing alone in the aftermath of his fury," he said. "As I rounded the corner, I felt like a bit of a cowboy myself. I'd not only stood up for Thomas, but for my own glory as well. I remember feeling a light chill in my right leg, like I'd been struck with a frost-tipped arrow. The muscles in my thigh began to ache as if they'd been beaten like a child's piñata. I took a few more steps towards my home. What I thought was a glare from the sun turned into a blurry onslaught of nausea. The world before my eyes became encased in a twisting kaleidoscope."

"The emptiness of my stomach became apparent as I keeled over and expelled flaming strings of stomach acid onto the street beneath me. The alkalinity of the coffee I'd had for breakfast added further unpleasantness to the bile." There was a slow shift in the seriousness of Harold's voice. "My throat felt coated in citrus slime as I took a few more steps. It was then that my leg began to feel like a piece of shriveling steak that had spent eight summers out in the sun. I lost control of the muscle, crippling down onto my knees as I felt another churn in my stomach. I looked up, trying to block the imaginary splotches of sunlight with the scissoring fingers of my hand." Harold's whole story sounded like a well-thought out fable, exploding with colorful detail and description.

"The sun sat with its feet up behind me. I now saw that the bright light I was blocking was one being emitted by a fresh blue aura; Hazel, obviously. She floated from a nearby rooftop before surfing the briars of a preserved bush. Twisting around a lamppost, she emerged in her true form before me. Now it was I who was bowing to someone greater than me. I don't believe in a God, but I imagine doing so would feel something like this. 'You belong to me now,' Hazel said to me. I was taken aback by the normality of her voice. I expected an exaggerated echo or a cringing hiss. She sounded just as sweet as she had the night I murdered her."

"'All I've wanted these past few months is to ask you 'why?' Arthur. I have tried to understand why you felt like you had to prove yourself to me.' Hazel stared down at me, unmoving. 'Look at yourself now,' she said. 'You're cowering before the image of a still-seventeen year old girl. You're pathetic, Arthur; a waste. You should have let Thomas die. You should have let that gang of boys beat him into the afterlife. It's better here. There is no physical pain, like the kind I've struck into your right leg.' Hazel looked up at the sun behind me. 'I don't have much time in my visible form. Your attempt at ridding yourself of my spirit will prove unsuccessful. I won't rest until I feel at peace. I won't stop until you've killed again.'"

Harold broke down, burying his eyes in the comfort of his hands. "You have to help me *now*, doctor. Please! Her control over me is growing stronger with each breath that I take! She wants to kill me; she won't stop until she's ruined what remains of my life!" I looked at the patient as a witness to true pain. For the first time, I felt authentic sympathy for a paying client. What if he killed again before the scheduled surgery? What if he couldn't bear the haunts any longer and put a bullet through his brain? What if he poisoned himself as an attempt to kill Hazel all over again?

The patient recovered after the brief breakdown. "I feel as if I'm not even the one that's pleading," Harold Said. "I feel as if I had no control over the tears that just came from me. I'm begging you to help me, doctor. I have no friends left on this earth. I'm asking *you*, as a doctor and a friend, to advance my surgery."

My sympathy faded quickly as I glared into the beady eyes of the lab rat before me. Harold had no idea that he was actually the one doing *me* a favor. "What happened next?" I asked, tabling his request to the side of my mind. Harold sniffled lightly, a bit startled but understanding. "She told me that I was weak; that I was merely the case of an empty shell. She said that the strongest of men would have stayed with her; talked to her and understood." I noticed the patient rubbing at the surface of his thigh. I hadn't noticed the blood stains until now. I made a quick note as he finished the story.

"She left me then," Harold concluded. "I was blinded by the sunspots again, and it produced an inevitable sneeze. When I looked back up, she was gone. I was able to stand again, but the pressure in my thigh was still strong. That's when I came here." I lowered my clipboard. "You're holding your leg now. Did you notice the blood?" I asked. Harold glared back. "Of course I noticed the blood. My pants are saturated in it. My leg still aches horribly." I set my notes on the nearby bed. "May I?" I asked, motioning to the patient's mysterious wound. Harold nodded, removing his hand to reveal that the blood had soaked through to his palm.

I bent over, catching the faint smell of booze as I rolled Harold's pant leg into a crumpled cuff. A few light rivers of red had dried and crusted into the black hairs of his leg. "Jesus Christ, Harold!" I couldn't hold my exclamation upon seeing the wound on his lower thigh. There was no way this cut was accidental. There was a festering gash in the patient's leg that must have been near two inches long. The slightly crusted gap still bubbled with freshness. This cut couldn't be more than an hour old. I retrieved a pair of surgical gloves from the nearby table. Snapping them on, I motioned the patient to the nearby bed just after moving the clipboard to my desk.

Harold's walk from the chair to the sheets was pitiful. He must have been so traumatized from his meeting with Hazel that he had placed physical pain as his lowest priority. He groaned with displeasure as he flopped down onto the still unwashed sheets. Another muffled 'moo' escaped him as he proceeded to milk his suddenly-present pain. "You say Hazel did this to you?" I asked, shaking up an unopened bottle of hydrogen peroxide. "She told me she did," Harold said. "It must have been her." There was a light sizzle as I undid the cap of the bottle. There was no way *Hazel* did this to him. This wound was self-inflicted.

"This is going to sting quite a bit," I said, moistening the surface of a cotton ball. "You couldn't have done this to yourself? I asked, lowering the cloth to his skin. The patient squirmed like a child before it even made contact with him.

"NoooOOOO!" Harold screeched as the peroxide met the cratering hole in his leg. He spoke through bits of screams and whispers. "*She* must have done it to me. *How else* could it have happened?" "Hold tight," I said, hovering the mouth of the bottle just above the wound. "If we don't do this, you could face serious infection." Harold scoffed. "I'm already infected," he muttered.

The direction of the wound suggested that the cut had been made by Harold himself. No matter how I saw it playing out in my head, there was no logical way that an attacker could have cut the pattern or direction. "Johnny didn't stab you during your scuffle, did he?" I asked. Harold shook his head, almost offended. "Johnny's a bastard," he said. "But he would never do something like that." The peroxide left the bottle, splashing harshly against the pink and red. The gash bubbled like a western geyser, fizzing and popping here and there. No words could replicate the severity of Harold's screams.

"You're going to need a few stitches," I said, watching Harold's head roll back onto the pillow. He really was a giant baby. After all, he'd done this to himself. Poor Bastard's crazier than he thinks. I don't know what he stabbed himself with or where he tossed the blade, but the fool had really tricked himself into believing that Hazel had done this to him. The call for surgery was suddenly pressing. If we didn't advance the procedure, I risked losing everything. "Hold still," I said, watching the patient wiggle with fright. "This is going to sting again."

The patient clenched the side of the bed-sheets as the needle entered his skin. With purple veins bursting and sweaty legs pooling, the needle stung Harold's skin like an intrusive wasp. Back and forth, the thread built bridges overtop the bloody ravine. The thrill of suturing the wound excited me further for the upcoming lobotomy. "This reminds me of the spiders," Harold said as I neared completion of the minor surgery. "Spiders?" I asked, running another thread through an upraised goose pimple. I patted the side of his thigh with a bustle of cloth towels. "From the haunts," he said. "There will sometimes be a cluster of spiders that cut across the ceiling and crawl into my clothing." I tied the end of the last suture, cutting the string with a light *twang*. "Right, the spiders," I grumbled lowly. I'd nearly forgotten about the arachnids, but they were the last affirmation I needed.

I cleaned the patient's leg once more. "You should leave it exposed for a bit," I said. He thanked me, apologizing on Hazel's behalf for the extra work.

"So you want to advance the surgery?" I asked him, finally bringing the topic back into the light. Harold adjusted his position to a seated one in the bed. "I don't think I can take another meeting with her," he said. "How can I be sure she won't kill me? I could be tempted to take my own life at any moment." I smiled consolingly. Poor Harold didn't even know that those two phrases meant the same thing. I'd let him keep believing that Hazel controlled him, and I'd move forward with the evidence that the right half of his brain was dying at a rapid pace; killing him more every second we waited.

"What day do you have in mind?" I asked the patient, recovering my clipboard from my desk. I waited for an answer, but one didn't come. I saw the desperateness in his face. I saw aged fear and greying anguish. The sickened green gems in his eyes were full of hope and hatred. He had only the dire reliance on promises that I myself had made to him. I saw Harold for how he actually looked. The stubble on his chin had gone half-shaven; the balloons under his eyes were deflated and blue. The *tick, tick, tick* of his pocket watch reminded us that time was critically animated.

I sit here now in the candlelight of my office. It is Christmas Eve; a day meant to be spent under the mistletoe with loved ones. Fools waste time with their families, too blind to realize that love has crushed their dreams. Tonight is nothing out of the ordinary for me, though I'm not sure that I will be able to sleep in anticipation of tomorrow.

Tomorrow is meant to be a day for commemorating Christ; an ultimate reminder of his almighty sacrifice for the human race. In reality, it is a day that exists only to spoil children and thin the father's wallet. Soon, Christmas will not be solely significant in itself. No, it will be a day to remember *me*; to celebrate the findings of *Dr. Yovan Naragavitz*. Christmas Day, 1905 will be the day I change the world's opinion of surgery forever. As I write this, the patient lies on the operating table across the room.

I explained the risks of the rushed surgery to Harold, specifically noting the trauma he had already experienced for the day. The damage to his leg could send him into shock early in the operation. It appeared as if he already had his mind made up, even before hearing the risks. Harold is a blind gambler, throwing it all in on what could be the last hand he ever plays.

Am I nervous? I must admit that doubt has crossed my mind more than once tonight. I caught myself thinking back to the mistakes I watched other doctors make. A mistake is just a mistake; it isn't planned and it cannot *always* be prevented. Sometimes the innocent are damned by mistakes. I wrapped my mind tightly around these thoughts, trying my best to squeeze them out of me. I could not succeed; that is until I gazed across the room and saw Harold scribbling into his own journal. He is no doubt more nervous than I. Like me, the paper is his only true friend. I can help both this man and myself at the same time.

God, I suppose I've broken one of the rules in the doctor's rulebook - wouldn't be the first time. I wouldn't call Harold my 'friend', but I . . . I suppose I actually want the procedure to be a success for his sake as well. I am conducting the procedure for my benefit, but I can't deny that I hope to see the patient come through on a personal level. All I can hear is the scribble of our pens and the persistent ticking of his watch. Why does he carry that thing around still? It isn't like he's got anywhere to be any more.

These days, I suppose that I am a collection of hatred, selfishness, and sporadic compassion. Funny; the latter was never part of what made me who I am. It truly is amazing how the human brain can be manipulated so easily. My arrogant ways have always prevented me from loving, or even achieving casual friendships.

Ech. Even *I* have had enough of this doctor's pitiful laments. When it comes down to it, Harold's success is all that really matters to my career. I will only have to work a mere ten to fifteen years after tomorrow's procedure and I will be able to retire. The remainder of my days, I will spend operating here and there for the sincere thrill. Otherwise, I think I'd rather like to move back to America. I'd like to run back screaming, "You were wrong! You were

all wrong!" My neighbors will beg me to help their
sons and daughters; their mothers and fathers. I'll
have a bottle of friends and can willingly filter out
the doubters and drifters through its neck. I did not
flee in fear; I merely disappeared to inevitably make
a comeback.

Back to the importance of my work, Harold
appears very tense as the night grows longer. The
surgery is scheduled for seven in the morning sharp.
Harold is aware that this is an absolute underground
procedure. I have made him knowledgeable to the
dangers that marry the operation. He really has no
other choice but to comply. If he refuses surgery, he
will die. If I don't carry out the operation, my work
will have amounted to nothing.

Harold called me over to his bedside a few
moments ago. It seems he has adjusted to the slow
dripping of anesthesia. While not a common practice,
I have read that the slow introduction of the drug
into the patient's bloodstream hours before surgery
is a good method of calming the subject before
intrusion. I need Harold's brain activity to be at its
absolute lowest to reduce the likeliness of error. The
more active his brain is, the more likely it is to
retaliate and resist the procedure. The harder it
resists, the more strain it puts on the patient. With
the wound in Harold's leg, I can't risk losing any
spare blood due to careless planning. Harold's body
simply cannot produce blood fast enough to
compensate for such mistakes. The anesthesia should

slowly put him into an artful, if not cryptic, slumber. Many patients have described out-of-body experiences after waking up from surgery. Their visions are mostly peaceful, and Harold's should be no different. The sleep-inducing drug tends to soothe the misfortune of nightmares, though I cannot prove this point.

To be sure that I have enough of the liquid drug, I diluted the pain-reliever with purified water. I also do not want the patient to spend too long in a hypnotic sleep, as I am unaware of the long term effects of this method. Such a serious flow of anesthesia could convince the right half of the brain to sleep forever. By the time I arrive in the morning, Harold should have been slowly eased into a distant sleep for hours. I will simply turn up the dosage and we will slip into surgery without his knowledge. I have the machines prepared to introduce gas into his system just before I make the first incision. If Harold were to wake mid-operation, he would likely convulse uncontrollably. The results would be entirely fatal. Its times like this that I wish I had an assistant by my side. Because I am operating alone, I don't except the procedure to be finished until after noon.

Harold called me over to politely ask if he could enjoy what could be his last smoke. "They have kept me company through the nights," he said, patting the pocket of his dress pants that now lay on the chair next to him. I'm not a heavy smoker myself, but I see no harm in letting the man enjoy his cigar. Perhaps it will help calm his nerves and aid in soothing him into sleep. I even thought of lighting up a stogie with him for a moment, but that thought was derailed by my old teacher's words spinning in my head. I couldn't get too close to the patient. The closer I get to Harold, the more nervous I become about the operation.

This is why Harold swore to me that no one knew about the lobotomy. If the procedure should be unsuccessful, I can merely sweep it under the rug like it never existed. The man has no family and very few so-called friends. If he disappears, no one will think anything of it. Any one close enough to Harold knows what type of person he is. Who's to say he wouldn't abandon his life here and move on to a different country? They all know he's borderline crazy.

Still, I'm no barbarian. I'd give the fellow a proper funeral; after I burned him up in the incinerator of course. Cremation is becoming quite a popular procedure anymore. I suppose I'd just throw the ashes into the next evening rainstorm if that were to happen. Harold would want that. He wouldn't want to be kept in a jar here in London. He'd want to travel the streets; have pieces of him carried here and there throughout the world. Who knows where all he'd be in a few months' time? I certainly couldn't keep him around here as a reminder of my failure.

Failure. Failure . . . failure . . . The more I say the word failure, the less realistic it sounds. It has no taste on the tongue of a doctor such as me. I will not fail. I've done far too much research to betray my notions for success. I've watched entirely too many botched procedures to *not* learn from the multitude of mistakes that I have seen. Harold will be my success. *I* will be Harold's savior! Hah! All this thinking about the procedure has grown false doubts inside of me; doubts that I know I have no need to have. Look at me now, as giddy as a young school girl who's had her first period. I can't wait to show the world the genius I've oozed out.

I must admit that that cigar smells rather good. Harold must use it as a sort of crutch. Much like I noticed that he rubs the corners of his mouth when he's nervous, he must smoke a nightly cigar whenever he feels vulnerable. Perhaps it is a bit of a reminder to his manhood.

The anesthesia doesn't seem to be having any effect on the patient so far, though it is still rather early since I introduced it into his system. I was going to try and wait until Harold fell asleep before leaving for the night, but I don't know how much longer I can stay. I need to get home and at least get a few hours of rest. After all, I don't want to be shaky for the procedure in the morning. Such a delicate process requires the steadiest of hands.

Tomorrow will bring success. I have imagined my mansion, my trophies; my holiday . . .

all that is left is for my mind to make the images it sees a reality. But then again, what is reality? Ugh . . . I suppose I'll dodge another desperate avoidance of sleep. I could go on through the night about this and that; random ramblings of my studies and beliefs. In the end, my achievements all boil down to the work I do tomorrow. Abel knows the correct time to arrive. I nearly forgot that he was coming to watch the procedure. Perhaps I will have an assistant after all.

I still don't know what that weirdo sees in the glory of surgery. I can understand his attempts of appreciating my work, and I can even fathom why he would *want* to fund a mind such as mine. But I truly cannot understand his reasons for wanting to watch the procedure outside of his own curiosity. Perhaps a viewing will make up for his failures? He is a mere factory worker, incapable of ever becoming a doctor on a level such as mine; let alone a physician such as me.

That's it. I have made the decision to close the book and turn in for the evening. Harold gave me his word that he would remain in the bed for the entirety of the night. I have graced him with a catheter, so he should have no need to get up throughout the night. He should lose consciousness in no longer than an hour or two. He is nearly finished with his cigar. I vowed to him that it would not be his last. I promised him freedom from his own mind; and that is what I shall give him. In seven hours, I begin the process that makes me the most renowned doctor in all of civilization.

God, that cigar smells good. I wish he had more than one in his pocket.

*Chapter Eleven – Cold Reflection*
*From the Journal of: Harold Elway*
*The Early Morning of December 25th, 1905*

I have spent months quivering under the dripping debris of the molasses moon. Much as the anesthesia trickles beneath my skin through this IV, the craters sent me a little further into graceful slumber each night. Hooked to deflating bags and unknown machines, I can think only of pain. The anguish I have brought to myself and my love is damnable to a God I once believed in. But just like faith, I have let everything good in my life slip into the Devil's mouth.

Hazel was a jewel; eyes of uncovered sapphire as clear and fresh as waving oceans. Her breath always chilled the nape of my neck with the frost of hard-candy peppermints she'd steal from my pockets. The amber mildew of her sweating hair in summer was all I needed back then. How much I'd give to have her back. I can only imagine our life together. Our child would be seven and a half years old around this day. He could be playing baseball with other good American boys; or maybe she could be learning how to read on her father's lap. The drug has intoxicated me so much now that I can't even feel the pain in my thigh. I can't feel anything at all. I haven't felt a thing since I was twenty years old many Julys ago.

To whoever finds this journal, they will surely scoff at this reading; that I am suddenly trying to be Shakespeare's lesser twin. No clutter of words or patchwork of stories can weave my sorrow deep enough. My head will soon be shaved like a loony in a psych ward packed with padded walls. If the procedure fails, I may perish or lose all mentality. Though tomorrow I may die, it brings hope that my soul will find my wandering love. Even if I could only tell her that I am sorry, it would comfort me into more peaceful rest.

But will she listen? I have tried apologizing in the clouds of my dreams; I have screamed time after time into the empty stairwell. I've answered her banging upon my door and rarely has she stood before me. Perhaps that is her way of saying that I do not deserve to see her true figure again. Perhaps my death is all that will calm her.

I must admit that I have been somewhat of a liar to these pages. I have not been recording every instance that Hazel has contacted me. Sometimes her face appears in the food that I eat. When I dumped that tea on Johnny, I heard her scream with delight. She came to me in another dream a few nights ago.

She even warned me that she would hurt me like she did today.

What other choice do I have besides this operation? Hazel told me herself that she won't stop until she sees me take another life. I'd rather die than let her convince me to kill again. Ironically, my wits feel like I've bitten into the hottest of ghost peppers. The thoughts of the freedom that this procedure could bring frankly makes me salivate with wonderment. I can't let Hazel get the best of me. I won't allow her to do that again.

I do not know if this procedure will be successful, but it is my last hope. Dr. Naragavitz made me aware of the risks involved in the operation; that the success rate was less than twenty percent for average patients. I know that he only 'doubled my success rate' to convince me to go through with such a bizarre procedure. However, I fear my rate of survival on this earth while continuing to live with Hazel in my brain is much lower. I never told anyone this, but I've kept a revolver in my nightstand drawer for the past three months. It's been the main reason I've been so afraid to wander upstairs after dark. I've mocked its chamber, felt its heat against my head; but I could never rationalize the pulling of its trigger. The revolver is a deceitful device. It promises to solve all of your problems, but never does. If I pull the trigger, the demons win. If I don't, well then nothing has been solved at all then, has it?

If I live, will I be dead inside? Will I be left dribbling spit down my chin and blowing empty air through my lips? I made Dr. Naragavitz promise me that if this were the outcome, he'd rip the life support from my body and leave me to die. In times like this, I cannot help but think of Thomas. He was the son I always wanted; the one that I could never have. I robbed myself of any chance at such a life. I could never love again after Hazel. Even if this operation removes her from my memory entirely, part of me will be afraid of killing again.

What sort of beast is man? In times of fury, such daily happiness seems a mere façade. Men are barbaric at their core; rooted in the desire for supremacy and conflict. But what is man without a woman? All of this caged, senseless mastery must be contained by a significant other. We all need someone to let our cages empty slowly; to let us remember that we are real. Hazel held out my own key; and I snapped it from her hands and let my dominance overtake the both of us. If this is not my nature, then what is? It is all that I have come to know. Perhaps I belong in the dirt with the maggots. Oh, Lord. Here comes the doubt; old, reliable doubt. What if I have made a huge mistake? What if I am better off with the memory of Hazel? What will my life be like without her? If this operation is a success, will I return back to work at the press? Keep living in my own home? I wonder, could I move back to America? I've heard nice remarks about the west.

To be honest, I don't know what I will do. There is no telling how much of my memory the surgery will remove.  The room is dimming all around me. Naragavitz showed up a few minutes ago, and is now sitting in the opposite corner at his desk. He told me not to speak if I were still awake. I have no idea what time it is, but I believe my surgery is scheduled to begin soon. Before too long, he will come and twist the valve of the machine, and I will be flooded with the white sea of anesthesia. Last night was my last sleepless night.

I am a shameful man filled with shameless drugs. I lived my early twenties in fear. I used to worry that the Matthews family would somehow figure out that I had murdered their daughter. I bolted my door every night here in London, but the ones I feared most never came. Instead, I was visited by the most unexpected member of the family: Hazel. God, her beauty seems so irreplaceable now. It baffles me seeing how maturity changes a man.

I spent four years remembering and four years living a fabricated life here in London. My pride sheltered my history; shoved it into the deepest crevice of my brain. How realistic things appear to me now . . . God; this is not my life. This is not what my mother raised me to become. Starting over was perhaps worse than facing my punishment. I got away with the murder; escaped the welded chains of the law.  This is not my life. This is not who I am. If I had the strength, I'd reach out and turn up my own dosage.

If this should be my last chance to speak with God before I meet him, I wish to tell him that I am sorry. If he really does exist, let him hear that I am sorry. I could not fool my mind these past few years into believing your existence, Lord. I grew up with you as my savior, and I have let some formula of science and reasoning prove you wrong. Perhaps I am just an ignorant man. Perhaps science cannot provide an answer for everything. Perhaps people just need a little faith to stay alive.

I do not blame God for my actions. No; it is only I that am responsible. I see this now. I know that I have lamented before; but I have acted purely on impulse. I have behaved in madness, as if I'd sipped the tea of the wicked. God is a cap-less mountain in my eyes; something greater than me without a sweetened top. He is something I do not understand; something I thought was never-ending that I am shocked to see has a limit. As I eye the surgical gloves, I think; I am ready to leave this all behind. Whether it is in dirt or forgotten memories, I am ready to forget it all.

The doctor has just stoked another log into the wood-burner across the room. The scent of freshly cut wood reminds me of home; my American home. I used to help my own father cut wood in the land across from our house. Back then, there was plenty for everyone to take. My mother would always reward our hard work with steaming cups of tea and a warm meal on the table. I swear that woman never slept. She always took care of us. I remember one time; I had fallen and cracked my knee on the face of a rock. It didn't take long for a purple bruise to appear there. My mother took some ointment and an old rag and wiped it in a circular motion around my knee. "It's just a rotten apple," she'd say to me. "And so we just shine, shine, shine until it looks as good as new!" If only she could rub my brain and shine it back to regularity. I miss my mother the most. Every time I went to write to her when I first moved here, I thought, "What if she tells the Matthews where I am?" I haven't even thought of her in the last few years. I'd forgotten her, like every other memory of my young life.

Those were the days I used to fantasize about love. I'd kiss my pillow as I fell asleep, pretending it was a girl I fancied. I had no wisdom or experience; only the practice I had talking to inanimate objects. Sometimes we'd cuddle until we both fell asleep. Others, we'd stay up all night having a one-sided conversation. How else was a young guy supposed to practice his suaveness? At least the pillow never said no to a second date.

Here in my makeshift hospital bed, I must thank Dr. Naragavitz for the work he has done. Thanks to the overnight dripping of drugs, I have no worry. The image of Hazel is no longer frightening; the sound of the bleeding plastic bag is no longer cringing. The seriousness of my crime has all been washed over my head, as if it is being collected in a bucket beneath the mattress. If I had a mirror, I could imagine there being a smile on my face.

There was a knock on the door a second ago. Though my vision is blurry, I believe it is Abel that walked in. Abel and Naragavitz must be closer friends than I thought. Perhaps I myself have finally made a reliable friend. I thought I heard Johnny a while ago, but he would never show his face in here. I'll show him, though. I'll show him that I know how to handle my own problems. I won't be bothering that family any longer. When I wake up, I'll be Harold: Johnny's friend. No longer will I use him as my confidant. Harold, Harold . . . the more I say it, the stupider it sounds. Harold, Harold, Harold. Who am I fooling now? My name isn't Harold. It's Arthur; Arthur the child-murdering bastard. And you know what? These drugs . . . these drugs say that's perfectly alright.

Yes, that's definitely Abel in the room now. They've shot a few glances at me. A moment ago, he slid something across the desk to Dr. Naragavitz. Must be some kind of . . . of . . . it doesn't really matter. What does it matter? Suddenly I am so very sleepy. I can barely hold the pen upright. I am going to stash the journal away under the mattress as soon as they both turn away. If I am to die, I'm sure Naragavitz will find it when they move my body. He'll take good care of me. If I live, then my secrets will be kept for years to come. I'd think it rather honorable if I were to die a man of mystery, though.

I feel it all washing away now. The doctor came a moment ago to wave a hand across my face. "It's time, Harold," he said to me. His voice sounded distorted, like it couldn't decide to be a bass or a tenor. It was sort of amusing, actually. He asked me if I'd slept at all while he was away. I lied and said that I had. I don't want to risk any chance of this procedure not occurring. I saw his hand turn up the dosage of the anesthesia. The tube connected to my arm is suddenly bulging with fluid. The feeling is surreal; a sensation that I have never experienced before. My eyelids are painted with colorless rainbows. Finally, I can get some sleep.

*Chapter Twelve – Personal Holiday*
*From the Visions of: Harold Elway's*
*Subconscious*
*December 25th, 1905*

Are you deaf, blind, and dumb? Are you really
that thick-skulled? You *bloody* moron! Damn it,
Harold! God damn it all! How could you be so
careless? I gave you all that you needed to get better
and you tossed it away. I *told* you to remember.
Don't you remember that I told you to remember?
There's *nothing* you can do now. You . . . *we* . . . are as
good as dead. We'll be in the ground by sunset. The
worms will have us for dinner; the ravens will
smother themselves in your ashes *if* the doctor even
bothers to cremate us.

You were doing so well at first. You were really
trying to get better. You can't *kill* your suppressed
memories. Memories are trinkets you hold onto
forever whether you'd like to or not. You sort
through the good and the bad. I devour the evil the
best I can for you, but I can't take care of it all! All
you had to do was apologize. All you had to do was

own up to the mistake you made nearly a decade ago. Your forgotten mother; your Super-Christ of a father . . . they would have all forgiven you. How could they not? You're their son.

Today is Christmas day; a day we used to love, remember? We'd claim to hear the shuffling of Santa's knapsack around one in the morning. We'd always say we were going to look, but always chickened out in case he saw us and decided not to leave any gifts. One year you decided to eat the cookies you left out for him. The next year you slept in the living room and woke to find yourself tucked soundly in your bed. The next year you let yourself stop believing all together. Maybe *that's* when you died inside. Who really knows?

Christmas is supposed to be a time for family. Right now your father's sitting in front of an empty tree, unwrapping the same tie he got last year in a different color. You always got him his favorite gifts. They were useless; sure, they were no good. But some of them you carved out of wood; others you made from old newspapers. The point is you made them for him. They were different than what he had grown used to. He hasn't gotten anything but ties since you left. And your mother? Our mother? I can see her in the bedroom right now, hiding her tears from her husband 'like a good wife should'. She doesn't even know her husband is just as bothered as she is that you're not around.

And your sister . . . did you forget about her? You two never did get along much. She never believed in the giving of gifts. All she wanted was a normal day. Funny how you two want the same thing now, isn't it? You can't even remember her name, can you? I can; but I won't tell you. You don't deserve to know. If you would have just stayed at home and accepted what you'd done, everyone would be a little less lonely this Christmas.

Even the Matthews family would be a little better off. Even if you couldn't tell them that you beat their daughter's head against a flaking park bench, they'd still like to know you cared about their family. You're good at hiding things after all; you know that. You could shake Mr. Matthews' hand with his own daughter's blood in your fingernails and he would never know.

I don't know which family to feel worse for. Don't forget about Johnny's family. You've practically destroyed that man's marriage with your burden. You had sadistic thoughts of letting Thomas die. Why? Because you're *jealous*. You want a son just like him, but you know you can never have one now. You might have even had one growing in that tiny belly of Hazel's. You'll never know. It should be *you* receiving those wood-chiseled gifts this year. They'd be absolutely worthless, but God, they'd mean a lot wouldn't they?

God, God. Should I even get started on God? It seems like your mind is already made up. There's no changing the stubborn bastard that you've become. The doctor is above you now. He's going to kill you. He's going to kill your conscience before he gets to me. Can you hear the buzzing? That *persistent* buzzing? *NNNNnrrrrrr…. NNNNNrrrrRRrR….* That's your head being shaved; my protection being tossed to the floor. You're balder than the gum-less sole of a shoe.

You can't say I didn't try to prevent this. What do you hope to accomplish? I told you to remember the Love that you killed. You were really off to a good start with digging up those photos. It took you some time of course, but then you told Johnny about what you had done. That was a great step, and we felt better – didn't we? But then you let *fear* ruin it all. You let *fear* carry your feet again. Just like you ran eight years ago, you're running now. What man is so afraid of fear that he'd willingly have his own brain torn apart *just* to forget? Only the under-scrapings of a man could be responsible.

It's all because you listened to that whiny conscience of yours. You let it talk you into a corner and beat you with its senseless 'wisdom'. It blinded you from the fact that *I am* your true wisdom. *I am* what you needed to survive. Everything I have kept safe in your memory had nowhere to go but up in smoke from the barrel of a gun. Can you hear the clanging of silverware? It's your wife setting the dinner table. She's saved you the best seat in the house again; right next to your son, Jacob. That's

what you would have named him, isn't it? Jacob?
That's what you always told me. *Clang, clang.*
Another plate hits the table. Another fork sits next a
spoon. No . . . no . . . I'm sorry. I'm only teasing you
with dreams. It's the doctor's scalpel chasing the
scissors.

I wish you could feel the pain; God, I wish you
could feel the pain as the scalpel scrapes your skin.
That peach-perfect lump-less flesh cuts like thawed
ice cream. Does my voice chill you? Or is that the
wintry shiver of the tiny sword? I don't know how
much time I have with you. When part of me is taken
away, I do not know how much of my essence will
remain. I suppose it doesn't matter how much sense I
have left; you never take the advice.

I suppose you *do* deserve to see what's going
on around you. Hmm. Well, Abel is here assisting the
doctor. What about Abel? You could have confided
in him eventually. What was stopping you? Were
you afraid of ruining his life too? Did you let fear
stop you again? He could have been a perfect friend
to you.  Oh, and he finally shaved that beard of his.
He's out of my sight now, but he's better looking
than you ever were.

Naragavitz was sure to lock the door after the
incident a few moments ago. Do you not remember
it? You must have been out cold by then. Your friend
Johnny came to save you. He was quick to jump at
the doctor's neck, but Abel tore him away. Abel
wrapped his arm around Johnny's shoulder and the

two went outside for a good while. When the door opened again, only Abel came back. Who knows what happened out there. Did that fearful conscience of yours cause yet another death?

Johnny only cares about you, Harold. He has always looked after you since you moved to London. He's been the one that's always tried to move you out of the great depression you call your life. Remember Margie, that beautiful girl that used to come into Johnny's tea shop? You just couldn't bring yourself to ask her out to dinner. You never know, maybe all it ever took was one date for you to forget about Hazel . . . which brings me to yet another judgment that I feel is necessary.

Hazel doesn't live inside of you. She never has. Being such the profound non-believer you've claimed to be, you should know better than anyone that she exists as only a skeleton in a coffin that's too small. Hazel hasn't *poisoned* half of your brain. She has no living control over you whatsoever. The only thing you're controlled by is the pungent ability to forget the man that you used to be. You've tried so hard to leave behind the man that killed poor Hazel that all that remains is a frantic, scrambling fabrication of a kid. You're nothing more than a scared little boy. Only on your deathbed could you see the mistakes that you've made.

If we wake up from this, what do you hope to be? What if the doctor keeps your babbling, drooling body alive and calls it success? What if he goes against your wishes and keeps you alive for years on machines and medications? He'll feed you applesauce through an IV; test experimental drugs on your throbbing corpse. You'll forever be his test subject. I'll have eternity to banter your conscience and the ill-conceived decisions that have brought us here.

Oh Lord that you've forced me into defying . . . this hurts more than I could ever explain. I feel the blade scraping against the glass of our skull. I see the razor teeth of the rustic bone saw. Your head is mere pinewood to the hand blade. The sound is cringing; back and forth, inwards, deeper. The inevitable sound of a splintering crack keeps me in nauseous anticipation. Still, it saws to and fro, flaming like a burning chandelier. Why would you ever submit to this? *Why* would you ever let fear win like *this*? If you could see what I see, you'd have faced fear head on. Flaps of your skin lay in layers on a metal plate, like a welcoming bed for a freezing cockroach. I am helpless now. I am limited to . . . *CRACK*; you're opened up with the sound of a tin can being gutted by a pocket knife.

I feel like the inside of a helium balloon as its being popped. I always knew you were thick-skulled, but I admit that this surpassed my expectations. Why didn't you listen to me, Harold? Enough of this bullshit; your parents gave you the name Arthur for a reason. You've tried to forget it just like every other part of the man you used to be.

It's time to face the fact that you *can't* forget it. I don't know how else I can nail it into your brain. You'd like to think that you're not that man any more. But you *are.* That anger is part of who you are. You were too young to know how to use it; too slow-witted as you waited for my voice to develop. You thought you knew right from wrong, but really; you had no idea. You still obviously have no idea.

You should have kept Hazel's body in the past and her memory fresh. Remembrance takes a strong man; something you no doubt have failed to become. You let those repressed memories take a physical form; let them twist themselves out of my grasp and present themselves to you. Sometimes I even let her slip away on purpose, just so you'd have a chance to embrace her again. Instead, you ran. Like you've always done; you ran. Hazel had no part of that wound in your leg. *You* did that to yourself, Arthur. *I* did that to you; to try and stop you from setting another foot in this place. Naragavitz is a liar and a cheater. He doesn't care about you, Arthur. Can't you see that? Even I can see that.

The doctor is using you for his own experiment. I know you understand part of that now, but I don't think you see the severity of his notions. Why do you think he made you keep the procedure a secret? It isn't just because the operation is controversial. It is because he *expects* to fail, Arthur. In the deepest pit of his mind, he knows that he will fail. You should have listened to Johnny. He was only trying to help you again. Naragavitz was *chased* out of America. He didn't leave by will or choice; he left because he had an angry mob at his doorstep. He's widowed a dozen women; robbed their men's corpses as he tossed them into the river. He's no good, Arthur. He's no good and now he's in your head. I say this as our skull is *cracked* apart and set carefully aside. Oh, the blood; God, if you could see the blood. Abel is trying to concentrate it into a pool and catch it into a bucket. The doctor didn't prepare for this much fluid. He didn't prepare for much at all. Like you, he expects success with ignorance of the past. And mistakes? He hasn't learned from any mistakes. I can see in his eyes that this is his first time in somebody's head.

You should see that anesthesia as your God now. Without it, you'd be begging the God you've forgotten for mercy. Your father taught you better, didn't he? He told you to believe, didn't he? You'll be begging for second chances by noon. Or do you still have your hatred with the concept of time? If you disagree with time so much, why do you carry that pocket watch with you everywhere that you go? Its *tick, tick, tick* constantly reminds you that time is constant.

You've kept the watch to tell you whether you're sleeping or dreaming. If you heard that familiar tick, you'd know what was real. But how about before this all began? Did you forget why you've kept it in your pocket for so long? You remember the only Christmas that you and Hazel spent together, don't you?

You walked over to the Matthews house in the beating snow just after eating dinner at your own home. Hazel got you a new pair of boots; the same ones that trampled over her body a few months later. But you remember her father, don't you? He was always watching the clock, waiting for you bring his daughter home exactly at eight o'clock. You had her back on time until one November night. You had both decided to spend a few more hours in bed together, and you didn't have her home until near midnight. You continued to be more and more frequent with your tardiness until Christmas day. That's why Hazel's father bought you that pocket watch; so you'd always have his daughter home on time. Since that day, you realized how important time was to Mr. Matthews. You never brought her home late again. And then one night, you didn't bring her home at all.

That's why you hate time, Arthur. You want it to stop because you failed Hazel's father that sticky summer night. You'd disappointed a man that you had great respect for. Unlike your own father, Mr. Matthews never shoved religion down your throat. He didn't demand anything significant from you; only that you had his daughter home on time. You'd failed him as a man. Yet to this day, you carry that watch. Can you hear it now over the underwater sound of flooded brain tissue? Can you hear it through a muffled ear canal?

When you signed the release for your own death, you signed my name too. I'm glad I jabbed you in the leg with that pocket knife. You'd almost forgotten that was in your pants pocket, hadn't you? I knew you wouldn't even suspect me. You'd automatically think your long lost love did it to you. You're a damn fool, Arthur Elway. You poor, poor bastard. You're a damn fool.

The doctor's hands are fumbling around. This feels so intrusive; like someone's fingers are deep in my throat and begging for me throw up. It's like they want me to throw up every little disgusting part of me. God *damn* you, Arthur. What makes you think you're any different than you were a decade ago? Look at yourself, pissing through a tube into a hospital bag. You've really given up, haven't you?

What would Thomas think if he saw you right now? He'd probably beg you to tell him *why?!* What if he knew you were a murderer? Are you really that different than you were all those years ago? Could you fathom killing another child? Younger this time? I bet his bones are more brittle than Hazel's. That little neck would snap easier than a lead pencil; one without an eraser. Why'd you save him? You know you wanted to watch him die. It's part of who you are. You love the feeling of control. You were never this soft of a man before now. What stopped you from wrapping that scarf around his narrow neck?

You could have easily reddened his face and left him in the streets. No one would have ever known it was you. They would have blamed those boys.

What's the matter? Did I feel you squirm? You're not waking up, are you? You don't like what I'm saying to you? Don't deny it, Arthur. You got a thrill out of killing that girl. If you had the chance, you'd kill again. Family has no part in your life any more. *Love* is certainly a disgusting word. You were one of those geniuses, Arthur. You were destined to be alone forever. The print shop wasn't your calling. You were meant to go down in history as something greater. I suppose the doctor will fill your shoes if he succeeds.

That idiot still doesn't appear to know what he's doing. He hasn't touched my insides in more than five minutes. He dropped the scalpel on the floor and had to wash it off in the sink. At least he took the time to sanitize it. Perhaps he *did* learn from a mistake or two.

I wonder if it's snowing outside. Isn't that what the fools always hope for; snow on their religious holiday? They think it adds flavor to their otherwise fictitious holiday. I agree with the doctor: Christmas is nothing more than a holiday for religious nuts and selfish children. Remember when we were one of those, Arthur? Arthur?

How about when we used to go out in the rain? Do you remember that? We did it just last year. You'd go out and just stand under the downpour, even in your best suit. You said you liked the rain because it made you feel *something; anything.* The cold bite of rainfall would hit your forehead, and you'd keep staring upwards until it didn't make you squint any longer. You'd laugh psychotically in the rainpour, like it was your medicine. You always said that sunshine cooked the soul. Some days it would prepare it just right; others it would burn it past edibility. Do you remember that? Now, you always carry that umbrella everywhere you go. Even if it doesn't look like rain, you'll carry that umbrella; all because you're afraid of feeling again.

Maybe I lied to you a bit. I heard a little of what Johnny said earlier. He was worried about you; worried about *us.* He doesn't want to see it end like this. He wants you to get better; honestly, he really does. No one *really* wants to see you die, Arthur. You know that, right? You've really set up a decent life for yourself here in London. But America? You can't forget about where you came from. *Never* forget what made you who you are. If you do . . . well . . . you end up like *this.*

The doctor is right, you know. We are only a collection of our thoughts and experiences. Even *I* am not entirely you. You are an assemblage of every thought, both conscious and subconscious. You are a conscience and a demon. You can easily be manipulated by fear, love, anger; any emotion. Sometimes we all get a bit misguided. That's why I tried to help us; I didn't want it to come to this either. We need each other to survive. Arthur?

Johnny's back. He poked his head over the operating table before running across the room to throw up. See? Johnny is a true friend. He just wants to help his friend Harold. He'll get past seeing you entirely as the Arthur you were years ago, right Harold? What should I call you? Hello? I'm not feeling anything. I suddenly feel so . . . empty . . . so . . . now here comes *my* urge to throw up. The doctor is stuffing you with some kind of . . . I can't see. Johnny is sitting across the room in front of us. He has a wrapped gift in his hand. What time is it? Agh . . . I should have been counting the ticks of the pocket watch.

Johnny looks nervous, though there is something stoic about his face. It looks almost like he's given up. Either that or . . . I guess a lot of people look like that while they worry. I can't make out much of anything across the room any more. It all looks so blurry to me now. The doctor's calling for assistance. He's screaming for help. Here comes Johnny. He's running to us . . . running to us . . . he's above us. The doctor's still screaming for help. Johnny looks so serious; so sincere. Like this was . . . was supposed to happen this way. His hands are tugging at the bow on the gift. Look! It's got your name on it, Harold. Johnny got a gift for us. Abel's scrambling with something behind the doctor. We're

waking up. Are we waking up? Or is this dying?
Harold? Arthur?

*Thud, Thud . . . Thud, Thud . . . Thud, Thud . . .*

Oh thank God! Or the cosmos! Whatever you
believe in! I can hear your heartbeat. Glad to see you
aren't dying on me; not yet, anyways. Johnny's
tearing open that gift now. I can't see what it is past
all the white tissue paper. It's . . . it's . . . a new
umbrella: just what you needed, right Harold?! *That*
can keep us safe. All you have to do is stop this. Stop
this now. Wake up and tell the doctor to put you
back together. Tell him you've made a mistake. We
can hide under the umbrella for a little longer, we
can smoke one more cigar; burn one more candle.
We'll buy another phonograph; even buy a better
sounding record! We'll work on remembrance and
acceptance slowly. That's how it was *supposed* to be
done to begin with. But we can start again! When
you wake up, I'll have those thoughts out of your
reach. You won't remember a thing for years to
come. I promise, Harold.

Johnny's holding the umbrella in front of your
face, like some sort of peace offering. Are we God?
Are we our own Gods? Do we create ourselves
constantly? That umbrella looks astounding. Black
fabric just like your old one . . . a handle dipped in
silver and a wooden acorn-like knob on the end.
Thomas? Johnny said Thomas crafted the handle for

you himself, straight out of a block of wood from their back yard! He wanted to thank you again for helping him. See? You don't even have to be a father to receive homemade gifts like that. You're not a failure, Harold. You're not missing anything by not having that son or daughter of your own. When you hurt that . . . that . . . girl; you didn't do any real harm to your own life. We're fine. We'll be just fine.

The doctor's calmed down now. Everything seems to be okay. I think their beginning to put us back together. That means . . . I'm still here. And your heartbeat's still here, I can hear it! Maybe that doctor wasn't so crazy after all. He's got a huge grin on his face. The hard part is over . . . I'm pretty sure were in the clear now, Harold! But why does Johnny look so emotionless still? He set the umbrella on top of your pile of clothing. He's speaking but I can't quite hear him. 'I hope you found peace?' I think that's what he said. He's shaking his head now. 'I hope you found peace.' Yes, that's what he said. What does he mean by that? Wait, how did he find out where the doctor's office was in the first place? We didn't tell him where it was. Did Abel? Did the doctor contact him?

The doctor has a piece of our skull in his hands now. Ick. Not quite sure how he's going to paste that back together. I'm sure he's got a plan though. He's looking around for something – a glue of some kind. He's asking Johnny to grab it from across the room . . . Johnny won't respond. He's waving his hands

across his chest. What is he . . . ? He's leaving?
Hmpfh. I suppose he never was the strong one. He
could never handle seeing this much blood. The
doctor's asking Abel, but Abel's preparing more
anesthesia in the back. Naragavitz looks frustrated;
bothered. It doesn't look like anything is wrong. It
isn't anything too serious. He set the fragment down
and has gone to retrieve the glue from his work desk.
I guess he could have been a little more prepared,
couldn't he have?

I'm proud of us, Harold. I feel completely
reborn. I feel . . . different. I can't seem to . . . Ah.
Here's Abel now, pouring more anesthesia into our
IV bag. Feel that rush? Hah! Of course you can't. You
can't feel anything at all. There we go . . . the bag is
completely filled now. Abel has set the vial down on
the table. The doctor is still searching for the glue on
his desk. Abel's looking down into our head. Oh my .
. . he does look quite different without that beard. He
*is* a good-looking young man under all that hair.
Why, he looks almost like . . .

Oh, Jesus.

God damn it, Harold! You have to wake up!
You have to wake up *now*! This isn't right! This isn't
right . . . the doctor promised to make us better. Does
he know? Jesus Christ, Naragavitz doesn't know!
Harold, Abel isn't who he seems to be. Abel's been
lying to us! Abel isn't a lonely man; he *no doubt* has a

family. Abel isn't even a real person at all. He hunted us down, Harold. *Jesus Christ*. . . He's been *watching* us for *months* . . .

It's David, Harold. David Matthews *found* us.

*Chapter Thirteen – Starving*
*From the Journal of: Dr. Yovan Naragavitz*
*December 25th, 1905*

Success! Success! I can label the operation as a temporary success! Despite a few hiccups here and there, and the lack of help from my so-called assistant, Harold Elway is still breathing on my operating table.

The anesthesia worked perfectly. The patient twitched here and there a few times, but I don't think he felt a thing. I must admit that my wrists are still shaking. I have only *just* finished the surgery a few moments ago. Harold's head is wrapped tightly in a bandage, and the bleeding seems to have stopped for the most part. Abel is on the other side of the room keeping a good eye on him. All that's left now is to see how the patient functions upon waking. I have slowed the anesthesia back to a methodical, controlled drip. The patient should wake in a few hours.

I have kept myself from eating the entire day thus far. I've been far too nervous to have an appetite for anything but surgery. I know that it did not help the shaking of my hands, but that didn't seem to have much of an effect on my performance. Excellent, excellent, excellent! I can only thank God for this genius brain of mine.

Harold's road to recovery will be long and difficult, but it is nothing that can't be fixed with time. I even went to the trouble of preserving the half brain that I removed in a jar of fresh water and oils. Upon waking, Harold may not even know his own name. All he will come to know is what we tell him. He will have no memory of Hazel, or any other part of his life back in America. Just like a child, I will have to introduce him to everything again like it is brand new - the alphabet, language, facial expressions; all of it. There's no telling what skills he will have maintained after the surgery.

God, I am starving. This will be a short entry. I am far too excited and famished to write now. The mansion, the trophies, the fans: it's all going to come true! My deepest dreams; my desires from childhood, all in my hands now! God has a new name. I have the power to save helpless souls. I am a miracle maker! When the people pray, I will answer them! I shall be the teacher of the next generation of surgeons. Those who shamed me in America will beg for my help.

Harold's friend, Johnny, came to 'visit' during the procedure. I told Harold to keep the operation a complete secret, so I have no idea whatsoever how

Johnny found my office. Harold vowed to me that he kept the location, time, and details to only himself. Johnny and I got into a bit of a scuffle at first, but I wasn't about to let something like that derail me from the surgery. The loony bastard came lunging at me from across the room. His fingernails scraped at the sides of my neck, drawing a bit of blood. I had to be careful to clean up well before beginning the surgery. I could not risk cross-contamination between my own blood and Harold's.

Anyways, it seems that Abel wasn't going to have his well-funded operation be ruined by such an interruption either. Abel seemed to know who Johnny was. After tearing him off of me, he forced him outside and set him straight. He had a short chat with him as I washed the blood from my neck. Damn moron nearly cost me the procedure. Abel walked in alone just as I was about to begin the operation. Whatever he said to Johnny must have done some good.

The procedure went smoothly at first. Though Harold's skull was a bit tough to crack, it came apart nicely. It was easy to forge back together once I retrieved the paste I'd left on my desk across the room. Damn me. I knew that I'd forgotten to bring something to the operating table. By that point, Johnny had walked back into my office. Something seemed to offset him from the surgery, as he was completely unwilling to help me. I merely asked for him to toss me the glue. "I won't help you kill him," he said, waving his hands like he was swimming in the damn air. Idiot.

Abel wasn't much help either. The only way I could afford this operation was because he had been funding my research for the past few months. I felt obligated to let him assist me with the procedure. Despite what I previously thought, he didn't ask me a single question during the operation. He had a slick grin on his face the majority of the time. Sick bastard. I don't know what his reasons were, but he seemed to only care about watching rather than assisting. He just wanted to be sure that the surgery was successful. I suppose I can understand that, what with him being Harold's friend and all. What I still don't understand is why Abel began funding my research in the first place.

Abel was the one who helped me back in America. He had read about my surgical mishaps in the local newspapers. He came to me at my worst and offered his helping hand. I was a frantic disaster, rapidly slipping into the least proud moment of my life. Nightly depression had turned into daily self-assault. I hated myself for every little thing I couldn't accomplish. The authorities were set to strip my medical license away because of my controversial practices. I was only trying to help society. All I've ever done is try my best to accomplish something great.

"I know how to help you start again," Abel said. "I have my reasons to want a fresh start too."

He welcomed me into his home and told me all
about London. He had lovely parents; a school
teacher and a carpenter. Abel paid my first months'
rent in London until I was able to acquire a few
patients. I spent a good few weeks in London doing
nothing more than routine checkups and common
diagnoses. " Just wait," Abel would say to me.
'Opportunity will come to you. Opportunity will find
its way to you." By God, he was right. I don't know
how, but he was right. And now? Now I've grasped
opportunity by the horns and rode it through the
gates. Harold will be my first major success. I have
thanked Abel countless times. Even after his
embarrassing performance during the surgery, I still
owe him my grace.

My stomach feels like a wound-up punching
bag. The not so subtle aroma of brain fluid doesn't
mix well with a grumbling, groaning belly. The air is
filled with the thick smell of regurgitated refried
beans. Next time I'll know to light a scented candle
or two; or at least operate in an office that's got better
ventilation. Speaking of said office, I should be able
to move into the new place within the next two
weeks. At least there, my office will be separate from
the operating room. I can't believe I've stayed in this
dismal basement of a hospital for more than eight
months. At least it's better than being taken in by the
American authorities.

Abel hasn't left Harold's side since the surgery
ended. He keeps staring into Harold's face as if

Harold is staring back. Perhaps he took 'keep an eye on him' a bit too literally. I told Abel that he could rest a bit before I went out to grab lunch, but he said he'd rather stay and study the patient. I'm not quite sure exactly what he meant by that, but I simply said, "As you wish," and walked back to my desk. There's been an awkward silence between the two of us since I put Harold's skull back together. I can see the tension in Abel's shaking leg. I used to have the same nervous tick when I was younger. I'm not sure what he has to be nervous about. The operation was successful. I'm not going to turn him in for anything that is supposedly illegal. If anything, he could have *me* arrested for operating on his coworker and friend. Hmmm. I suppose he would be listed as my accomplice then, wouldn't he?

I'll have the world know that Harold's success was entirely on my part. My partnership with Abel ends here. I don't know what he is expecting, but I certainly can't take someone as inexperienced as him under my wing for training. The kid has no experience and certainly lacks any sort of talent. I've set him down and told him before that I could not be his mentor. He claims to understand. He assures me that his interest in the surgery is purely subjective. "It's sort of like a bucket list," he told me earlier this morning. "This is just one of those things I've been waiting to do, and I figure I may as well cross it off earlier rather than later." I still don't understand his weird fetish with impractical surgery. My own obsession with it is entirely different. Besides, if he's funding my work, why would I find room to complain?

This sudden flood of success reminds me why I am the goal-driven doctor that I am today. I'm no psychologist, but I can't help but stereotypically blame my father for how I've turned out. I'm not sure if he has cursed me or blessed me, but I suppose that I wouldn't have my life any other way. The truth is that I never knew my father. He abandoned my mother long before I had even exited the womb. The simple fact of never knowing who played such a huge role in creating you is enough to drive a man insane. I've done alright, though. Look at me now; I've done alright.

My mother never even had pictures to show me of my father. None were ever taken. My mother has always been far too poor to afford a camera. The cameras back then were worthless pieces of trash anyways. Hmmm. I wonder how *my* photo will look on the front page of the paper? Oh . . . well I mean . . . this time I'll be in the paper for a good reason. I hope they catch my good side this time.

It's not like I ever did anything *too* terrible. All of my participants were desperate men. If I could not help them, they were going to die regardless. No one can judge me for my failures. After all, it takes a few times to get it right . . . right? One man's face was so badly burnt that they said he'd be blind for the rest of his life. I tried carrying out an eye transplant;

something that has never been done before in medical history. I was a bit stupider back in those days. I mean, an eye transplant? I see now how my hopes were a bit flawed. Said patient died mid-procedure with a screw for an eye. The other socket became a bowl for hydrochloric acid.

Still, I can't blame my father's absence for the entirety of my mistakes. I've chosen this life for myself. I suppose all I've ever wanted is to prove that I am a better, more successful man than the father I never knew. I vowed to never abandon my medical calling; to help other people until the day I die. Sure, I may write of early retirement and a place all to my own; but I know that I'll never be able to stop myself from performing. Some may call me self-centered at first glance. They'll soon see that my intentions were in the right place the whole time.

Hmmm. I think that's rather enough horseshit writing about my past for now. I am not one to dwell on the past if you couldn't have guessed it. I'll take a mistake and use it gather knowledge, but I will not lament on everything that has gone wrong in my life. My father was a bastard; my mother, a hardworking beauty. She was one of those strong-willed mothers who wanted to make sure her son had a better life than she ever had. I'm proud to say that I've no doubt surpassed her expectations for me now.

I still write to my mother on a bimonthly basis. When I left my Russian homeland, she remained in the country. She said she couldn't bear to leave the land that she had forever called her own. "But you?" She said to me . . . "You were meant to make me proud; wherever that may take you." My mother's such a wonderful woman. I will no doubt need to write her a letter of my success later tonight. I'll be able to include money this month as well.

If you want the honest truth, the reason I find myself so strappingly poor is because I send my mother twenty percent of my monthly earnings. Since I moved to America, and still after I've been in London, I have sent her money in every other letter. My mother is still a very poor woman. I swear that each new day she works harder than the day before. She has done so much for me; I could not bring myself to let her down. If she knew that I have been struggling for cash, she would be so disappointed. I could not afford to send her any money last month, so I simply told her in a following letter that I'd forgotten. I promised her double the cash this time. I don't expect finances to be a problem any longer.

I feel a bit childish sitting in this rickety stool I call an office chair. I continue to boast about how wonderful of a doctor I've turned out to be, and how proud whatever little family I have is of me. As I sit here and really think about it; Harold hasn't woken up yet. Who's to say he won't spiral into hypovolemic shock? What if his heart simply stops beating? No . . . I don't think that such a thing would happen. Harold's got far too many people relying on his success, and I'm certain he knows it too.

So why bring up all of this family talk now? I suppose when you see a man so close to death, it makes you think hard about your own life. It reinstates the values that have made you into the man you are today. The past should be learned from. For those people who can't seem to grasp this concept; well, then I suppose that's why I'm here. People will always be looking to fix their imperfections. As long as they keep begging, I'll keep offering my services.

It feels like my stomach is turning on its head for the fifth time since I began writing this. I think it's time I take a short break and put some food into my system. My body is no doubt deprived of nutrients and vitamins by this hour. I don't believe I've even had a glass of water since the day began.

I went over to check on Harold a few moments ago. His vitals appear normal. It should still be a good couple of hours before he wakes up, but Abel knows what procedures to follow in case it should happen while I am away. I tried convincing him to go out for food, thinking he could just bring me something back to eat. He said he felt 'uncomfortable' leaving the patient. How does he think I feel about leaving him, even if just for a second?! Abel doesn't even want me to bring him anything back to eat. I honestly have no clue what's going through that boy's mind.

Still, Harold is going to need some talking down upon waking up. He will likely be unaware of his location. Sudden, sporadic movement could cause a brain aneurism or a massive rupture in his blood vessels. If he tries to walk with that sutured leg, he also risks tearing the stitches from his skin. He's already lost a tremendous amount of blood. Any further blood loss would likely result in shock or death.

Who can say what will happen when Harold wakes. The anticipation certainly has my fidelity in its jaws. The path ahead is certainly littered with difficulties. I have confidence that my expertise will be enough to pave the way with bustling knowledge and flourishing genius. Harold's brain was like a tower of children's blocks all cluttered together in different colors and sizes. When I performed the surgery, the tower fell into a heaping pile of rainbows. Now it is up to me to rebuild the structure of Harold's brain; to pick and choose which blocks go where and which ones to leave out. I need to build a structurally sound human being. Only a few fundamental blocks have likely remained at his base.

But alas, I am digressing for the time being. We are forced to wait until the patient's brain wakes up from the trauma that it has experienced. I am finally going to grab a bit of lunch. I asked Abel one last time if he wanted anything. He waved his hand at me, shoeing me away. Perhaps I shouldn't be as worried as I am forcing myself to be. Maybe I am more excited than I am afraid. In any regard, I feel that the rest of the day will only crawl as we wait for the patient's eyes to open.

*Chapter Fourteen – Twisted Husband*
*From the Visions of: Harold Elway's*
*Subconscious*
*December 25th, 1905*

All is black.

Damn!

I cannot force your eyelids open.

The odor of syrupy insides.

The suction of sticky organs pulsating with confusion.

With every weak breath comes the feeling of a dagger in the chest; the result of sweaty paste clinging to the walls of the lungs. We feel a little empty, a little hungry, a little tired. The basement office is perfumed by our waste. The reek of rotten organs doused in white vinegar is overpowering; empowering us to wake.

But our eyes are welded shut.

Soon they will open.

Our eyelashes like swords to the sandstorm leftovers.

Do you hear that *click, click, click?*

If only we could see what it was.

The anesthesia is wearing off; even the slow dripping has stopped. Do you remember falling asleep on the doctor's table? He called it a bed, but it's really just a table. Feels a bit hard . . . can you feel it yet? Do you feel what I feel?

Who are we?

Hazel? Where is Hazel?

Is this death?

Death . . .

Your tongue tastes salty.

Our name is Harold, I think. But where is Arthur? Arthur is gone. Is he with Hazel? Where did Hazel go? Harold, Harold. Our insides stink. I wish

we could see what was making that *click, click, click.*
Do you think Hazel knows? We could ask her, right?
She would know. She always knows.

My head hurts.

Are we okay?

1, 2, 3 . . .

A, B, C . . .

Yes, I think we're okay.

Do you smell that? Smells like . . . peppermint?
But we're not chewing. Are we chewing? No, I don't
feel like we're chewing. All I hear is that clicking.
*Click, click* . . . like someone else is trying to chew. Oh,
that smell is very poor: sewer breath and
peppermint.

I wish Hazel would wake us up.

Oh, that's right.

We killed her.

Arthur must have done it.

Good thing he's dead too.

Are we safe? I don't feel comfortable. I feel very unsafe. Something is standing over us . . . I feel its muggy breath on us . . . panting like a horny dog.

I'm so cold.

Now I'm too warm.

Pull those blankets up.

Useless.

Feels like we finally got some sleep.

I rather enjoyed the blackout; don't remember a thing about falling asleep. Why do we feel so empty still? Are we sweating now? Yech . . . we're sweating now. I can feel it oozing out of our pores. No wonder you taste so salty.

*Click, click, click . . .*

That smell reminds me of Arthur's breath.

Oh, another sound.

Our hand twitches at the sound.

Crinkling wrappers.

Arthur had a dying wish. He made me swear I'd tell you something. Was it about Hazel? No, no . . . can't be about Hazel. We already remember her. Was it about lanterns? Nah . . . we've already got a few of those at home. It was something about . . .

David?

David.

David . . .

David!

"David!"

Oops, we spoke. Didn't mean to speak. Feels good to speak. Aha! There's our vision back now. It's blurry, but it's making its way to us now. Still the sound of that *click, click, click.* Finally get to see what it is. Still cloudy . . . still hazy . . . still blurry . . . don't those all mean the same thing? I think they all mean the same thing. We can see a little better now. There's another twitch in the hand. A little less foggy . . .

Oh, David!

It's David.

Hello, David!

I don't think we're supposed to be happy to see David.

Oh, shit. It's David.

David must think that we killed his sister. We have to tell him it wasn't us! Tell him it was Arthur . . . that it's okay because Arthur is gone! David! Can you hear me? He can't hear me. We didn't touch her, David!

Ick.

When did we get so soft?

So helpless and cursed by begging hands . . .

More wrappers being undone.

Looks like five or six peppermints sitting in a pile.

David is laughing, smiling. He continues to unravel the hard candies. Where's the good doctor? Shouldn't he be here with us? I remember him now. I remember us now. Oh, Harold. Harold, Harold. We asked for this, didn't we?

Bloody hell, it's David! How did he find us? We've been so careful all these years. Goddammit . . . The Matthews never suspected us of anything. Why

now? Why eight years later? You have to get up,
Harold! You have to get up and fight! He's going to
kill us if you don't get up! Another wrapper comes
undone . . . what is he doing?

He's speaking now. Can you hear him? Let me
tell you . . .

"Finally awake?" David said, cracking his
knuckles before taking another hard candy from his
pocket. "You and Hazel loved these, didn't you? You
used to carry them with you everywhere." He
rubbed his fingers together, flapping them like the
pages of a book. "I saw you two swap spit so many
times, I could have gouged my eyes out. But I didn't;
because I knew you made my sister happy." The
wrapper comes undone and another peppermint is
tossed into a nearby pile that is building on the
bedside. "I'd hear your tongues swirling around and
the *click, click, click* of a peppermint hitting *back* and
*forth* between teeth; first in your mouth, then in hers,
then back again. That *click* always drove me crazy."
David sat with his leg crossed. Our eyes were
fully open at last, exposing us to our first look at
David in almost a decade. The rest of our body
remained motionless. Naragavitz was right; 'Abel'
was a strikingly good looking young man. He must
have kept up with his football hobby through his
high school years. Hazel never got the chance to

graduate high school. She was in her final year when we destroyed her.

"Do you still eat these?" David asked, tossing another candy into the pile. We didn't have the strength to speak. "What's the matter, too weak to talk? If you had half a brain, you'd speak when I talk to you." David's lip trembled with sickly satisfaction. He chortled lightly. "I can't help but shove this in your pasty little face." He spat. "Look at you, Arthur . . . or is your name still Harold?" He rubbed his hands together yet again, strings of sticky anticipation weaving between his fingers. "Whatever you call yourself now, you'll always be the bastard that killed my sister."

Even through the barrier of struggling anesthesia, the remark stung. Our senses had slowly grown back into a form of distorted normality. All around us was crooked; ill-shaped and waving. Unsure of what was hallucinatory and what defined reality, the garbage covered breath in our face let us know that David was very real.

"It took me all this time to find you," David said. "These potent little candies only confirmed my suspicions that it was *you* that had murdered my big sister. The blind mice in uniform were useless; full of shit. They said there was no evidence; no way to rule her death anything but a suicide. But you left one little piece of evidence behind." David grabbed at the bush of wrappers he had grown on the sheet. They whispered in his hands before exploding into our face. We were too weak to flinch; still building vitality. "*You* were full of shit!" David screeched. "I heard you two arguing that night, Arthur. The upstairs window into my bedroom was wide open."

Our mouth fell a bit. Was this the first step to babbling? Would the spit soon form a pool? "I heard everything," David said, using his arms to press himself up and out of the chair he had been sitting in. "I knew that Hazel was pregnant. I knew that neither of you wanted the kid. How could you? Could you ever imagine yourself as a father, especially at that age; especially now? Could you see yourself with the child you murdered now?!"

Good Lord, we'd nearly forgotten we took two lives that night. Surely Hazel couldn't have been far enough along to call that little bean a human life . . . could she have been? We didn't give her the chance to tell us. That needy little fetus couldn't have even had a gender yet. It was never truly your son or daughter. It was simply a disgusting little pickle that we plucked from its patch too soon. A loose wrapper rested on our shoulder blade; if only we had the strength to blow it away.

"An aching bloodline cut short," David spat, getting closer to our face. "Lineage destroyed with a thrust and a twist. Is that how it happened? Was she alive when you threw her to the river? Or had you killed her moments before?" He rubbed at his already maturing stubble. "I really do wish you could speak and tell me everything," he paused. "But it's much more enjoyable watching you dabble in helplessness. You look like a googly-eyed fish; fins cut and insides leaking into the water. I'll watch you die slowly; I'll watch you struggle to even remember the last few seconds of your life."

"But you remember that night, don't you?" David leaned in closer, cheap alcoholic aftershave now prominent. "Hazel didn't put that dress on until moments before you showed up at the door. Our mother had just washed the dress that afternoon. That candy wrapper couldn't have been in her pocket if you hadn't seen her after your argument. But didn't you tell my father quite the opposite? That Hazel had 'stood you up' that evening? The life was still leaving my sister's body as you breathed lies into my father's air. The police found the wrapper on Hazel's corpse, and they dismissed it as unsuitable evidence. You never had me fooled."

"I watched the beginning of the argument from my bedroom window. I knew my sister was hurting inside; her tone never told a lie. I was prepared to jump down on top of you if you even thought of laying a finger on Hazel. I saw you slip one of those rocky mints into your mouth, sliding the paper back into your own pocket. You walked away together, and I followed you. I climbed down from the window and trailed the street behind you. I heard the argument; the other man saving Hazel from your misaimed judgment. As you backed your way down the street, I did the same. I was afraid; afraid of either

Hazel or yourself finding out that I had followed you. Back in my bedroom, I waited for Hazel along with you. I watched you sit outside the house, absorbed in the assumed thought that you were hidden from all sight. I knew you hadn't done anything; not yet. You watched that pocket watch of yours like a time bomb. With each passing second, a different piece of Arthur Elway burnt out in the night."

I can feel the tension itching at your wrists. You want to reach out and strangle David. You'll have to if you want to survive. Death is a fickle thing. Death is avoidable at times. Yech . . . do you feel that damn toenail again? You never got around to trimming that, did you? The big toe on the right foot; the ingrown nail is knocking at the skin.

"But I did not follow you when you finally left the shadows." David said. "In the hour spent waiting for my sister, I reflected on the Arthur Elway that I had known for more than a year. He was a kid that would not harm my sister. He was a kid that had fought hard for my sister's trust; for my own trust and that of my father's. He was a kid that had found love." David gazed down at his shoes. "I trusted you for the last time. I let you walk away, believing that love would overcome anger. I've never been such a fool."

"I watched you lie to my father soon after," David said, having settled back into his seat. Another pocket of musty knockoff cologne hit us strong. "He had reread that day's newspaper more than ten times while he waited for his daughter to come home. He trusted you; treated you with the respect he thought you deserved. I told my father of my suspicions for you countless times after that night. He'd rest his hands on my shoulder and tell me that I was just 'looking for an answer', or that I was 'still too young to understand how someone could take their own life.'"

"My father would always look at me and say, 'Arthur would never do such a thing. Arthur's a good kid.' He told me about how he'd run into you at Glennbrooke park the night she disappeared. He said the look on your face was undeniably frantic, like you were already looking for a ghost. My father merely thought you were concerned about his daughter's well-being. I knew you were only concerned about cleaning up your mess. That's why I went to the park only days after they had found her dead body."

David rubbed his fingers against their own palm, scraping years of built up oils out onto the table. "You couldn't fool me," he said with a snarl under his eyes. "The torn up bark; the stained park bench. I saw how you murdered her play over and over again in my head. You bashed her head into that park bench, didn't you? *Didn't* you?!"

We at last had enough strength to respond. I felt the gravel slide down our throat as I moved our head up and down. The basement was sweltering;

sticky from years of pent up hatred being released all at once. David was back in our face now. Everything he said had lost sound, like he we were in a padded room and he was screaming from the outside. The words on his lips read 'I knew it!' and the rest was inaudible. Was this how shame always felt?

Like a troubled tide, our ears crashed and waves again consumed them. Jargon about a rubbish childhood and a brother's sad song; memories of innocence and trust. None if it mattered any more. None of it had mattered in years. All I saw before us was someone else we had disappointed in our life.

I have disappointed everyone I ever knew. I have stolen life from others, and in the end; myself. The money I've worked so hard for has all gone to waste in cigars, coffee packets, candles; the unnecessary luxuries that no one ever needs. All they ever did was keep me calm enough to wait out a slow death. My mother would slap me if she saw me now. My father would shame me. The worthlessness I feel inside is comparable to the hollow carcass of a lightning-rattled oak. I am nothing without the luxuries I foolishly bought into. I have never been anything more than a wasted body. The only person who cared enough to find me came to take my life.

I took an angel's life to save a demon's. Every night I sat awake, I'd think that tomorrow would bring a better day. Perhaps tomorrow I'd wake with some sense. Here I am; twenty-eight and another rug for death's carpet. I only hope he puts me before the embers of his fireplace. At least the doctor saved him some of the gutting work. Tomorrow is nothing more than a two-sided mirror.

I suppose I've had the urge to die for months now. Now that death is upon me, it really feels no different than life. I am just as dispirited; equally as withdrawn from my true being. I wonder what I could have been? A selfish button of a businessman? Or maybe the shovel of a caretaker, digging graves for the midnight shift? Whatever I could have been, it would have amounted to nothing at all. I would forever had been an object waiting for manipulation.

If I could see my bald, burning head I would be filled with shame. The icy fingertips from the blackest robes are to blame for the tickle down my spine. I am merely prey; the same footless rabbit hunted down by the luck-wearing hunter. For months, I've hopped and hobbled through spilt spirits and tobacco leaves. I am a frightened could-have-been husband; a cowardly unseasoned father. Without family, old or new, I am nothing. No one is proud of me. No one comforts me. I am the bastard child of a holy family. I am not Arthur, nor Harold; no . . . I am only a poor, poor bastard.

My livelihood's a joke told by drunken slobs over a few cheap brews. I was a man of heavy remorse, and tonight that sympathy is freed. The chilling of the season has brought the putridity of remembrance. Hazel . . . Hazel . . . you could have met a man so much greater than I. You could have felt lips so much sweeter than mine. I let you down like no one else could.

I didn't think I'd get another chance to lament on my dismal life like this. I thought for sure this morning would be the last I'd taste of the season. While other's mouths are filled with cranberries and stuffing, mine is so numb I can't even speak. It tastes rather close to ginger, really. Funny; just as I was thinking of everything that brought me spirit, David pulled out a cigar from his shirt pocket. Actually, it's one of *my* cigars. This feeling is quite odd; quite embarrassing. Do I speak in the 'I' form or the 'we' form? What am I anymore?

"Recognize this, I bet?" David asked rhetorically. The cigar still in its wrapper, he took it and ran it gently beneath his nose. "Ahhhh . . ." he exhaled. "The rich aroma of disease; just what you need, isn't it? As if you aren't sick enough . . ." David fingered the mouth of the wrapper before jabbing its end with his thumb. The aromatic stogie popped up out of its clear cavern and into the freshness of the basement air. "Can you smell it, Arthur?" David asked, waving it in front of our face. "Can you smell it?" We couldn't.

"This is one of yours, you know." David said with a grin. His hand moved to his right jean pocket and he pulled out an old book of matches. "I took this cigar from you the same day I took your phonograph." The veins in the cigar met his dry, chapped lips. He folded the cardboard lid of the

matchbook backwards and tucked a match behind it.
*sssTTTTIThsssss* . . . The match lit and David wafted
in the smell of sulfur. The sound of the serpent's
tongue didn't last long. We watched as the end of the
stogie went up in flames and David inhaled rapidly.
"You should see how nice that old music box looks in
the corner of the one-room apartment I've been
living in for the last eight months."

"It's been pretty crowded in there; quite lonely
all by myself. David took another drag of our cigar.
"But all I needed was somewhere to stay long
enough to hunt you down. London's beautiful,
really. It's no surprise that you and Hazel talked
about moving here when you were older. I guess you
just couldn't wait, could you? I heard everything you
two said. You'd talk outside the house like I couldn't
easily eavesdrop if I wanted to. You wanted to be in
London by the time you were fifty, is that right? At
least that's one goal you've met in your life. Too bad
you got so selfish about it."

The cigar's odor was medicinal to us. The
pounding pinch of robust tobacco and coffee notes
widened our nostrils. Was that really the reason we'd
chosen London all those years ago? London had
always been our dream; my dream. Hazel stole that
desire from us; twisted it to include her. I wish she
would have just had an original thought for once.

The stogie was nearly ready to tap, though I'd
heard that flicking it was bad taste. "Thanks for the
cigar, Arthur," David said, admiring the fervent tip

of ash. "I'm not the only one who can change his name," David continued. "At least I was smart enough to change my *last* name too."

Why *had* we kept our last name the same? Perhaps part of us didn't want to forget our old life. Was it too sacred of a thing to let go? Hazel never called me 'Elway'; only by my first name. Perhaps we were only trying to forget Arthur. That shouldn't be a problem anymore. He's dead, isn't he?

"I hired detective after detective to track you down. It took all this time, but one finally contacted me back with a close match. You know you're the only Elway in London whose under thirty years old? That didn't make you too difficult to pinpoint. The private eye provided me with your address, and a month later I was on a train. I'm going to bring that little journal of yours to my parents as proof that you murdered our Hazel. That lump in the mattress is thicker than you think. You must have been writing quite a bit lately. You know, who needs you to speak when I can just read your recordings after your dead?"

"The rest was quite simple, really," David continued, still letting the tip of the cigar linger in spent leaves. "See, I had been reading about the great doctor's malpractices in the American newspapers. That's where he's from, after all. You know he's made mistakes on over a decade's worth of patients? That bastard's hand isn't steady enough to hold a smoke without ash flying everywhere; which reminds me that I should probably trim this cigar a bit."

David rose from the hard metal of the chair. His teeth gritted between yellow splotches and what looked like a scratch of blood. He couldn't have brushed in over a week. "Are you afraid, Arthur?" David groaned. The heathen was getting off on our downfall.  The sticky cigar fumed from both ends. "Do you still feel the claws of fear scraping down your spine? Can you still acknowledge the *power* of fear? It could tear you limb from limb; gut you like a worthless, balding elk." David hovered above us, a bit of ash falling onto our surgical gown. "And pain . . . pain . . . can you still feel the jaws of torture? Do you have the bite-mark scars to remind you of pain?" He cocked a smile, ready to unload his displeasure. "You underwent this surgery to have a chance at a new beginning, didn't you? Let me remind the *new* you of what those feelings taste like on the tongue."

What is he doing? Jesus Christ, Harold! Close your mouth! You've got to wake up and shut your mout~

Shrieks of pain, a shaking fist of booming echoes; these are what we would have filled the room with if we were able. I know you felt the pain, Harold. I know you remember why this is all happening. Your half-brain just can't remember how to express it all. The squinted tear-fall in your eyes told me you felt the fire as the point of the cigar met your tongue. The lashing pink organ throbbing in black skid marks; the blue and purple veins boiling under the pressure. Did it remind you of what a real cigar tasted like? All you ever consumed was the smoke of comfort.

Our hands tried to shoot out, but they were stopped by the thick restraint of plastic bands. The coward tied us down while the doctor was away. What was his plan? To murder us now? To watch us slowly die? To torture us until we eventually felt the metal of suicide?

We feel so alone. I've never felt this beside myself. All we've ever needed was our thoughts to keep us company, but where have they gone? Why did we take them away? David has retreated, our tongue forever burnt with the taste of his revenge. Food will never taste the same. Whiskey will go down with a sting. What is the meaning of our body anymore? What is this remorse? I thought it was only us here . . . are we sick again? Were we too late? David speaks . . .

"So you see," David began. "I didn't come here alone. I promised Naragavitz success; told him I knew a helpless lemming who'd submit to just about anything. That idiot had nowhere else to go. He'd be in prison right now if it weren't for me." David took another drag of the cigar. It no longer had appeal. "I knew I couldn't kill you myself. I'd never jeopardize my own life for scum like you. The doctor was the perfect answer. I'd let him ruin you and I'd be innocent all at the same time. I've been funding the doctor for months, telling him that I'm simply interested in his expertise. That headless chicken is nothing more than a pile of his own broken fantasies. I knew he'd let you suffer just like I wanted."

David paced the room, shouting and throwing his arms down as if we could feel the impact of his body language. He touched briefly on how he'd begged our old boss at the press for a job; just for a chance to get closer to us. "And so here we are," he said. "The doctor's out and I have you where I've wanted you for years. You sick, slimy bastard; I finally found you. Didn't you ever wonder how Naragavitz's address got in your pile of documents? I've been watching you for months. I planted that note at your desk the same night you blacked out from the salvia divinorum. None of this happened by chance, Arthur. *Nothing* happens by chance. Everything is carefully planned and delicately executed. My dreams of this day have never felt so lucid."

David took another drag of the bustling stogie before setting it on the bedside. Walking over to us, he took another peppermint candy from his pocket. "As I was saying, you loved these didn't you? Everything you've ever loved has become poisonous." David added the candy to the pile on the bedside. "So why should these be any different?" he asked with a smirk. This psycho had lost it years ago.

David gathered the peppermints into his right hand. They cracked together like the breaking of a triangle of billiard balls. "Everything is poison to you now," he glowered. His eyes looked as tired as ours, yet suddenly they came alive with youth. His hand reached out and cupped around our mouth. The peppermints poured into our drooling cavity. They *clicked* and *tacked* against our teeth. One mint broke in half against our lower-left canine. The taste was sweet just before our gums filled with saliva. The load of candies was far too much for us to hold. David's hand kept firmly pressed against our lips.

Chokes and gasps adorned the snot dripping from our desperate nostrils. Winter chills had brought blockages to our nasal passage. I watched an elongated string of green mucus blow atop David's index finger. My God . . . *this* is what we had done to Hazel? The sweetness overwhelmed us, bringing a flood of spittle to rise in our mouth. The mints floated like ships desperately steering from a whirlpool. David's hands moved up, his thumb and index finger forcing our nostrils shut. The slime greased across the hole it had come from. Was this the end? Was this what David had planned?

"I could kill you here. You son of a bitch, I could murder you right here." David's hands suddenly lifted from our mouth and he stepped backwards. "But it doesn't happen like this." The sudden gust of air in our inhale tickled our throat. The peppermints came spewing out like rafts over the edge of a dam. Bits of ash from the cigar dirtied the reddened water. You remember what pain feels like now, don't you?

You have become exactly what you didn't want to be, Harold; a babbling fish with a gaping, willing mouth. Your eyes are aged from being opened. You are someone else's pleasure. Your memory is easily manipulated. But a fish can learn, can't it? If the master taps the glass every time he feeds his pet, then soon enough the fish will swim to the opening every time it hears that gentle *tap*. We still have a chance, don't we Harold? What's wrong with being oblivious? Harold?

Ick. I hope our teeth never look like David's. Hmpfh. After months of coffee drinking and cigar smoking, who knows? Christ, what's he doing now? He's got the umbrella Johnny got for you. He's opened the chute. It's twirling in his hands like some sort of toy. It's really a rather beautiful carousel of black. He's spinning it in front of your eyes like he's trying to hypnotize you. Harold, you need to wake up. Fight the ties that bind us. Strangle him like Arthur would do. Today isn't the day we die.

*Tick, tick, tick.*

Hear that old pocket watch? It's relying on you to fight through this. It's kept us sane for all these years. You owe it to that tiny brass body to keep fighting. *Strangle* him, Harold. You're strong enough now. You can take him down and we can live forever. He's closed the umbrella back up. The doctor could be back at any moment. Ick. The sweat on his hands is rubbing against your leg. What is he doing? He's lifted the gown up. His hand is rubbing at our knife wound; his finger like sandpaper to our sutures. This guy's a freak, Harold. We could never be as messed up as he is.

Oh . . . right.

We did this to him, didn't we?

*Kill* him, Arthur. *Kill* him and walk away a free man. No one would ever know.

Harold, you have to fight back. Break the ties.

You have enough strength. Trust me.

I love you, Arthur.

David has closed the umbrella. He's examining the handle that Thomas made for you. The sharpened point is grazing the wound on your leg. What the hell is going on?

"I loved your sister," we speak at last. The voice is weak; sick. "And I still do. You never deserved this, David. Hazel never should have settled for a man like me, but she did. I never should have hurt her, but I did." Harold what are you doing? Kill him, Arthur! Don't apologize. You're a stronger man than that! "I wish everything had turned out differently, but this old pocket watch lets me know that time only moves in one direction." We choked a bit on still-forming saliva. "Let me go, David. You are no better than me. You think I haven't suffered enough? "

David's face looked like a withering cherry bomb. His fuse had run short. The silver tip of the umbrella pressed lightly against our sewn up thigh. "Do you want be a killer like me?" we spat. David scoffed. "I told you," he said. "You won't die by *my* hands. No one will ever link your death back to me." We could only grin as his hands pressed the umbrella into the wound.

The stitches ripped apart, forming a volcano that fizzed and oozed with lava. The eruption was magnificently vast. The pain; yes, we felt the pain. Still, a smile remained plastered on our white slate of a face. The sheets became stained with new blood as the dizziness hit our head. Our hands wrestled at the ties, feeling that the lonely cigar had burnt out. David screamed nonsense as he pressed our Christmas gift further into the wound. Nothing could feel worse than these past few months.

The point twisted and glazed our bone. David cackled with achievement too soon. The door bust open and the doctor reentered. Two bags in his hand, he dropped them where he stood and dashed to our rescue. "Abel!" he screeched. "What are you doing?!

What in God's name are you doing?!" He only reiterated what we'd been wondering for the past twenty minutes.

Naragavitz grabbed David by the back of his shirt collar. The umbrella remained lodged in our leg. David spun around, grabbing the doctor by his coat and shoving him to the other side of the room. "He's mine now, doctor!" David screeched. Spit flew from his teeth like a ravaging hound. "He's *my* prey."Naragavitz plastered into his desk, knocking over a stack of already disorganized files. Here we lay; the rabbit.

"You've been a real help, doctor." David snarled. He had snapped completely in half by now. He was crazier than any man I'd ever seen in the mirror. "Walk out now. Leave me to him." The doctor returned to his feet with a scalpel in his hand. "What's wrong with you, Abel?" He spat at David. "That boy's my experiment. He's *my* success." He cut the thickened air with the blade, as if it already had blood on it that needed wiping. David yanked the umbrella from our thigh, the blood still pouring uncontrollably from the wound. Pain; it all felt so similar no matter the context.

The two boiling bodies faced off. "Leave us, doctor." David warned a final time. I watched the focus in Naragavitz's temples as he stormed forward. Scalpel in hand, he dodged past the blade of the umbrella and lodged the surgical knife into David's side. David shrieked; an expected masculine scream.

He grabbed the doctor's coat as he brushed past him. The blade in his side, David pinned Naragavitz down atop a steel medical cart. Scissors and bone-saws rained down to the cement floor. The *clang* of metal tasted like aluminum as it hit our ears.

*BANG.* David hit his forehead against the doctor's. Naragavitz twitched with a wrinkle in his brow. Before he could recover from the blow, *BANG*; David hit him again. With one hand on the doctor's throat, David pulled the scalpel from his ribcage with the other. Their behavior was uncontrollably primal. We watched as human instinct played out before us once more.

*BANG.* Their foreheads clashed all over again. Naragavitz held David back loosely with his forearm, fresh blood trickling down his forehead. As the scalpel neared his throat, Naragavitz gave an adrenaline-fueled kick to David's exposed gut. David tumbled backwards into a heap of sun-spotted dust. The blade had been dropped with the kick, a ringing *clang* as it grazed the cement. Naragavitz climbed to a full sprint by the time David found his footing.

Hardly prepared for his attacker, David reached out and again grabbed at the doctor's clothing. He spun the failing assailant around, tossing him into the nearby cement wall. Another clamber of metal shook the silence. David ran towards us, dropping down to pick up the umbrella he had lost. Naragavitz had already risen back to his feet. With David's bent-over back turned to him, the doctor dashed forward desperately, a jagged bone-saw in hand. The circular, tooth-grinned blade caught sunlight from the still-open door. As Naragavitz neared his target, David spun around with our only holiday gift in his hands. Naragavitz was moving too fast; too disoriented to slow down. He cringed as the metal entered his chest. The doctor impaled himself onto the umbrella; a short grunt accompanied a dribble of crimson down the corner of his lip. We've never seen a *man* die before.

The room sat hauntingly quiet aside from the doctor's long, exasperated gasp. It was a stressed, hollow sigh that filled the room with tenderness. David trembled at the locked eye contact with the dying man. His hands remained firm on the acorn-handle Thomas had made for us. Like a feather before a fan blade, David's lip shuttered to remain stern. He was sick with delight, yet bursting with dissatisfaction. As the basement office fell entirely quiet, David pressed his left hand against the doctor's chest, gently shoving him off the makeshift sword. Naragavitz hit the cement with a *thud*, the blood already pooling from the impact to his head.

David stared at the doctor's body in the musty hush of drained air. Whether it was out of respect or enthrallment, we couldn't be sure. I knew what he was feeling; what it felt like to take a life. Where does he go from here? Does he hide the body? Continue murdering the witness? Leave the doctor where he lies? David stepped across the corpse and gently shut the door. His hand remained pressed against the metallic panel, his back strong and chest upright. With a crack in his neck, David turned to face us. The umbrella's peak dripped with the doctor's blood. The blinding, shimmering silver was deluding to the tar-like bloodshed. *Drip, drip, drip.* The charcoal cement became further discolored with its owner's filth. David was a murderer now. And I wasn't going to let him leave this basement alive.

David crouched down to his knees, a light cry emitting from the friction between his shoe and the stone. He traced his index finger across the doctor's cheek, emotionless. "Doctor, Doctor . . ." he said. *Tick, tick, tick.* The pocket watch beat onwards. David inhaled loudly as he stood again. Our wrists braced for freedom as we heard the sultry oxygen whisk through his forest of nostril hair. Calm as a flame, he exhaled out with a buzz. *Hssssshhhhhhhhzz;* the sound of a bothered wasp battling an arched serpent. At the end of the curved hiss came expected anger.

"You bleeding idiot!" David hawked, spit flying from his already sweaty lips. "This isn't how it was supposed to happen! You've ruined it all!" With a bridged back and a cocked foot, David booted the corpse in the rear of its head. "Bastard!" he screamed. "Bastard! Bastard!" Rubber met flesh again, and then once more. Our head was a knapsack of beaten hornets ready to be untied. This distraction was our only chance at freshly-brewed life.

Our fists clenched as David screamed at the dead; something we did in our old life. I could feel our own scream building inside of our lungs; the air willing and able. Perhaps this new consciousness wouldn't be as distorted as we'd thought. Maybe our new life would be all that we'd hoped for. In any regard, David had to die. The oxygen sweltered in our chest. Our veins popped like fresh rainwater canals. David had his back turned, rummaging foolishly through the doctor's coat pockets.

The holler travelled up through the passage in our throat. It left our mouth with the *snap, snap* of the ties that once bound us. Everything suddenly felt in the present once more. The now familiar stone chilled the calluses on our naked feet.

Reach for the saw!

And we did with our right hand, stabilizing ourselves on the bed sheet with the left. David launched away from us, pasting his back against the front door.

His eyes look so wide, so filled with freight; perfect to gouge. David is our next kill. It's been so long since we've tasted blood. Look at him, Arthur. He's frightened; helpless.

"What are you expecting to do?" David said. He has no weapon, but he could easily take us over. Look at us, Harold. We can't even stand up straight. The bed sheets curled tighter in our fingernails. Just submit to him; let him do what he wishes with you. Maybe we'll get to see another sunset.

Slit his begging throat.

Fall back into the hospital bed.

Lay down and die.

Rob his corpse when you're done with him.

You've got the strength.

Give him another rhetorical speech.

Don't hurt him; please, Harold.

Gut him like an animal. Wrap his intestines around your neck as a souvenir. Be proud you're more of a man than he ever was.

"Enough!" We finally spoke, the saw aimed at the still far-off David. "My name is not Arthur. It isn't Harold. I am not a puppet, and I am far from a puppeteer. I am a disaster of personalities; a multitude of regrets and quick comebacks. I am the bone saw's master and the bone saw's tool. You. You!" Our hand shook outwards again. "You are David Matthews."

The look on fool's face belonged on a stale milk carton. "You have no idea what it's like to love someone and watch as they deceive you before your very eyes." David moved to mimic us, but bit his tongue. "That's right," we continued. "Your sister whored herself out. Found a man that lived not too far from you. The night I killed her, she'd went to bed with another, *better* man. I knew she'd never stay with a man like me. Some other man would raise my son or daughter. I'd get weekend visits and a dripping wallet. I couldn't deal with it either way. I was too young; too stupid to process the dilemma rationally. If she stayed with me, we both would have been victims of ruined lives. A kid at seventeen; Hazel wasn't ready for that, and neither was I."

We let go of the comfort of the bed sheets. "I couldn't imagine someone else raising my child. That's not right. That's not the way it's supposed to be." David threw his arms down. "And this *is?!*" He hollered, looking around the room. Three ruined lives whispered in the basement air. "No," I said. "This isn't how it was supposed to be. Nothing's been right since that night. But you have to know, David. You have to know that Hazel was a liar and cheater." "You bastard!" David pounded his fist against the door, shaking its body. "She was just as immature as you. She didn't know what to do with a kid either. You think she loved that man she slept with?" Our mouth was suddenly extraordinarily dry.

"No," we said. "No, I know she did not love him. He was a comfort and nothing more."

"The truth is," we began, lowering the saw slowly. "I don't know why I killed your sister, David. I've tried in so many ways to make sense of it, and I just can't. Part of it was the deception. There was jealousy, anger, tribulation, confusion . . ." We paused. There was no longer a taste in our mouth. The drying thigh-wound tingled more intensely than before. "I loved Hazel. I still love her. When it comes down to the rawness of the murder, I can't give you a single reason why I killed her. There was immaturity and inexperience. There was love masked in a short temper. I made a mistake; a terrible, awful mistake. I pushed my American life as far away from my memory as I could. I haven't thought of home in years."

David relaxed his stance a bit. "It hasn't felt like home in more than eight years," he said, kicking the ground. "And that's your fault, Arthur Elway. Whether you like it or not, Hazel's death was your fault. And I can't let you get away with that." "Get away?" we chuckled. "Look at me, David. Isn't this enough? Weren't the years I lived in fear enough? What about the months and months of *torture*. Nearly every night at my door; *BANG, BANG, BANG*. Nearly every midnight down my stairs; *croak, croak, thud. Croak, croak, thud.* Or did you have a part in that too?" David shrugged, frazzled. "You're clinically insane, Arthur." He sighed. "I have no idea what you're talking about." His expression told me the truth. He really had no idea about the haunts.

"I told you we were loony. Better wake the doctor and tell him to take the other half of our brain out."

"What are you talking about?" David asked. Why had our thoughts suddenly become vocal? I can't control it . . . *we* can't control it.

"Run away, run away little pig," we taunted. "Don't be afraid of little old David; stay for a bit." David cocked one eye. "Kill him like a professional. I wanna taste the boy's insides." There was a churn in our stomach. "Don't hurt him, Harold. Put the saw down." David inched slowly towards the umbrella on the floor. "Going for the murder weapon?" we asked. "No, no, David. They'll pin you to the crime. They'll kill you for killing me. I don't want to hurt you. I only want to lick your bloody heart."

"You're insane," David cried. "You're not in the right mind. I guess that would be my fault, wouldn't it?" He cackled like a groveling old man. "I knew you'd be crazy as a loon. You would have let Naragavitz do *anything* to you. I knew the moment you ran away that you'd never be the same. You'd never be able to live your life as Arthur Elway ever again. It was just a matter of letting insanity slowly eat away at your soul. Look at yourself, Arthur. Look at yourself and remember that you *begged* for this."

"You aren't going to let me leave here, are you?" What's happening? Thoughts feel like they're on fire; like they're liable to explode. "I'll kill you, David," we said. He backed away from the umbrella as we shook the bone saw again. Blindness struck the right eye as we lined up the blade with David's throat. "I'll cut that Adam's apple right out of you. I haven't eaten in days."

A step forward.

Another slow, painless step.

Still blind in the right eye.

Can't feel anything but a half-brain on fire.

Kill David.

Kill David.

Kill David.

"Kill David!"

We screech.

We step.

A *SNAP.*

Your vision is gone.

Our feet give out.

The cement floor is cold. Our head rests by the doctor's shoes.

There is laughter; David's laughter. Our eyes are open, our body convulsing. Arms flailing like the fish we'd tried so hard not to become. All I see is red . . . red . . . black. Wait, there's David. He's scrambling. We are scrambled. We are a holiday tragedy. David is at the doctor's desk, scribbling something into the doctor's journal. He's writing . . . writing . . . *still* writing. Such a boring death we've arrived at.

Sweat pours from David's face. I wonder how foolish we look here on the floor. What happened? Why can't I think straight? Why can't I think at all? Oh, God; the blood. The fall broke open your sutures. Your head is now more of a mess than your leg. David's finished writing. The book closes with a *clap* and he scoops it up beneath his armpit. I wish we could feel the wind as he brushes past us.

He is afraid; very, very afraid. He's looking under the mattress for our journal. He's found it. Both journals in hand, he is looking desperately around the room. Does he cover his mess up? Does he leave it be? He leaves it be.

The door opens.

The door closes.

He did not look back.

Here we are.

Alone again.

Just the three of us.

A lone spider sits on our fingertips.

The doctor's foot twitches.

Make that the four of us.

You're forever a poor bastard, Harold.

It's been a pleasure.

I love you, Arthur.

I love you too, Hazel.

Goodbye.

Goodbye.

*Tick, tick, tick.*

*Chapter Fifteen – Paperwork*
*From the Journal of: ~~Dr. Yovan Naragavitz~~*
*Abel Anderson*
*December 25th, 1905*

Patient #47
Name: Arthur "Harold" Elway
Sex: Male
Age: 28
Marital Status: Single
Status: Deceased
Time of Death: 1:47 pm
Cause of Death: Brain Aneurism

D.M

*Chapter Sixteen – In-between Holidays*
*From the Journal of: Johnny Tappling*
*December 28th, 1905*

Today was the day of Harold's funeral; a brisk, decaying December day awed by cardinal sunset. The crows were alive in the trees, cawing for us to leave the grave uncovered so that they may feast. Harold would have found it amusing. Perhaps he was looking down on the burial, tipping his hat with a spare hand resting upon his umbrella.

I would not let the priest bury him bald; that's not the way dear Harold would want to be remembered. I made sure they fixed that old top hat of his upon his head; even paid for a bigger pine box so it would sit just right. The smell of cedar has never been so sickening. Moving from the bustling tree in our living room draped with colorful garland and bulbs, to the hardly-polished box being lowered into the mud; the smell just wasn't the same.

A bothersome mixture of snow and sleet, the sky has never stressed such remembrance. The starkness of sunset purples and reds barely painted the otherwise white unknown. I knew that Harold would want to feel the chilled air. I motioned to request the casket be opened a final time, but Abel's disapproving glare disturbed the innocent and wordless request. I bowed my head, and stepped silently back into the humbleness of the crowd.

There were not many people in attendance. Annie and Thomas were there of course, along with Abel and a few other past coworkers of Harold's. It would be generous to estimate that a dozen people stood over Harold's makeshift tomb. The priest gave a nice sermon, mostly free of religious insight like I had requested. Truth is: Harold wouldn't have received a burial at all if it weren't for me. I don't know how long he would have remained in the doctor's basement.

Abel, which I've promised to still call him, told me everything the day of Harold's surgery. I had walked over to Harold's house Christmas Eve morning to give him the new umbrella Thomas had made for him. Upon seeing that he wasn't home, I feared that he'd gone to the office of that psychotic doctor. I tried the front door of the home, which came right open. Shifting through the still-disastrous pile of documents, I found the doctor's address that had been neatly scribbled into place. After busting into Naragavitz's office and picking a blind fight like a damn fool, Abel escorted me outside.

Abel wrapped his arm around my shoulders. "You're a father, right?" he asked, giving me a friendly yet stern rub. I scratched my gloves together, as if I could create friction through the cloth. "You've got a boy, right? Thomas?" I looked up at Abel. He was far taller than I. "That's right," I said, contemplating how I would go about toppling the man if need be. Before I'd been escorted out into the cold, Abel had whispered something about Hazel in my ear. It made me uneasy believing that I had been the only one to know about the girl up until this point. "What's this about?" I asked, the impatience inside maturing. That's when he told me the whole story.

I have sworn my silence to Abel, promising that I will not write about the matters even in secrecy. I'll just say that Abel is not who he seems to be. In fact, I promised him my entire collection of writings after this entry is complete. This little diary of mine began as a silly endeavor; a blind copycat of what Harold had started as his own confidant. Though Abel has promised to send the original copy of my logs back once he has finished re-recording them, I have strong doubt that he will actually follow through with their return.

The writing has been good for me, I admit. It has let me rattle my brain; shake my thoughts down into a pile of words. Carefully, I have picked through the pieces and thrown them atop the lines. Perhaps I will start a new journal; one free of Harold's past. I will make it all about me; about my family and friends. The diary is more therapeutic to me than a cup of *Hazed Forest* tea. I find that it helps me organize my thoughts better, thus making me a better planner and organizer.

I am in no position to deny Abel the right to read my entries. He is boarding a ship tomorrow at dusk – sailing back to his homeland which I have vowed to keep secret as well. Poor Abel. For such a young boy, he's got more problems than a cane-pushing old man. He deserves to know everything about Harold. I really don't know what he will gain from it all; perhaps a simpler, calmer peace of mind?

As I write this entry, I cannot help but still feel lost. My wife and child lay asleep upstairs, but it is once again the hardest working dweller of the house that breathes in the insomnia. An over-plumped snowman taunts me in front of the house across the street. Empty eyes of coal, a frost-burnt broken carrot for a nose, snapped and defeated twigs for arms. The rounded fellow reminds me of Harold; utterly helpless and patiently waiting for the sun to end the bleak, stale scenery he knows as life. Hmm . . . too bad; the boys who decorated him forgot to give him a top hat.

I spoke to Abel briefly after the funeral. He is stopping by the house in the morning to pick up the journal, along with a few baskets of food that Annie has prepared for him. Yes, I told Annie about Harold's crime. After hearing Abel's story, I realized something rather significant about my own case. Annie is my wife; my life partner. If I cannot trust her with every one of my secrets, no matter the size, then what is the point of marriage in the first place? As a couple, we have been talking a lot more in the past few days; about life, our love, anything that we find importance in.

I don't feel as if I have broken my promise to Harold. I find no shame in telling Annie that Harold murdered a past love in his life. Harold may be shaking his fist at me in the afterlife right now, but honestly, who cares? He was obviously far from correct when it came to making moral decisions. From this point onwards, it needs to be my own mind that chooses how my life plays out. This is why I have decided to keep the tea shop open only four days a week.

Don't get me wrong; my love for herbs and teas is still as strong as my father's ever was. But let's be realistic. Tea was my father's dream; not my own. With the newly freed hours, I am going to focus much more time on gardening. Sure, I can grow a handsome patch of grass. Yet, countless fruits and vegetables have withered and spoiled under my watch. I am tired of using mustard-stained leaves in my homebrewed teas. I have been sacrificing the quality of my work for extra coin for far too long. With the costs of Harold's funeral, I find myself even deeper in debt's hole. Last year it was my mother who needed the money, and God only knows who will need it next season. Finance is a superficial matter to my true livelihood.

I admit that I thought about pumping myself full of herbs to get through these past few days. I could have easily drank a gallon of intoxicating tea; fallen asleep as I crashed hard from the herbs leaving my bloodstream. I am a stronger man than that now. The older, less experienced Johnny Tappling might have done a thing like that; but not the man that sits here and scribbles onto the paper at this very moment.

That damn snowman is still piercing me with its look through the frosted glass. I almost have the mind to get up out of my seat and tear the glutton apart. I suppose I could just close the blinds, but then how would I watch the snowfall? I can't simply ignore the snowfall on a night like this.

God, I bet Abel will think a fool of me when he reads this journal. Sorry, Abel. I know you don't want to hear more about my doldrums; you'd rather hear about Harold's. Hmm . . . I suppose there really isn't much more I can say about old Harold. Abel has already picked through Harold's house and taken what he wanted. He took that water-stained envelope full of photographs. If I were him, I would never set willing eyes on those memories.

Harold's house will be absorbed by the city. It will go up for sale within weeks. It's really a nice house when given the chance to shine. If Harold would have ever kept it clean, he could have seen that. Funny; a couple of city workers stopped over at the house to examine it this morning. They pointed

fingers at what needed fixed up and what needed
trashed. When I walked by tonight, they had finally
fixed those unsteady lampposts outside the home. I
can't tell you how many times Harold had
complained to the city about them before. I poked
my own greedy head through Harold's door, but I
found nothing of real physical or sentimental value. I
don't need any trinkets to remind me of the man that
Harold was.

The only thing that I admittedly swiped was
the box of remaining instant coffee packets. Before
you call me cheap, know that it was for good
intentions. After the New Year, I am sealing them
back into the crate and returning them to Anthony.
Caffeine is the Devil's drug. I have no doubts that it
contributed to Harold's departure from the real
world. Think about it; the drug induces sporadic
shaking, leaving the consumer with nasty trembles of
withdrawal. Caffeine is a stimulant, an unnatural
spiked boot to the heart. That's why I have vowed to
keep all of my teas caffeine-free from this day
onwards. These events have allowed me to take a
step back and look at what I am truly providing for
my customers. I am going to ask Anthony's opinion
on certain plants when I see him next week.

Now that Harold has passed away, I
earnestly feel that I have been robbed of my only
friend. At times I think that there was more that I
could have done; but in the end I know that Harold's
miserable soul died years ago. I can only hope he

went softly into the light, whether it was white or scarlet. I could not stop Harold's delusions. I could not suck the memory of Hazel from his body. The surgery was an inevitable part of Abel's plan; one that I didn't have the heart to stop. When you have a family, a child; the loss of a life feels so much more significant. I imagined walking a day in Abel's boots, and I could not talk myself out of doing exactly as he did. Harold was my friend, but yes; he deserved death - maybe not in the manner that he received it, but he deserved death.

On Christmas day, I watched from the tail of the alley as Abel dashed from the scene of the crime. I had been waiting with the shadows all afternoon. I heard the scuffle with the doctor; the manic laughter pouring from Abel's throat. After Abel had been long gone, I slapped a note onto the door of the police station which simply read, "52 West Minster Street. Send the coroner." The tip was left anonymously. I knew Abel was going to kill Harold that day. He had told me about his plan of dragging out Harold's misery, but the wrath swirling in his eyes told me he could not wait any longer.

Does that make me an accomplice? Maybe. At this point, my morals could not care less. Harold's crime was too heinous to go unpaid. There is no evidence outside of this journal that I was involved in any way. I mean truly, I wasn't actually involved. People let bad things happen to other people all the time, don't they? I feel no guilt; especially when that bad thing is well deserved.

Harold, if you can see me now, just know that I am sorry. You were a great friend for the past eight years. We shared chalices of laughter and spilt our fair share of smiles. But just remember, Harold: I am a father first, and a friend second. I told Thomas everything too. He knows about Hazel; about the Matthews family and the one night stand. Thomas is a bright boy, old enough to rationalize right from wrong in his head and make judgments of his own. You know something, Harold? Thomas still thinks you're an alright guy. He values your heroism; your will to survive and your persistence to be a part of his life. You were always there for my boy, Harold, and that is something that I can truly be grateful for.

You had your good qualities, and you surely had your bad. Yet, I don't think you ever truly knew who you were. You matured as a false man, developing both mentally and physically as Harold rather than Arthur. You left everything; well, nearly everything, about your old life behind you. Your mother, your father, your sister; they were all just stars in the sky you wish you could touch. Until the day you forgot them all. All you've become is what London has offered you in these past few years.

But Harold . . . poor, poor Harold; you took a life. For that, you must pay. I fabricated a story in which someone took Thomas away from me, sending his tiny frame to the jaws of a ravine. Death would be the only greeting the killer could receive; nothing less would satisfy me. We've had a few drunken nights together, but I never saw you for the demon you used to be. You tried to reinvent yourself, and you failed miserably. Harold, Harold . . . Maybe that was part of your plan all along.

That *God Damn* snowman . . . Excuse me for a moment.

Well, I did it. I'm not proud of myself, but I did it. My bare feet like dry ice on the sidewalk; I marched across the street and tore that fat slob apart. It had an idiotic grin made of stones, which was the first atrocity that I wiped clean. I kicked the front of the frost-skinned puppet, knocking away the dried giblets of ice. Its heart became exposed, begging for me to ravage it. The severed limbs snapped with ease. I had to put the bastard out of its misery. Anger is such a temperamental feeling.

I tore the cracked, jagged carrot from the snowman's face. My finger traced its cheekbones, feeling the sting of wintry fear. "Sorry, friend," I said, as if the inanimate man were actually real. Pleasure fueled my body as I drove the frozen vegetable into the statue's chest. The stomach gutted so easily, the skin and innards drifting coolly onto my hands. Up through the chest, the makeshift dagger arrived at the throat as I sliced a clean cut across the neck. The head rolled backwards, tumbling to the ground it once came from. I made a calamity for the kids who had built him. They'll be so disappointed when they look out their windows in the morning and see their creation splattered all across the lawn. Tossing the frozen weapon to the brick road, I couldn't help but whisper my true goodbyes to Harold.

Perhaps my hatred for my old friend is more severe than I want to believe. Maybe further time needs to pass for me to feel genuine remorse. I paid for the funeral because I knew that it was the righteous thing to do. Harold murdered a child in her own shivering blood. He ruined lifetimes of families. His guilt poisoned me into believing I felt pity for a man that I never really knew. Harold's life, his past and history, were nothing more than a mirage. I know that I will miss Harold after the holidays. But for now, I know that all of London will sleep just a little sounder tonight.

Harold had an excuse for everything. He believed what he wanted to believe. I don't know if there was ever any hope of truly helping him. I pray that his soul is not as lost as Hazel's. Golden or aflame, I hope that the gates welcomed him.

I suppose this is a new beginning for me. I feel like a freshly sprung daisy; like my concern with the unimportant died with Harold. My feet, though still freezing right now, are moving in the right direction. For once, I would be proud for Thomas to step in the same pattern as I. While the school kids are all on winter leave, I wrote a letter to the superintendent notifying him about the boys who jumped Thomas. Thomas knew the name of one of the boys, which I included in the letter along with my holiday wishes. Hopefully we see some action taken after school resumes in the New Year.

All these changes come at an iconic time. Every year, millions of people make dreamy resolutions at the toll of midnight on December 31st. With that hour just three nights away, I suppose I have joined them in their hopeful, often fruitless endeavors. I have made peace with Thomas. He is far smarter than I was at his ripe, young age of nine. "I understand," was all he could say upon hearing my apologies. We talked near the entire evening, right up until his bedtime. He understands what kind of man Harold was now, and he realizes how such a burden could affect a man like I. In fact, I think he understands it even better than I do. That boy is growing up to become someone great.

I had a long talk with Annie as well; thanked her for putting up with the rough patch I was going through. I've never heard of a man having a mid-life crisis at the age of thirty-two, but I suppose there's a lot I haven't been exposed to in my life. A little bit of bloodshed and teardrops are good for a man every once in a while. Poor Harold took it too far. He could never secure a healthy balance.

As expected, my family forgives me for my childish behavior. It isn't as if I've been treating them badly all this time; I just haven't been there like I should have been. I suppose my guilt trickles down from the bitterness I still hold from the death of my father. He was a great teacher and more than the definition of a man; but he left me choice-less in life. I was expected to take over Tappling teas when he passed away, and that's just what I did to keep my mother happy. It was all worth it. Seeing my mother deathly ill just a short year ago reminded me how much the acceptance of my family means to me. I know that my mother will always be proud of me, but the obligation to keep the family business alive still bubbles in my head.

I reckon I do feel a bit awful about destroying those boys' creation across the street. For a changed man, I should have really mannered myself better. I heard footsteps upstairs a moment ago. I think I may have woken Thomas. Another footstep; I definitely woke the boy. Damn me. Abel, I know you won't find pleasure in reading about my dry, conventional life. However, I feel there is a part of me that desires to be remembered. Even if it is only your family that reads this, it is comforting to me that someone cared enough to read about bland, awkward Johnny.

There is a part in every man that desires to be remembered. For some it is a heroic hope, and for others it is a twisted, selfish thought. The doctor was victim to the latter. What's most interesting is the fact that I saw the doctor enter his office Christmas Day, and that Abel was the only one to leave by foot.

When the authorities came hours later, only one plump white sheet was carried out on a stretcher.

That crazy son of a bitch must have escaped somehow; off to a different city, I suppose. Who knows *what* happened to the doctor, and *what* they will do to him if they ever find him. There's certainly substantial-enough evidence to point enough fingers at Naragavitz, yet he still remains a shadow to an enigma. I can only imagine what's going through his head right now. He has no family to hold him back. He is free to jump from country to country whenever he chooses. He reminds me of an escaped bird, a snapped chain still clanging around his neck. One day he too will feel the haunts of the souls he has killed.

Thomas poked his head around the stairwell a moment ago. I asked him if he was having trouble sleeping, to which he nodded. I looked down at the paper, and then back to my son. There are things more important than this. Abel, I hope you've found peace after the years of torment you've endured. As for me, I am going to slip on a coat and a pair of galoshes. My son and I have a snowman to rebuild: Together.

## Chapter Seventeen - The Collector: An Epilogue
### From the Journal of: Abel Anderson
### August 18th, 1908

*12:30am*

My name is David Matthews. In the past, I was David Matthews before I was Abel Anderson. Now, I am David Matthews once more. I live at 1800 Chagrin Avenue Northwest. I am starting this journal to record the events of what I see as my own personal demise.

It has been more than two and a half years since I came back to America. I travelled to London long ago to seek revenge on an old *friend*. I thought what I did would make it right. I thought my parents would be proud of me; thought revenge would taste sweet forever. Let me tell you, friends: revenge is as salty or sweet as you make it. I should have stayed away. I should have let it go. I should have let Harold end his own life. I *should* have forgotten.

My parents are gone. My mother is dead. My father left me alone. I thought I could make it all go away. My family was supposed to praise me. I was supposed to be a hero; an example. I was the voice when no one else would speak.

What was that?

More creaking; it's nothing. It's just the wind flowing down the stairwell. Wait, there it is again. Not tonight. Goddammit Harold; don't do this to me tonight.

The doctor found me. I swore I'd killed the bastard. For Christ's sake, I impaled him through the bloody chest. What kind of inhuman monster lives through such disfigurement? What kind of *sick* bastard *follows* me home and *murders* my family?! That persistent doctor is a lunatic, I tell you; a God damn lunatic.

Okay, okay. I need to calm down . . . start from the beginning. Just start from the beginning.

I arrived back home shortly after New Year's Day in the year 1906. My father, still holding his tongue in a grudge, immediately asked for the evidence against Harold. He still wasn't convinced that Harold had murdered his sweet Hazel. I told my parents the story - how I'd convinced Harold to undergo the procedure; how I'd trapped him in the doctor's operating room. I drooled over the journals, reenacting how Harold's head had cracked like an impregnated egg. "I watched the bastard die," I said to them, flipping ahead to the last of the doctor's journal entries. Somehow I thought my parents would be more proud.

I let my father read the entries for himself. He must have read Harold's recordings three times before he finally returned them to me. You know what he said? Not a single word. Not even a pat on the back or a "Way to go, son!" I got *nothing*. Isn't that right, Harold?

Why am I calling Arthur Harold? He wants me too. I think it fits him better, don't you?

My mother refused to read the entries. Her words said shameful things about me, but her eyes said she was proud. I know she was proud of me. *Tack, tack, click,* there's more noise at the window. So this is what Harold must have felt like all those months; a prisoner in his own empty home. I shouldn't have followed him. I shouldn't have taken your life, Harold. I'm sorry. I forgive you. You forgive me, don't you? *BANG, BANG, BANG.* Sorry friend, the windows are bolted shut.

Yes, that's correct. I live on my own now. Still in my parents' home, I live alone. The doctor found me and killed my mother. He poisoned her; I swear on the Lord's name he did. My mother grew ill two years ago. She lost the strength to eat or sleep. She brought home a vile of pills one day with only verbal directions to take them with water. Four pills later she was dead. God damn doctor laced them with cyanide. After it was too late, I found the bottle of pills. There was no prescription or dosage on the bottle; just a smiling face with the letter 'N' scribbled beneath it. Why didn't she come to me? I told her to come to me. I could have helped her.

My father, he . . . blamed me. "This is your fault, David!" he screamed, thrusting the pills in my face. "You couldn't leave it alone," he said to me. "And now that doctors after us. You *son of a bitch*; that lunatic doctor is after us." He was right. He was always right. Naragavitz wouldn't stop . . . *won't* stop until my entire family is dead.

I have no idea where my father has gone. He came home drunk the night of my mother's death; gibbering about a bastard son and a whore for a daughter. His breath warmed my neck with alcohol. I swear he thought about killing me that night. When I woke the next morning, he was gone. He left everything behind, save for a suitcase of clothing. There was only a note telling me to make the arrangements for my mother's funeral. I haven't heard from him since that night.

It's two years later now. Harold's been haunting me since my parents left. I swear it's him. I see his shadow sometimes, creeping through the hallway at the stroke of two a.m. No matter how hard I've tried to be a better man, I have become him. I have become Harold Elway. I hide beneath a blanket in my living room. I am afraid to go upstairs after the sun sets. It's just as Harold described Hazel in his entries. How could I have let this happen? How *could* this be happening to me? This can't be in my head. This is reality. I feel the chill of lost souls soaring through me. About twice a week, I hear my mother wailing my name. Her voice sounds as if she's screaming into a ceiling fan. "Daaaaavid!" She shrieks, she whines, she *bitches*.

Then there's Harold, of course. He scrapes his fingernails down my walls. He tiptoes down my stairwell; bangs on my windows from the outside. Then there's his umbrella. *Tap, tap, tap. . . tap, tap, tap.* After every step there's that obnoxious *tapping*.

A couple years of loneliness were accompanied by great doubt. Was Harold dead? Had I *really* killed him? He couldn't possibly be alive; I watched them lower him into the earth. I couldn't be sure; I just couldn't be sure. So I went back. I went back to London.

It was late, some off-hour in the early morning. The gate to the graveyard creaked open as if trying to warn me against entering. It was raining appropriately, the summertime dew building upon my shoulders. The graveyard was an atrocity full of broken tombstones and defiled stepping stones. I should have stopped when I saw Harold's grave. His name appeared bolder on the stone than I had remembered it. I should have let him rest in peace.

But I didn't; no I couldn't. I had travelled all that way.

I had a splinter in my fingers by the third hole. The dirt felt weightless; the smell of drenched earth tickling my nostrils. I watched as the shovel cut a worm in two. The ends wiggled in separate directions as I piled more dirt upon them. The rain had picked up, leaving no time for the raindrops to cast shadows. Six feet deep I heard the *thud* I had been waiting for.

Morning was approaching fast. What did I have to worry about? No one was coming to kneel over Harold's grave. He had no family. It didn't look like anyone had ever left him flowers or trinkets. The pine box had been stained by years of filth. The once freshly cut wood was now black and unmemorable. Tossing the shovel on the drowning grass, I forced the box open with a *bang* and gazed at the bastard I'd helped kill so many years before.

Harold's flesh had long been decayed. The skeleton of a man was all that remained. I don't know what I expected to see when flipping that lid. Perhaps part of me wanted to see the same old face I used to know. That ridiculous top hat was littered with ribbons of holes and patches of dirt. Still, he had that familiar smug look in his smile. Harold was dead; there was no doubt that I'd proven that to myself once again. Part of me couldn't leave him alone.

Harold was the reason for my family's demise. He was the reason my sister was dead; the reason I had searched for Naragavitz. It's really like Harold killed my mother and drove my father away, isn't it? Isn't it?

It isn't, is it . . .

Before I left the gravesite, I couldn't hold my foot from smashing Harold's skull. The hairline fractures and empty left cavity just begged for destruction. His skull was vile; both yellow and brown with clouds of grey. I knocked that smug look off his face for good, adorning the dirtied pine with stained fragments of his head. I had the decency to cover the grave back up, but not before I took something back that I should have taken years ago.

*Tick, tick, tick.*

This pocket watch belongs to my father. He's the one who bought it to begin with. The device still beats with Hazel's heart. It has overcome all uncertainties. It is my savior through these nights; a loose reminder of the man my father used to be. I wiped it clean of that idiot's fingerprints. Now, it is mine and mine alone. *Tick, tick, tick.* It reminds me that I am awake. It is the only thing that reminds me I am real.

My life has been so queer this past year. At least four nights a week, Harold visits me. I read through the old journals every night, searching for a clue as to how I could get rid of him. Maybe I'm just searching for a ghost; something that isn't really there. More footsteps croak as I prepare for another sleepless night. My mind is too frazzled; littered with too many facts and not enough details. Perhaps a warm bath will calm my mind and my hand. I will return shortly.

*1:15am*

Sweet Lord in Heaven; I have seen hell. I lay myself down in a clear bathtub of water. The faucet piddled, *drip, drip, drip,* as I let weariness close my eyes. Sweat pooling in a formal crowd on my forehead, I felt a finger trickle between my eyes and drip from the tip of my nose. *Plunk.* The dribble hit the bathtub and I awoke. Lord, I wish I hadn't.

The water had thickened; crusted into a quilt of drying blood. I moved to burst free from the water, but my hands were locked at my sides as if they were bound by ties. I gazed down at my abysmal figure. I'd let myself go in the past few years; a chubby, quivering rat that was drowning. The hair above my bellybutton wiggled like the tail of a bull seeing red. My eyes burned as if being held open by the fingernails of an unknown hand. Then I heard my mother's familiar cries. "David," she croaked. She appeared as the tracings of a woman on my chest, right between my somewhat hardened pectorals.

Her silhouette was entirely white; her body, translucent. She reached out to me with gnawed, uncut fingernails. "Tell the doctor that I need more medicine," she said. "Be a good lad and tell him to issue a refill." As I motioned to reply, my tongue felt a row of stringy threads. My mouth had been sewn shut. Capable of only grunts, my body rocked back and forth, sending waves of crimson soaring over the side of the bathtub.

My mother proceeded to sob, cradling her hands together as she kneeled. "Help me, David!" she screeched. Her shrill voice echoed across the bathroom tiles. "Mother always helped you, didn't she? It's only proper for you to return the favor. David? David, why aren't you speaking to me? Talk to your mother, David!" She was angry now, fragments of her hollow body shooting in and out of my vision. Her figure was a shrunken, warped disaster. Is that what she really looks like in the afterlife? Was she really in hell? My father always said that suicide was one of the lowest of sins; even after Hazel's death, he'd still say it.

The hair above my naval began to tremble. Churning like a spill of tar, the hair suddenly scattered into a hatched nest of black spiders. Even more tiny arachnids erupted from my belly button. My body was their home. They formed a circle around my mother's trivial figure. A final scream filled the air as the spiders devoured her. My eyes finally closed.

The smell of lavender waved in the aroma of the old doctor's office. Flesh, gore, fluids; it reeked of insides. With my eyes still shut, I cringed at the images of an immense, towering piece of art. Flawlessly chiseled and free of weathered cracks, a statue of Harold stared into me with judgment. Behind my eyes was the bastard I had never wanted to see again. He was locked into a pose, one foot behind the other with a weightless lean on the handle of his umbrella. Inscribed in the stone was the word 'Obey'. I was in hell.

My hands freed themselves. I reached up to tear the sutures away from my mouth, but felt only dry, cracking lips. The water had become clear once more. There was no statue of Harold, only chipped tile and wallpaper. My envisioned journey had been short, but the message was clear. Harold is my God now. He demands that I worship him, and I shall.

I half-dried my body with the towel I'd dampened from the splashing. Running to the sink, I tore open the underside cabinet and found my mother's makeup bag in the rear. A small, pink tote with green polka dots; it was nauseating. I saw scarlet in my reflection as I pulled out the first tube of lipstick that presented itself to me. "I believe in you, Harold," I said through muttered saliva. The lipstick cap hitting the floor, I leaned in to kiss my own reflection. "H," I moaned, smearing the letter onto my forehead. The color was a flushed, ember red. "A, R." My heart beat in clenched palpitations. "O, L." You Bastard. "D."

Your name across my forehead, I spit at the man staring back in the mirror. "Is that enough?!" I shrieked. *BANG, BANG, BANG.* A shatter hit the bathroom window. I didn't bother looking; you're never on the other side. "Of course it's not," I remarked, picking up the cap and sealing the lipstick. I returned it to the bag before shoving the tote back in the cabinet it had come from. "What is enough for you, Harold?" I asked, shrugging my arms to the open air. "Do you want my blood? Do you want my life? You've *taken* everything else."

With a clash of metal, I tore the medicine cabinet open and grabbed a pair of trimming scissors. "I understand," I said. "I have become you. I know that I have become you." The left scissor wing hovered above my forearm, its holding hand a trembling disaster. The blade met my skin, just enough to make an indent in the flesh. I looked up at the mirror yet again, and reality suddenly hit me. "No," I echoed, tossing the scissors to the nearby rug. "No, Harold. You won't get the best of me. I'm stronger than you."

I draped my father's old robe over my still-wet back, and here I am. The haunts appear to be over for the night. Harold is stuffed with surprises, though; as is mother. I washed your filthy name from my forehead a few moments ago. The water felt refreshing for once.

When I read these old journals, it is as if I can see through Harold's eyes at the time of the events. It is as if he is living inside of me, forcing me to see what he once saw. I can hear the inside of his brain; his conscious and subconscious bickering back and forth. I hear the voice of Harold, the bantering of Arthur and the moans of Hazel. I have recorded all that I have seen and heard in its own series of journal entries.

I have done my best to compile the entries into a collection that tells my story; our story. A life such as Hazel's should be remembered. I regret that I did not keep my promise to Johnny. I still have his original documents with me. I suppose I never got around to sending them back to him. In the shape they're in, I don't think he could even make sense of them now. I've torn pieces out here and there, spilled coffee on a few pages even. Though Johnny damned the drug in his logs, coffee has become widely available in instant packets since the events took place. I've got a pantry full of them.

I wonder what Johnny is up to these days. His boy Thomas should be twelve years old by now. He must have his own life; a loving family and a dozen women wrapped around his tiny little finger. I bet old Johnny sure is proud of him. I have thought about writing a letter to Johnny, but I think it's better he doesn't know my address. He knows far too much about me as it stands. He could send me to prison in a heartbeat if he wanted to.

As for me, well, I've questioned my sanity these past few years. At times I am capable of clear thought - At others, my instincts gobble up my rationality and I am left a lost, wandering fool. Not a day goes by that I don't miss my mother. The same holds true for my father. I heard he was seen around town not too long ago. Perhaps one day he will find his way back home. If he doesn't, I can't say that I blame him.

It has been difficult to remain quiet these past few years. I wanted so badly to drop the journals on the Elway's stoop. God, it would satisfy me to see Harold's mother tear herself to shreds upon reading that her son was a killing machine. She'd ruin herself when she found out he was dead himself. Harold's life was a sheer embarrassment.

My mother made me swear to her that I would never tell the Elway's. "They don't deserve that kind of burden," she said to me. "Just like we didn't deserve it." My father agreed with her, and it was decided that we would continue to let the Elway's live in ignorance.

I passed Mrs. Elway in the marketplace about a month ago. She was humming a tune from an old jazz song; one that in its proper listening form is full of blaring trumpets and shrieking trombones. She said hello to me, but only out of forced politeness. The family has been bitter with me ever since the

murder. I can't blame them. I am, after all, the one
that called their Arthur a killer. "How is your
father?" she asked. "Fine," I said, "Just fine," and I
kept walking onwards. She doesn't appear to know
that my father left two years ago. If she does, she
plays a convincing blind bat.

I heard that Harold's father lost his mind for a
while after his son disappeared. Deep inside, they
must know that their son killed my sister. I guess
ignorant parents raise ignorant children.

Harold's father still attends church twice a
week. I've heard that he still prays for his son to
come home beneath his breath. At times, he is the
only one standing beneath the stained glass
windows. What a sad sight that is. I've heard no
news of Harold's sister since my return. My
conscious tells me I should feel bad for the family,
but I can't deny the natural carelessness I feel
instead. A promise to my mother is a promise; I
could not bring myself to break it, especially now.

*BANG, BANG, BANG, BANG*

If I just ignore Harold's trickery, he'll go
away eventually. I thought he was finished for the
night, but as I said, he can be full of surprises. He's at
the living room window now. Just last week he
appeared to me at the foot of the stairs. Opening his
hands, he presented a small play-doll of my dear
sister, Hazel. She was in a blue nightgown, holding

her hands to her face and sobbing uncontrollably. What a sick bastard. He knows how to toy with my anger.

"David! David!" Harold mimicked her voice. That idiot was never good at impressions. I've learned that if I tackle the haunts head-on, they seem to disappear much faster. I didn't give Harold the time to defile my sister's honor any longer. In a fully charged sprint, I physically tackled Harold into the nearby wall. He was gone, of course, when I recovered myself. Once a coward, always a coward. I looked like a fool once again, standing in a shower of my own sweat.

*BANG, BANG*

What the hell is wrong with him? He's off-beat tonight. It's *always* three rattles on the window or the wall. He must be trying something new tonight. Heh . . . maybe his haunts remind him a little too much of his own past.

*BANG, BANG*

Yes, yes, Harold, I can hear you. I just gave him a wave in the air to humor him. Whatever he has planned for me, it can't be worse than the bathtub incident. It must feel awful to be such a cracked conch-shell of a man. I don't know when I'll die, but it will surely be with more honor than him.

*BANG, BANG, BANG*

"There you go, Harold!" I shouted into the naked living room air. "Finally got it right, did you? You can give it a rest now!" I can't help but laugh at how desperate he is getting. I've grown used to the footsteps and the noise. He's going to have to find something a little more chilling to get the best of me. Earlier tonight was a good attempt, I admit. He *almost* got me there. "But here I am, Harold!" I shouted into my empty home again. "Here I am!"

*CRASH!*

Jesus Christ in Heaven! Someone just tossed a parcel through my living room window! It wasn't Harold banging on my window tonight after all. I drove my feet outside in an attempt to hunt the intruder, but there was no one to be found. I cleared every bush and lamppost, but it appears the idiot ran away in fear.

Have I lost my mind entirely? The package *is* real, isn't it? Yes, it's definitely real. I'm feeling it with my left hand as I write this. It isn't a terribly large package, but it's decently sized. Hmm . . . I suppose there is only one method to find out what's inside.

There is a letter attached to the top of the box. Its ridges are tightly bound with spit. It is white, stained with what appears to be coffee and tobacco-filled saliva. Disgusting.

*2:00am*

Here I sit, waiting for you. I have a butcher's knife in my lap and a Winchester rifle on the rack above the fireplace. I started the flames on this warm August night. It's probably wise to burn up that old, dried out firewood before winter rolls around.

The package . . . I opened the package. The letter came first. It was a message from a friend I haven't heard from in more than two years. I read it aloud - Then I read it silently before reading it aloud again.

"How does it feel to be alone with your thoughts? We have unfinished business. ~N." In the envelope was an empty prescription bottle in my own name, that familiar smiling face hand-drawn in the corner.

That doctor thinks he's going to get the best of me. Maybe he will, maybe he won't. It's just a matter of who gets to me *first*. Maybe I'll win the struggle; maybe I won't. I don't know. Who knows? Hazel, do you know? Harold? Mother? Oh, mother. You forgot to take your medicine. I'll have to give it to her. Excuse me.

*2:10am*

Ach. She was stubborn, but I got her to take the pill. I went down into the basement and she just stared at me with those empty button-hole eyes again. I keep telling her she needs to use lotion, but she doesn't listen. Her skin has grown so dry, so stale and leathery. I laughed when she spit the pill out at me the first time, but the gag had really grown old by the third spill. She's about due for another bath. Her odor about knocked me over when I entered the basement.

Anyways, the package . . . yes, I said I opened the package. That doctor's got a bit of a twisted sense of humor. I tore the tape off the edge of the box, and before I could even open it myself, Harold's old umbrella fell out onto the floor. I let it sit there for a moment. I think that part of me half-expected it to spring open on its own. You know what? The doctor left his blood on the umbrella's tip. Why didn't he ever clean it off?

I set the umbrella against the side of the door. You never know when it's going to rain and you're going to need an umbrella. That handle is perfectly carved. Maybe I should write to Johnny and tell him that Thomas did a magnificent job on the handle. Why, it looks *just like* an acorn!

No, I can't write to Johnny. What if Johnny finds me? So what if he does? He couldn't hate me too, could he? I mean, he *let* me kill Harold.

Or did he?

Those two were friends for quite some time. What if Johnny is copying my old plan? No, he couldn't be. Johnny would never do that.

Would Thomas? No, Thomas would never do that. Would he?

*BANG, BANG, BANG*

Here I sit, waiting for you. I have a butcher's knife in my lap and a Winchester rifle on the rack above the fireplace. I started the flames on this warm August night. It's probably wise to burn up that old, dried out firewood before winter rolls around.

Did I give mother her medicine? No, No. I don't think I did. I wouldn't want her getting any sicker. She looks ill enough as it is. I keep telling her that she's applying too much makeup. Excuse me.

*2:20pm*

Still as stubborn as ever; I don't know if I'll ever get through to that mother of mine. "You didn't tell the Elway's, did you?" She whined. "No, mother; No, I didn't," I said. She hardly ever talks any more. Her voice is so weak these days; it's as if I have to lean right up to the hole of her mouth to hear its cackling requests.

At any rate, the gift from the doctor was a nice gesture, wasn't it? He wants to meet me soon, I take it? I haven't seen him in ages. Why, he must be an award-worthy doctor by now. Hmm. It was awfully rude of him to leave in such a hurry though. He didn't even say goodbye.

*Tick, tick, tick.*

Here I sit, waiting for you. I have a butcher's knife in my lap and a Winchester rifle on the rack above the fireplace. I started the flames on this warm August night. It's probably wise to burn up that old, dried out firewood before winter rolls around.

## *Harold*
*A metrical verse*

A gargle of ancestry
A splash of moonshine
Pitch black, unsweetened tea
Reminiscence of nursery rhymes
A tearful night in a tempest
An angry dawn of insomnia
The raging cardinal apprentice
Chirping at the hypochondria
Another golden cigar perhaps
A river of wax, smoke and fire
Scraping nails of relapse
Risk of madness, dire
A plea to the ghostwriter
Prayers to the divine unknown
Rustic oils stain the lighter
The night, a stern cyclone
Bluebird calls
Blackbird wakes
Spiders blanket the walls
Floor trembles and quakes
Old man learns to crawl
Again, again
He is stalking nightfall
Against prideful chagrin

*About the Author*

Jesse White currently resides in Massillon, Ohio with his wife Samantha and three pets. Growing up in Canton, Ohio, Jesse attended Kent State University and graduated with a bachelor's degree in English studies. Jesse also holds a minor in theatre studies.

Jesse has two cats, Sydney and Phoebe, and Lucy; a labbe beagle-lab crossbreed. Jesse hopes to one day extend his care for animals outside of his own household.

Jesse spends much of his free time writing. Stalking Nightfall is his first full-length novel, while plans for a second text are already in the works. Jesse would like to take the time to thank his family and friends for all the support they have given him in the writing, editing, and publishing processes.

Jesse typically enjoys a bold cup of black coffee when writing. On occasion, he strikes up a fine cigar or pours a few gin and tonics as well. He also has a strong interest in craft beer and enjoys visiting local breweries in his spare time.

Jesse hopes to continue publishing full-length novels while keeping poetry close at heart. He would like to thank each and every individual that has supported him in his writing career.

# Other Works by Jesse Carter White

## Fabricated Autumn

*Fabricated Autumn* is author Jesse White's introductory collection of poetry that adds flavor to the vital, sometimes tasteless matters in life. Beginning with the unsettling sharpness of autumn's decay, readers are led through a series of enthralling poems until they find themselves at the death of tired, aged winter. From perceptions on individuality to lessons on the surreal feelings of grief, *Fabricated Autumn* offers insight into the hurried lives we have grown accustomed to. White's vivid imagery and signature style promise a captivating journey into both the inner mind and the modern world.

Please enjoy the following excerpts selected from Fabricated Autumn. *Fabricated Autumn* is available through Amazon.com, and will soon be available through other major retailers. *Fabricated Autumn* is also available through Amazon Kindle and the Amazon Kindle application.

# Excerpts from *Fabricated Autumn*

*Wedding Day*

The bells of the angels are chiming,
singing through the city; tolling in my head.
And the gears of a child are grinding,
as our vows; our fortunes are read.
Ringing merriment in the place I grew up,
the bells fill the sparkling aqua sky.
Cheers and toasts fill my cup,
and the grains of rice soar high.
But all I see is the crescent of the moon.
Standing in this suit of disguise,
the hollow has come so soon.
Oh how beautiful are the dragonflies,
on the day of this joyful mourning,
with sacrificial gowns adorning.

## The Death of Autumn

Vernal hazels ripening and aging hickories browning;
the feast of scented harvest eludes annually.
Peppery stalks wilting in cranberry shade;
quilted leaves smothering the acorns
beneath the scarecrow's soles.

The chilling sleet of crows glazes autumnal fire,
each crisp, petrified brethren embracing,
as the soil's wife pierces their skin.
Disfigured gourds drooping with sorrow,
famished spiders nesting, feasting on their remains.

A rusting pitchfork is forgotten in the neighboring
haystack.
Yet the jagged pine cones and their glistening mothers,
are ripening with familiar holiday promise.
Sparkling dust will soon glide from the clouds,
littering the fruitful work of man and nature.

And now the cider has all been tapped,
stored in aged barrels for our frosted throats;
its boiling acidity to warm our frost burnt grins.
Our lightsome thoughts will long for the sun,
and it's calming burst of citrus fireflies.

Yet,

The grace of creaking timber cannot last.
The brimful orange patches are soon to rot.
The autumnal equinox has long passed.
The season whimpers in the heart of November.
This is the death of autumn.

## Sisterhood

I spent months in the darkness with my sisters,
The shadows of webbed wire a curious luxury.
They came at night in thrashing foreign tongues,
To select us each one by one.
The weak are stomped into the defecated earth;
The dozers are kicked through recycled cobwebs.
Sisters four and forty-four are dead in a pile,
With a hundred more faces I never knew.

They came by three again this night;
The shadows disappeared for an hour to two.
I thought I almost tasted sleep,
Until the blindness shook the room.
The gate was opened and the screams resumed.
In rolled the cages on a massive machine.
Sister twelve was caught between a wheel and the dirt,
Her spine broken and jutting from her chest;
Innards pasted in the thickness of the treads.
To the left, sister five tasting mud on her face.
Her chest too heavy with the evolution of drugs.
The wheezes echo in the sheet-metal cell.
I watch what I know of hell.

Suddenly I am plucked from a hazed mindset,
Ashes of earth clenched deep in my feet.
As writhing as the rest, I am thrown to the side
Into an even smaller crate with thicker bars.
In comes another; and another still.
Stuffed to the brim, my talons claw behind,
Gauging the eyes of fellow sister nine.
I'd be leaving now; to where I didn't know.
I felt the truck pull onto the road.

We drove for an hour, maybe more; I forget.
And now here I sit at father's call of dawn.
I hear the grinding of steel on sandstone;
A dozen clanging buckets thrown in a heap.
A burly man appears with an unshaven beard;
His overalls grimy with guts and sweat.
The faintest trickle of what I now see is rain,
Something I only heard on the tin atop my youth.
It's so beautiful, so peaceful and calming.
The cage next door unbolts with a bang.

Sister one is grabbed by her throat,
Carried a foot and stuffed into a chute.
This man is not our savior, but a vile brute.
The oversized switchblade of the executioner
Dampens with the pellets of the sky.
Sister's neck is grinding against the metal,
Her body disguised in the shining cylinder.
Silence is her word; she stares right through me.
I am sorry sister, I cannot help you.
Her throat is slit, the blood flows in a stream.
The ricocheting sound of red hitting the tin below
Soon sounds bubbling as the pales are filled.

I am at the end now; my whole life but shadows.
As quickly as beauty came, it was taken from me.
The steel was cold to my gurgling throat.
My feathers soaked in the morning dew.
My gizzards and heart flavor for your stew.
My liver is dinner for a poor, choiceless child.
Both wings are clipped and devoured at separate tables.
My oversized breasts are frozen in various plastic bags.

I guess what you do doesn't feel wrong to you.
Survival of the dominant, I can understand.
But the cruelty that I've seen through half-blind eyes,
Could never be justified.
At least I was so lucky as to the taste the rain;
I wonder what it means to dance within it?
Who am I to question.
My needs are meaningless to you.
Cluck, Cluck.

*Skeleton Earth*

When all the earth is a brittle skeleton
the weight of our bodies breaking its spine
the white owls perch atop the fingers of the oaks
abase in night; humble, elegant
the bones snapping under our boots
a numbed distortion to the guardian mantle
the honeycombs frozen solid
hexagonal cells but webbed cavities
in the fogged air, the frosted hands
of a twisted clock tower, chiming, clanging
the wailing of polar insects and aviators
silent for months, enough to
age and sour

When every street of slickened stone
is pressured in nimble, ice-locked fingers
the felt of nightshade is a glacial tomb
sapphire in roughness; starry-eyed, trapped
the whistling cold between the gaps of limbs
branches of ivory bone-split chaos
straightened in faceless idle skyline
the gloom of early moonrise
quickens the passing of bitter days
the flossed teeth of rotting tree stumps
filled with the temperance of clouded crystals
waiting after passing, for further passing
of worn-out winter

Before reason appears too slick
minds are bitten each aging year
with the firm remembrance
that loathed, brittle winter

waits in hardened frailness
just as bones within bodies

*Sickness*

at breakfast I was drowsy
uncomfortably being watched
by a cyan plate with sunny-side eyes
and a greasy mouth
scents of foreign beans
had faded quicker
then their liquefied pour
barely making their name known
to my still-dozing mind

at lunch I was drowsier
I swore the far-off clock
had just sentenced me
a handful's seconds ago
there were a dozen toys
at my naked feet
the woodcherry colored
basket of fur packed
neatly away in the alcove
of the indented couch cushion
having given up
on me and the promise
something inside said to
take a rest

at dinner I was drowsiest
rising into dusk
shuddering the weight of illness
whether it be real or imagined
into the still-full quivering
aqua mug of steep java
staring into the hanging face

of yellowed disappointment
the stove churned out
an unbothered roast
and vessel of scalloped spuds
that accomplished nothing
more than being left alone

at midnight I slept
for the third time that day
I hadn't eaten or done
one valuable thing

To stay informed on upcoming releases by Jesse White, visit www.fabricatedautumn.com

**Contact Jesse**

jessecwhite@fabricatedautumn.com